JACK McGUIGAN'S
DOG WALKER II
SHADOW PACK

This is a work of fiction. All of the characters, organizations and events portrayed in this novel are either products of the author's imagination or are used fictitiously.

GORILLA HOUSE
GorillaHouseBooks.com

DOG WALKER II: SHADOW PACK. Copyright © 2019 by Jack McGuigan. All rights reserved. For information, address Gorilla House, PO Box 893, Park Ridge, IL United States 60068.

Edited by Crystal Watanabe. (PikkosHouse.com)
Author Photo by Mike Pokryfke.
Black December Font by MDW.
Special Thanks to Will Haley, Mike Pokryfke, and Brian Wessel.

ISBN-13: 978-0999298206
ISBN-10: 0999298206

Ben Carter, pet care specialist, is hired to walk a Shiba Inu named Toby. Unbeknownst to Ben, Toby is no ordinary dog but an "inugami" – an immortal demon born in feudal Japan and bred for only one purpose: murder. Bonded by the power of the kakawari, their wounds are shared and their fates intertwined.

The doorway to Hell has been opened. A great darkness has been unleashed upon the Windy City, but even the dark knows to fear...the **Dog Walker.**

ONE.

The old woman took a long drag from her cigarette. She leaned against the windowpane and watched the sun set over the funeral home across the street. There was a chill in the air. She held her matted pink bathrobe closed. Above her, Shrek and Donkey grinned, each raising one eyebrow. Together they held up a big green "2."

Every inch of the storefront window was covered in faded posters—romantic comedies and kids' movies from a decade earlier. The small sign on the glass door read:

EAST WEST VIDEO
CLOSED
THANK YOU
FOR 22 YEARS

A brown Cadillac pulled up to the curb, and Det. Sarah Martinez stepped out of the driver's side. She gave the store a once-over, then reached into her sport coat and flashed her badge.

"Ma'am," she said. "You called about strange noises?"

The old woman exhaled a plume of smoke. Det. Jake Bolland—Sarah's partner—went directly to the store window without acknowledging her. He peeked in between the posters, stroking his neatly trimmed mustache.

"I live upstairs." The woman glared at Jake. "I own the building. The other two have been in there for three hours."

"Other two?" Sarah saw the empty squad car parked across the street. She pulled a walkie-talkie off her belt. "Adam four, code four. Respond."

"I can't be doing this all day," the woman said. "I work the night shift tonight. I'm supposed to be asleep right now."

No response on the radio. Sarah shook her head.

Jake turned to the woman. "They're in the store? Have you checked on 'em?"

"After what I heard this morning?" She tossed the cigarette butt into the gutter and headed toward the stairway to her apartment. "*I'm not going in there.*"

Sarah and Jake exchanged a look.

Thin strips of sunlight bled between the posters, blanketing the video store in an uneven grid of dusty illumination. Along the walls on either side stood white bookcases lined with empty cardboard VHS covers. At the center of the room were two smallish metal racks full of DVDs. Darkness loomed beyond a wooden counter with a cash register and an old tube monitor. The sun was shining in that direction, but the back of the store was pitch black anyway.

"Police!" Jake didn't get a response. He and Sarah crept deeper into the store, watching that back area. "What do you think?"

"Something ain't right." Sarah pulled out a small flashlight and scanned around the ceiling. "Posters in the window are from the mid-2000s, right?"

"What, *Shrek*?" Jake's arm rubbed up against one of the shelves. He brushed a thick layer of dust off his sleeve. "Probably. I guess so."

"Seems like a lot of spiderwebs."

"What spiderwebs?"

Sarah looked at him. "You don't see them?"

"Welcome to East West Video."

The two cops jumped, reaching for their guns. A pale woman stepped out from the shadows behind the counter. Long, straight black hair covered most of her face. Sarah aimed the flashlight at her.

"If you need help," the woman said, "let me know."

"Jesus, lady." Jake relaxed, fixing his shirt. "What are you doing in here? You scared the—"

Sarah grabbed him by the collar and yanked him toward the exit. Once they were safely outside, she leaned against the door, panting.

"What are you *doing*?" Jake said.

"You can't see the webs."

"What webs?!"

Sarah put her hand up, calming him. "What did you see behind the counter?"

"Skinny woman. Long black hair. Seemed to think the store was still open."

"Did she have a body?"

Jake started to answer, then stopped. "Is this one of those things?"

Sarah pulled out her phone. "Let me call my guy."

Jake closed his eyes and pressed his forehead on the glass door. "Not him…"

Ben Carter, pet care specialist, struggled to free himself from a tangle of leashes. The four gray miniature schnauzers at his feet—Rosie, Josie, Posie, and Rex—were in a state of chaos. Rex, the only boy, did a handstand while peeing on the building next to them. Rosie tugged hard on her leash from the other side of a tree, unable to comprehend why she couldn't move forward. Josie circled Ben, wrapping her leash around his shins. Posie was pooping. As Ben knelt down to pick it up, the dogs all turned and yapped at him.

"Yep. It's still me," Ben muttered. "I've been here this whole time."

The mini schnauzers had spent years as yard dogs, and they had just started going out in the world a few weeks ago. Their entire existence prior to now consisted of hanging out on the lawn and barking at everything that went past. Their walking skills were negligible. It took Ben forty minutes to get a few houses down.

These were not usually Ben's dogs. Kaylee, another walker, had a job interview. Or audition. Improv show? Something like that. Ben was covering for her. He was actually a little surprised she'd asked. Kaylee didn't like him. She was always pretty mean to him.

Ben stood, flipped the poop bag closed, and checked the color-coded leashes in his hand.

"Rosie, Josie, Posie…" There were only three. He looked up. "Rex!"

Rex cheesed it down the sidewalk, leash dragging along behind him. Ben tried to follow, but the other three dogs were all facing different directions, oblivious.

"Son of a—" Ben yanked at their leashes. No response. "Rex!"

Just as Rex reached the apartment building on the corner, two arms scooped him up.

"Hey, you! Where are you going?" Kaylee held the small dog. Rex's nub of a tail wagged as he licked her face. "Did Ben forget how to do his job?"

The other mini schnauzers swarmed Kaylee, silently wagging. Her reflective bracelet flashed as she set Rex down with the others. She always wore reflectors while she was on duty. It was a practical choice. Good for safety but very dorky. Ben handed her the leashes.

"I don't know how you do this every day." He spun the key to the mini schnauzers' house off his keyring. "How was your thing?"

"Terrible," she said, giving Ben zero hints as to what she did. She pulled her hand away as he went to give her the key. "Let's go on a date tomorrow night."

"You and me?" Ben said. "With each other?"

She laughed. "Yeah, playing hard to get clearly doesn't work on you. This is the direct approach."

Ben thought a moment, then smiled. "Okay. Sure."

Kaylee plucked the key out of his hand. "I'll text you."

"Text me," he repeated, slightly dazed as Kaylee led the mini schnauzers back toward their house. His phone buzzed in his pocket.

The screen showed a Shiba Inu silhouette in a circular yellow spotlight projected onto a dark night sky.

"Oh, hey," Kaylee said, turning back, "did you give them—"

Ben was gone.

犬

"All right." Jake checked his watch. "It's been long enough. I'm going back in."

He started toward the video store. Sarah tried to stop him.

"You can't go in there!" she said. "This is beyond our capabilities! You can't even see the perp!"

"We have a job to do! There are police in there!"

Brakes squeaked. A cherry-red Hyundai stopped in front of them and threw on the hazard lights. Ben got out of the back seat with what looked like a cricket bat strapped to his back.

"Sorry I'm late!" He ran around to the front passenger door. "I had to wait for a Lyft that would drive a dog."

He opened the door, and a chubby Shiba Inu looked up from licking his crotch and regarded the cops with a blank expression.

"Toby!" Sarah said. "Who's good?"

The dog gave her a slight wag. For Toby, that was a lot.

"What's the situation?" Ben said.

"Spiders," Sarah said. Ben made a *yuck* face. "And a floating head. It's definitely *yōkai* because Jake can't see anything. There are two unresponsive cops in the back somewhere. You still don't have a car?"

"I've been busy." Ben unzipped the carrying case and drew his weapon—a *macuahuitl*, an ancient Aztec sword. Small obsidian blades dotted the edges of the flat wooden club, which had been engraved with holy symbols from a wide variety of religions—a Christian cross, a Star of David, a yin-yang, a Shinto Torii gate, a skull with jewel eyes.

Toby hopped out of the car. He trotted over to the video store door and peeked in through the video-return slot.

Jake crossed his arms, glaring at Ben. "What does that do?"

"It's the Onislayer, Jake." Ben swung it around a little. "Demons burn at its touch."

"Uh-huh. The landlady complained about noise. Can you do…whatever it is you do quietly?"

Ben smiled. "Quiet as a clam."

He knocked over a rack of DVDs immediately upon entering the store. Plastic cases clattered to the floor. Dust clouded the air. The sun had gone down since the cops were in here, and the streetlights outside provided much less light through the cracks between the posters. Ben aimed the Onislayer at various points in the room. He saw shelves full of VHS boxes and an empty counter at the back.

"Hello?"

There was no sign of immediate danger. He lowered his weapon. Toby sniffed the dust-filled air and sneezed.

The dog's thoughts bounced around in Ben's mind. *BAD SMELL. BUG STINK.*

"Your nose works a lot better than mine, buddy." Ben stepped a little farther into the room, carefully avoiding fallen DVD cases.

USE EYES.

Toby was looking up. Ben followed his gaze. The surface of the ceiling was covered in a thick mesh of spiderwebs, which held three globular web pods the size of beach balls aloft.

"Are those egg sacs?" Ben exhaled through his teeth. "I'd better take care of those."

He turned to the bookshelf next to him, found a good place to grip, and climbed up a level. The bottom shelf groaned under his weight. Toby's ears twitched as he heard something Ben could not. He sniffed the VHS cover next to him.

Ben swung the Onislayer upward through one of the pods. It crackled, glowed slightly, and fluttered to the ground like tissue paper as it turned to embers. The pod was empty.

"We're too late," Ben said.

The VHS cover Toby was sniffing shook. He growled.

Every cover in the store rattled in place. Ben hopped down from the shelves and clutched the Onislayer tightly in front of him. A shadow, a blob of semitransparent darkness formed around Toby in the shape of a bigger, meaner Toby. The dog lifted off the floor and hovered at the shadow's center. Tentacle-like shapes grew from its surface.

The VHS covers stopped moving. Ben held his breath.

All at once, the covers tipped over, and thousands, *millions* of tiny black spiders skittered out. A shimmering wave of arachnids poured onto the dusty carpet and quickly encroached on the boy and his dog.

Ben speared the Onislayer through the nearest mass of spiders, straight into the bookcase. Flames kissed the spiders in its path. The boxes around it caught on fire. Ben went to pull it back, but the ebony blades were jammed into the wood. Ben put his foot on the shelf for some leverage and tried to yank it loose. A dozen spiders wriggled up his pants leg. He could feel them crawling around in there, biting his shins. Ben screamed, jerked the Onislayer free, and pressed it against his leg. The spiders burned through his pants. When he pulled the blade away, there were scorch marks on his jeans.

Toby hovered above the floor, encased in his larger shadow form. The tentacles of darkness growing off his back whipped around, swatting clusters of spiders en masse. When a clump of spiders near him got large enough, he turned and gobbled them up like kibble. As he did, Ben's leg immediately felt better.

Ben slid the Onislayer on the floor around him, carving a flaming circle of sizzling spiders. He kept hopping from foot to foot, always keeping one off the ground so the spiders inside the circle didn't get him. The next line of arachnids just climbed over the burning ones. This wasn't nearly as effective as Toby's method.

"I'm gonna find those cops!" Ben said. He headed toward the back of the store. Toby kept doing what he was doing.

As Ben approached the counter, a woman's face shot out from the shadows and floated up in his grill. She had long, straight black hair parted in the middle, covering her eyes.

"I'm sorry, sir," she said. "This area is for employees only."

Ben glanced down. Sarah was right. This head had no body.

He swiped at the floating head. The woman snarled. Her long black hair hovered upward into two thick tendrils, exposing two solid black eyes, which glared at Ben with lifeless rage. The hair whipped forward and sliced Ben's Onislaying hand off at the wrist. His severed extremity, still clutching the weapon, dropped to the floor.

Ben screamed, gaping at the bloody stump. Toby's front-left paw slipped off his wrist and landed on a pile of DVDs. The dog sighed, and then started eating spiders at a furious rate. Ben felt a tingling inside, like the chills he got when he heard a great song, but these chills moved from his stomach to his shoulder, down his arm, and into the bloody stump. A dark green gelatinous fluid oozed from his pores and his wound and, slowly but surely, his hand grew back: bones, then tendons, veins, meat, and skin.

"You have the *kakawari*," said the floating head.

"Complicates things, don't it?" Ben said, wiggling his fresh fingers. Behind him, Toby sniffed his brand-new paw.

"Complicate?" said the head. "No. Not really."

The woman's face drifted back into the dark, and less than an instant later, the wooden counter smashed to splinters as a ten-foot spider pounced upon Ben, crunching him into the fallen DVD rack. Its eight thick hairy legs stomped around, slipping on DVD cases, avoiding the growing flames. Ben held its huge pincers back as they snapped at his throat. He saw his own face reflected in eight tiny, asymmetrical eyes. A curved stalk grew from the center of the spider's forehead, like the glowing bulb on a deep-sea anglerfish. The woman's head bobbed at the end of it.

"I'll just have to eat you first," she said.

"Better do it quick," Ben said.

Toby hovered over next to Ben. The shadow form around him pulsed and solidified into coarse black fur. What stood there now looked like a cross between a wolf and a bear, with glowing red eyes, massive teeth, and a tangle of prehensile fur tentacles whipping around on its back. Toby the dog was gone. Only the *inugami* remained.

The inugami howled, a piercing shriek that made the windows rattle. Ben covered his ears. The spider staggered back, releasing him.

Outside, three different car alarms went off.

"Woman upstairs is *not* gonna like that," Jake said without looking up from his phone.

Sarah shook her head. She made a beeline for the store.

The inugami leapt upon the giant spider, biting at its neck. The spider managed to catch two of its back legs on counter rubble, and it slipped, briefly giving the inugami the upper hand. Ben stood and dove to the side, avoiding a spider leg and then a fast-moving inugami tentacle. He picked up the Onislayer and frowned down at his old severed hand, still gripping the handle.

The inugami rammed the spider into the shelves nearest to the exit. The wooden case collapsed around them just as Sarah went to open the door. She found it blocked.

"Ben!" she shouted.

Ben pried his old hand off the Onislayer and ducked another waving tentacle as he headed into the dark. The spider rolled, the inugami rolled with it, and they slammed into the opposite wall. The pockets of flame around them slowly grew larger.

The dog walker treaded carefully past shelves full of video tapes in clear plastic cases. There were empty cases strewn about the floor and tapes cracked open like eggs. Bits of black plastic crunched under Ben's feet. The magnetic tape had been unspooled and removed. There were a lot more spiderwebs back here. The air around Ben felt hotter and more humid.

"It's okay," he whispered to himself. "You chose this. This is what you do."

At the end of the tape racks, Ben turned a corner to the right. He gasped. Less than a foot from his face, two huge cocoons dangled from the ceiling. Viscous fluid oozed out from between the thick tangles of webbing and magnetic tape.

One of the cocoons moaned. Ben backed up and squatted down. He tilted his head sideways. Each cocoon had a human head poking out the bottom. These must be the missing cops Sarah had mentioned.

Their skin was pale, their lips were blue, but one of them had made a noise, which meant he was alive. Ben climbed up the nearest shelf and sawed at the top of one of the cocoons with his Onislayer.

The giant spider charged at the inugami, hissing, pincers pinching rhythmically. The inugami lunged to the side and clamped its jaws onto one of the spider's legs. The beast twisted its head and wrenched the leg from the spider's abdomen. The woman's head, still bobbing up and down on its stalk, wailed in pain.

Ben sliced the root of the second cocoon, and it dropped onto the floor next to the first with a wet flump. Ben knelt down beside it and pressed the Onislayer up to the webbing, right beneath the cop's neck.

"I hope you're not fatter than you look," he said.

He sliced down the center. A foul stench filled the room. Earthy, like rotten cabbage. Ben gagged. As he got close to the end, the cocoon split open, revealing the cop's body. The guy was pretty goopy but not visibly harmed. He didn't move. Ben grabbed him by the navy-blue vest, and it was like sticking his hands in warm Jell-O.

"Hey! Wake up!" He shook the cop. "You're being rescued! Wake—"

The cop shot up, gasping. His panicked eyes darted around until they settled on Ben.

"You all right?" Ben said.

The cop was young, around Ben's age. He felt around, shook off some of the slime. He nodded.

"Good," Ben said. "You can help me with the other guy."

The second cocoon began convulsing. That still-cocooned cop's mouth opened, but no sound came.

"Shit," Ben said.

The cocoon burst, splattering Ben and the cop next to him with webs, tape, slime, and blood. A mass of tiny spiders flowed out from where the second cop's body should have been. Next to Ben, the cop's eyes rolled back in his head, and he flopped into his cocoon.

Ben dove at the spiders, stabbing with his Onislayer and shouting obscenities.

The inugami and the giant spider were still fighting hard as Ben dragged the unconscious cop back into the front of the store. The flames from the Onislayer had grown into a full-blown fire. Smoke filled the room. Boxes and shelves burned. Everything reeked of melting plastic.

"Toby!" Ben said. "Time to go!"

The woman's head swung into view. "You! Human! What have you done?! Where are you going with my—"

Slice! Ben severed the connective stalk. The human head tumbled through the air and landed, bounced, rolled over by the remnants of the counter.

The spider slumped onto the inugami, dead weight. Orange mush seeped from its forehead stalk. The inugami wriggled out from underneath, bit through the spider's exoskeleton and started eating its guts. Ben felt the rush of energy he got when the inugami ate, then shook it off. *Gross.* He coughed.

The smoke was getting thicker. Ben couldn't see the exit. He grabbed the cop under the armpits and tried to drag him further but couldn't. He fell to the floor, coughing more.

"Toby!" he shouted. "We gotta get out of here!"

Laughter emanated from across the room. The woman's head propped itself up on spindly spider's legs made from its own hair. It wobbled awkwardly toward the back of the store. The inugami turned and dove to attack it, missing and catching only rubble.

"Help me!" Ben got up. "Toby! I can't move this guy!"

BEN GO, Toby snarled in Ben's brain. His thoughts always felt angrier when he was in full inugami mode. *TOBY KILL.*

"I'm not leaving without the guy!"

He got between the inugami and the escaping head. The inugami growled at him.

BEN GO! TOBY KILL!

"No!"

The inugami barked in Ben's face. *TOBY KILL! TOBY KILL!*

"No! Damn it! Help—" Ben coughed. "Help me save that cop!"

The smoke was completely blinding now. The severed head with the hair legs faded from view. Ben went into a full-on coughing fit and collapsed.

犬

Jake tried to calm the woman who owned the building, who was outside again, shouting in his face. Sarah waved the approaching fire engine toward the store.

"You burned down my building!" the woman said. "I'm going to sue the city! I'll have your jobs for this!"

"Ma'am," Jake said, hands up, "ma'am. If you'll just—"

The storefront shattered. Ben, Toby, and one of the cops rolled out onto the sidewalk amongst the broken glass.

Toby, back to his normal size and shape, shook like a wet dog. Bits of glass tinkled off his fur. Ben shot to his feet, screaming. He wriggled out of his flaming hoodie and tossed it onto the concrete, stomping on it until the flames were out. Jake, Sarah, the landlady, and several firefighters were staring at him.

"Hey," he said.

The woman pointed at him. "Who the hell is that?"

DOG WALKER II
SHADOW PACK

COPYRIGHT © MMXIX by JACK McGUIGAN
ALL RIGHTS RESERVED

TWO.

Jake had a look of defeat as he took down the landlady's statement, which involved the words "private property" and "gross negligence" and "sue your ass" at an alarming frequency. The firefighters hosed down the last of the fire. East West Video was now a charred, hollowed-out husk. No sign of the spiders remained.

Ben sat on the curb, swiping at his phone, looking for a Lyft to drive him and Toby to class. The nearest one was ten minutes away. Toby was curled up in a ball next to him, napping. Sarah plopped down on the other side.

"Is he gonna be okay?" Ben gestured to the cop he'd rescued, who was drinking coffee under a blanket at the back of an ambulance. He was staring straight ahead, his expression blank. He'd had a rough day.

"Better than he would've been. I think you pulled him out before the spiders got into his guts, but we should probably have him looked at. By *who*, I have no idea, but..." Sarah pulled out an envelope. "I've got something for you."

"No." Ben shook his head. "Sarah, we talked about this. I can't get paid for this."

"It's not taxpayer money," Sarah said. "Me and the other cops who can see things put it together."

"This is all my fault. The demons have been running rampant since I yanked Toby out of Hell. I opened something. They're here *because* of me." Ben petted Toby. The dog glanced at him briefly, then went back to sleep. "You guys do most of the work, anyway."

"Correct. But also, shut up. Take it." She forced the envelope into his hand. "Buy a vehicle. You'll be more useful. What are you doing Friday night? My cousin sells used cars. I can take you there and get you a deal."

"I can't. I have a, uhh…" Ben found it difficult to spit the word out. "…date."

"*What?*" Sarah smacked him. It hurt. "Look at you! Who is she?"

"She's a dog walker." Ben rubbed his arm. "We work together."

"That is your type. Are you sure you want to go down that road again? The last dog walker stabbed you and Toby to death."

"She was nice to me after that," Ben said, shrugging. He changed the subject. "I like your coat. You look like a grown-up."

Toby got up and stretched, yawning. He walked past them, heading for something on the other side of Sarah.

"I'm a detective now." Sarah pulled her phone out of her brand-new sport coat. "I *am* a grown-up. Nice try, but we're talking about this. Do you have a picture of this girl? What's her name? Are you guys friends on— Shit, I'm calling you."

She hit the End Call button. For an instant, she saw Ben's phone screen change in his hand. "Did you make a Batman signal with Toby instead of a bat and set it to show when I call you?"

"Uh, no," Ben said, quickly pocketing his phone. "Yes. Whatever. I'm allowed to enjoy this a little."

"Dweeb." Sarah laughed. "You know, the dog logo makes it look like I'm calling Toby. Like you're his sidekick."

A car horn honked right next to them. Toby was in the front seat of a dinky blue hatchback, paw on the steering wheel, standing on the lap of a very confused driver.

"Certainly no truth to that," Ben said.

Out in the northwest suburbs of Chicago, in a building that used to be a Pizza Hut, class had begun. The door was propped open to let some of the heat out, and a small fan blew the cool night air in. The floors were lined with gym mats. The far wall was covered in mirrors. A big banner above the mirrors read in red-and-green block letters:

DRAGON MASK LUCHA DOJO

"Niños! Niñas!" Tatsuya-sensei paced back and forth, hands behind his back. Dragon tattoos poked out of the sleeves of his T-shirt. "You have come here at a momentous time! Great evil has embraced these lands, but times of darkness bring opportunity for warriors! Are you ready to be warriors?"

"Si, Sensei!" the dozen children lined up along the mirror shouted in unison. They wore baggy white pants and black T-shirts with a little DMLD logo. They had their hands behind their backs just like Tatsuya.

"Are you ready to be samurai?"

"Si, Sensei!" the kids repeated.

"Dragon stance!"

They all got into position, knees slightly bent, right foot in front, left foot in back, dukes up.

"As samurai," said Tatsuya, "you must adhere to the code of Bushidō. You must always hold in your heart the eight virtues! Righteousness!"

"Hyah!" The kids punched the air with their left arms.

"A samurai knows when it is right to strike. Good! Courage!"

"Hyah!" They punched with their right arms.

"A samurai fights for justice without fear! Courage without honor is stupidity. True courage is doing what is right!"

Toby lay in his little bed on the counter, dozing. Behind him, Tatsuya's old luchador mask observed the proceedings from its protective glass case, surrounded by burning incense and photos of Dragon Mask's greatest victories.

"Compassion!"

The kids each took a step forward and blocked an invisible punch with their forearms. *"Hyah!"*

"You are samurai! Your fists are now weapons! This power should be used for good. You are the defenders of the realm! Respect!"

The students all returned to their starting positions then bowed formally to their sensei. Tatsuya looked over both shoulders, scanning the room.

"That one is for your parents, who are not currently here. Manners are good. Integrity is better. What is number six? Honesty! Kevin!"

A gawky ginger kid jumped, startled, standing up a little straighter. He pushed up his glasses.

"Did you eat fruits or vegetables with your breakfast?"

"No, Sensei!" Kevin squeaked. "Cap'n Crunch!"

"Captain Crunch?!" Tatsuya shouted, really leaning into it. "Too much sugar. You will be a fat samurai!" He slapped his belly. The kids laughed. "But you told the truth! That is the warrior's way. Honor!"

The young students turned away to face the wall of mirrors. They stared into their own eyes.

"You must be honest with others, but also to yourself. With honor, you cannot hide from yourself. Loyalty!"

"Hyah!" The kids spun back and karate-kicked the air in their sensei's direction. Having the kids kick at their teacher for loyalty didn't really make sense, but when Tatsuya first put the routine together, he thought it needed a few more punches and kicks. No one ever questioned it.

"Self-control," he said gravely.

The kids froze, each keeping one leg up over their waist. Ten seconds passed. Twenty. A few students wobbled. Tatsuya looked at the inugami. Toby opened one eye and glared back.

At the far end of the line, Ben Carter struggled to stay upright. He was twice as tall and twice as old as the other students, and the extra decade of pizza and video games had taken its toll. With a grunt, he fell onto his side, slapping loudly onto the mats.

"Ben fights first. *Again.*" Tatsuya sighed. "Everyone get your pads."

The kids bowed, shouting a rough approximation of *"Yoroshiku onegaishimasu!"* before heading over to the racks to get their head guards, mouthguards, and wrist pads. Tatsuya helped Ben up.

"Listen," Ben said, quietly so the kids couldn't hear. "I just came from a job. It's been a long day. This hand is new." He wiggled his fingers. "Maybe we can have the kids fight each other this time?"

Tatsuya nodded. "I understand. Ash!"

A short, skinny girl with a long black ponytail turned while putting on her head guard. She slapped the side to make sure it was on tight.

"Go easy on him."

Ashley Ocampo smiled, revealing her bright-pink mouthguard. The other students giggled. Ben heard rhythmic thumping and saw Toby wagging his tail against the counter. It was the dog laughter that hurt the most.

The kids all lined up against the mirror again, wearing their pads. Ben and Ash stood at the center of the room, facing each other. They got into their dragon stances. Ben didn't have any pads. He was the only adult student, and Tatsuya had neglected to order grown-up sizes.

The old luchador raised one hand and paused.

"Begin!"

Ash took a step forward. Ben stepped back.

"What's the matter, Big Ben?" Ash said, her consonants slurred by the mouthguard. She bounced from foot to foot. "Afraid to fight a girl?"

"Not really," Ben said, moving more slowly. "I just don't want to hit an eight-year-old."

Ash snorted. "I'm ten."

"Oh. Well. In that case."

He punched at her, way too high. She grabbed his wrist and spun, crouching as Ben flew over her head and landed hard on his back behind her. The other kids cheered.

"Boom!" Ash said. "Just like the real Big Ben!"

"The clock?" Ben wheezed. He rolled to his feet. "In England? That never fell down."

"Yeah, it did!" Ash said. "A spaceship smashed through it! The alien inside turned out to be a mutant pig!"

Ben squinted. "What?"

She swung at him. He blocked it with his forearm and shoved her away. Ash spun, kicking him in the side. She tackled him while he was off-balance and pinned him to the ground.

"Bueno!" Tatsuya said, kneeling, ready to slap the mat and count Ben out.

Ben lay there for a moment, defeated, embarrassed, before remembering that he was a grown man, with the proportionate size and strength of a grown-ass man. He stood easily, with the girl's arms still wrapped around his neck.

She kneed him in the stomach before letting go. He stumbled backward toward the crowd of kids, who dove away to avoid him. Ben flopped up against the mirrors and slid down.

Bam! A small fist clocked him in the cheek. *Bam! Bam!* Ash got him two more times. She went to do it again, but this time he caught it. She spun and kicked.

"Yamete!" shouted Tatsuya.

Ash's foot hovered next to Ben's ear. He leaned away from it. Ash smiled.

"Self-control," Tatsuya said. "Good."

Ash backed up a few paces and bowed to Ben. He nodded to her. Something dripped down his chin. He wiped it. His nose was bleeding.

Over on the counter, Toby stood, stepped in a circle, and lay back down, facing away.

Later, when class was over, the kids goofed around by the changing rooms as they waited for their parents to pick them up. A severe-looking woman in her fifties—thin face, pointy cheekbones, red hair that was unquestionably a wig—stood by the exit. She kept checking her watch. When Tatsuya passed her, she threw him a fake smile then went back to scowling. Tatsuya handed Ben a Pocari Sweat, his favorite sports drink from Japan. The old luchador had them shipped to Chicago by the crateful. The dog walker had a cotton ball stuffed in his nose.

"I am told you burned down another building," Tatsuya said.

"You gave me a sword that starts fires," Ben said. "It would be more surprising if I didn't— Ow!"

Ash slugged him in the arm. She held out her hand. "You'll get me next time, Big Ben."

Ben shook it. "Take it easy, L'il Ash."

"Ashley!" said the stern woman by the door.

"Bye, Sensei! Bye, Toby!"

Ash gave Toby a quick pat on his head, which annoyed him only mildly. Ben rubbed his arm. Ash had punched him right where Sarah had earlier. Why did girls keep hitting him?

"Ashley! Let's go!" The woman pointed at her watch. She noticed that Ben and Tatsuya were watching and flashed them that empty smile as she led Ash out the door. They were the last to leave. Ben and Tatsuya were alone.

"Tough kid," Ben said. He looked at his Pocari Sweat, frowned, and set it down unopened like he always did.

"Smart, too. She borrowed my book on Bushidō to read on her own." Tatsuya turned off the light in the changing room. "She lives in a foster home. Her parents died in a car accident. Very sad."

Ben went over to the window. He saw the stern woman close the door on a beat-up station wagon. She glared at Ben before he closed the blinds.

"I found her pummeling two teenagers senseless at the park and offered her free classes," Tatsuya said, closing the changing room door. "That kind of anger needs an outlet."

"Like my face?"

"If you cannot beat a little girl in a fight, what good are you against yōkai? I'm not making you fight children for fun, gringo. That is a bonus." He put his hand on Ben's shoulder. "You could learn from Ashley. You cannot do this with half of your ass."

Tatsuya cracked open a Sweat—his third—and chugged the whole thing down. Ben helped Toby off the counter. The dog felt extra heavy, probably from all those spiders he ate.

"Hey, how come you never put the mask on?" Ben pointed at Dragon Mask's mask. "Do some of your Dragon Mask moves. The kids would love it."

Tatsuya crushed the bottle between his hands.

"I never wore that mask sober," he said. "Only a madman would."

Three different cats bolted from the room as Ash entered Mrs. Greco's house. She was still in her uniform. Her backpack was overflowing with textbooks. Someone was watching a sitcom in the other room—one of the bad ones, where a hidden audience bursts out laughing between every sentence. Mrs. Greco closed the door behind Ash and locked it.

"Homework, then bed," Mrs. Greco said.

"Yeah, yeah." Ash switched shoulders with her backpack. It always felt heavier after lucha class.

"Don't you get smart with me."

Ash rolled her eyes and stomped into the TV room. Taylor was sprawled across the couch. She was a couple years older than Ash but only one grade ahead of her. She had an ice cream bar melting in her hand. She noticed a drop running down her arm and licked it, then each of the fingers on that hand, making a popping sound with her mouth at the end of each one.

"Eww," Ash said.

"Uh-oh!" Taylor said without looking away from the TV. "Don't hurt me with your nerd karate!"

"It's not..." Ash stopped before going in her room. "It's a lucha dojo. I'm a samurai luchador."

"That's two different things," Taylor said. "That doesn't even make sense."

"It doesn't make sense how fat your butt is," Ash said.

"Hey!" Taylor threw a pillow at Ash, and she dodged it.

"Girls!" shouted Mrs. Greco from the other room.

"She started it!" said Taylor.

Ash ducked into her room and slammed the door. The framed picture of her parents on her desk slapped down on its face. She lifted it back up and held in the urge to cry when she saw them. She missed her mom and dad. She hated this place. She wanted to go home. And she was so sick of crying.

She looked up at the wall, a thick slab of gray paint on brick. A streetlight glowed through a single small block window. Ash sat down at the desk and pulled out her math homework. Fractions. Okay. She was good at fractions. This wouldn't be so bad.

"A samurai…" said a woman's voice. "What a noble pursuit for a child."

Ash looked around. No one else was there. *Was that the TV?*

"In my youth, samurai were very well respected," the voice said. "Pillars of the community."

"Who's talking right now?"

"A friend." The sound was coming from the heating vent under the window. Ash squinted at it. Dark inside. "I'm here to give you a gift. Come closer, little samurai."

"Um…no thank you," Ash said, looking away. After a moment, she watched the talking vent out of the corner of her eye. Where did that actually lead? The furnace? Outside?

Mrs. Greco stormed in without knocking, startling Ash. She slapped a stack of papers and books onto the girl's desk.

"You need to do Taylor's homework, too."

"*What?*" Ash said. "Why can't she do it?"

"We've got to keep everyone's grades up or we lose your government money. You're better at school. This will be faster."

"That's not fair! You can't make me—"

"How about this, Ashley?" Mrs. Greco said, leaning in close. "You do this, or you lose your little wrestling classes."

"No!" Ash said. She felt that rage build up inside her again. She glanced at the vent.

"You think I want to drive out to the suburbs five days a week? You live in my house, you eat my food, you gotta pull your weight."

Over Mrs. Greco's shoulder, Ash saw Taylor in the doorway, sucking on the last of the ice cream bar, looking real smug. She turned and walked away, humming to herself.

"I didn't have to take you in. You need me. So, homework." Mrs.

Greco pointed at the stack of books. "Then bed."

She left, shutting the door. Ash smacked the textbooks off her desk. The girl rubbed her forehead and closed her eyes, running through the eight virtues. *Righteousness. Courage. Compassion.*

"It is not right, the way she treats you," the woman's voice said. "I can give you the power to fight her. Real power. No more 'home work.' No more sadness. That woman will never hurt you again."

"Who are you?" Ash looked up at the vent. "Are you real?"

"A samurai should not live here, like *this*. I offer you power and purpose. All you have to do is come closer."

Ash stood.

"Come closer, child."

Ash walked up to the vent. She peered inside. There was nothing in there.

"What—"

Poof! A cloud of green gas hit her in the face. It burned! She coughed, waving her hand in the smoke, stumbling back into her desk chair and knocking it over. As she rubbed her eyes, she saw the vent open briefly, then close. Nothing came out, but she heard the nothing skitter down the wall and across the floor behind her. There was a buzz inside her head, a high-pitched hum in her ears and fire inside her nose. She looked at her fists, where she'd rubbed her eyes. They were covered in green.

She tried to run, but she found that she couldn't move. Her arms dropped limply to her sides. She tried to scream, but she could only whisper. "H...Help..."

"Do not be afraid, little samurai," said the woman's voice, now below her. "All is as it should be. You are being reborn."

Ash felt something rub against her leg delicately, then wrap around it.

"Ascending to a higher plane of being." The creeping feeling went higher and higher, up Ash's back and onto her shoulder. "You will be strong. So strong. Your parents would be so proud of you."

Ash could see it reflected in the glass on the picture of her parents. A woman's head, with black eyes and sharp teeth and tendrils of hair quivering like insect legs. The hair wrapped around

Ash's neck.

"What do you want?" Ash whispered.

"For you to hold still."

The head snarled and bit down hard on the back of the girl's neck. Ash screamed.

犬

Ben and Toby trudged up the stairs to Ben's apartment. The light in the hallway flickered. The smoke detector beeped periodically, as it had been doing for a month. They stopped in front of Ben's place.

"You know, you could just stay with me if you want," Ben said, unlocking the door. "I got you a bed."

He opened the door. A red cushion sat at the foot of Ben's bed. It was on the smaller side of what Toby would need, but Ben had still had to save up for it. He gestured to it like *Eh? Right?*

Toby trotted two apartments down from Ben and scratched on the door. It opened.

"Toby!" said an elderly woman excitedly. "There you are! Let me fry you up some bacon."

The dog looked at Ben, then followed the elderly woman into her apartment. The door closed.

"I can make bacon," Ben muttered.

THREE.

Bailey the labradoodle dashed around a corner with Ben hurrying to keep up with her. What he had once assumed was puppy energy had turned out to be *Bailey* energy, which could never be extinguished at a mere walking pace. They ran every single morning, covering twice the distance Ben did with any other dog, but he was happy to do it, especially today.

Today was Bailey's last day.

She had been a puppy when Ben started, just after film school. Back then, her head was bigger than her entire torso, and her paws all flopped in different directions with each step. Ben had helped potty train her and had seen her grow out of two different collars. They'd grown up together, really, and now her owners were moving to Phoenix. It was going to be weird not seeing this dog every day.

Bailey stopped suddenly to sniff a tree, and Ben stumbled a few paces ahead of her. His phone buzzed, and he answered it.

"MADISON! DON'T DUNK YOUR BROTHER!" Children giggled and splashed in the background as Ben's boss, Mrs. McClanahan, spoke. "Ben, hi. Sorry. We've got the kiddie pool out. How's Bailey?"

"She's great." Ben knelt to pet the dog under her chin. "I'm gonna miss her."

"I bet. Listen, I've got a new one for you. A black lab. I already did the meet and greet. You just have to walk him…"

Ben gazed at the mailbox across the street. Up until recently, this was the corner where the blonde hipster girl would walk past, at the same time every day, and Ben would dream of their impending romance, formulating very elaborate plans for talking to her without having to walk over and actually do that. This was before he'd found out her name—Emily Gritz—and the fact that she was not, in reality, another dog walker, but the leader of a faux-Japanese death cult, spying on him in order to track down and ritually sacrifice one of the dogs on his route—Toby—so she and her followers could gain total control over one of the deadliest creatures in existence. Things had kind of gone downhill from there.

"...bad hips, so you have to go slow. You got all that?"

"Yeah," Ben said, blinking. "Bad hips. Got it."

"It'll be on PetDocs if you need a refresher. Good luck!"

She hung up. Windy City Waggers had converted to new software a few weeks ago, but Ben's dogs hadn't changed since before then, so he hadn't actually checked it out yet. He started to scroll through his emails to find the one with the login until he noticed Bailey staring at him. Her tail wagged, and she got in the play stance—front low, butt up. Ben slowly lowered his phone, maintaining eye contact.

"So that's how it is," he said.

He took off running, and Bailey followed, biting at her leash.

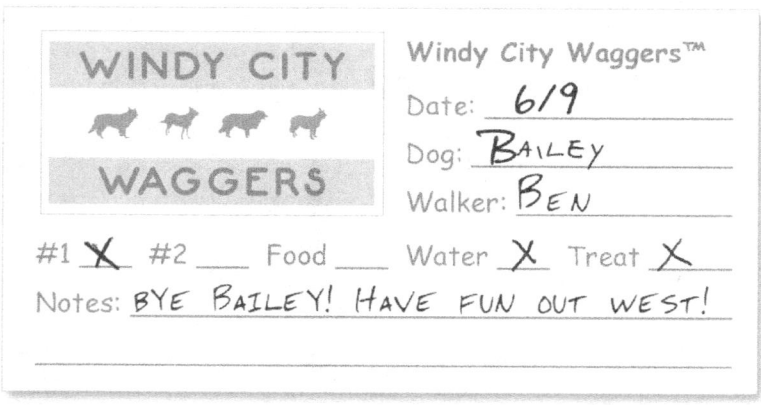

Fergie the greyhound barked furiously at a goose. The goose, which wore a yellow raincoat and matching floppy hat, was made of stone, so it didn't seem to mind.

Ben laughed. "I don't think it's a threat, Ferg."

The other greyhound, Stoney, drooled as he panted, standing at Ben's side. They were all the way around the block from the dogs' apartment. Ben had decided to go left instead of right at the corner to change up the walk a little, and Fergie was royally spooked by all the new sights and sounds. Stoney was his stoic, unflappable self, though he was slower than Ben would like. He was getting older. Ben had added ten minutes to his daily schedule to account for Stoney going up and down the stairs, and it was starting to look like he'd need more.

"C'mon, dogs," Ben said. "We gotta head back."

Fergie gave up on the goose and stepped forward. Stoney didn't.

"Stoney, come."

The old greyhound squatted to poop, smack in the middle of the sidewalk. He actually hadn't gone yet, which was unusual for a greyhound—especially this one. Ben whipped out a plastic bag and slipped it over his hand.

A liquid nightmare burst forth from the dog's bowels, a nameless and unknowable blasphemy against nature, an abomination, endless in its torment and destruction, the likes of which Ben had never seen and would not soon forget. It gurgled as it passed into this world. Ben and Fergie could only stare. When it was over, Stoney trotted past them and tugged the leash toward home. The loathsome puddle slowly expanded.

The dog walker frowned at the probably-insufficient bag on his hand and shoved it back in his pocket.

"Maybe it'll rain," he said.

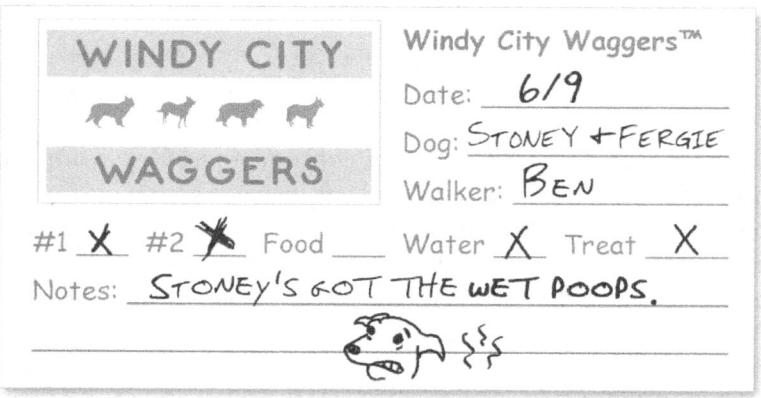

Libby the mini dachshund scampered down the sidewalk. She had just been to the groomers, where she'd had her nails clipped, her under-fluff trimmed, and her tail sculpted. She had pink bows on her ears and a bounce in her step. Three tough-looking biker dudes approached, heading for the dive bar on the corner. One of them glanced at Libby.

"She's, uhh...it's not my dog." Ben coughed, struggling to keep his voice deep. "They pay me."

The bikers ignored him, because contrary to Ben's suspicions, not everyone was silently judging him. Once they were out of sight, he knelt down to get a good picture of Libby. He and Kaylee had been sending each other cute dog pictures for the last couple of days. Hers were cuter, but she walked all the little fluffy ones. Ben usually got the big dogs with intestinal problems.

Libby sniffed the air. Ben lined up the perfect shot, backlighting the dog with the sun, mildly thrilled that he was finally using his film degree for something. Just as he was about to take the picture, he got a phone call.

Unknown Name, Unknown Number.

He hit Ignore. Libby realized he was down by her, and she padded over, wagging. Ben tried for a selfie, holding his phone up above them. Another call. The Dog Signal popped up on his phone.

"Ooh!"

Ben was excited to show off his new vehicle.

```
WINDY CITY       Windy City Waggers™
🐕 🐕 🐕         Date: 6/9
WAGGERS          Dog: LIBBY
                 Walker: BEN

#1 X  #2 ___  Food ___  Water X  Treat X
Notes: LOOKING GOOD, GIRL!
```

The brown Cadillac idled in the forest preserve parking lot. The park closed an hour ago, so it was the only car there. Cicadas chirped. Wind rustled through the trees. A lone squirrel picked up an acorn, sniffed it, ran away, then came back and sniffed it again.

Jake relaxed in the driver's seat, watching the squirrel while eating a hot dog. Sarah leaned in the passenger window from outside.

"Are you sure you don't want to come with?"

Jake looked at her, chewing. The high-pitched whirr of a small engine, like a fishing boat or a remote-control car, drew steadily closer. Jake glanced in the rearview mirror.

He rolled up Sarah's window.

An olive-green moped coasted into the lot and wobbled to a stop in front of Sarah. It had a big Windy City Waggers magnet on the front and a white plastic basket on the back. Toby sat in the basket, his paws clutching the corners for dear life. His eyes looked ready to pop out of his head.

"What do you think?" Ben asked, smiling like a kid on Christmas morning. He honked the horn. *Deet deet!*

"You bought a scooter," Sarah said.

"It's a moped! Isn't it great?" Ben hefted Toby out of the basket and onto the asphalt. The dog stumbled on shaky legs toward the nearest tree. "The guy downstairs sold it to me for two hundred bucks! I didn't get my motorcycle permit yet, though, so don't tell, uhh…you."

"I thought you were gonna buy a car."

"This is better than a car! It's got a basket for Toby and a perfect place above the engine to shove this." Ben yanked the Onislayer free, and it made a metallic screech as it scraped the scooter's frame.

Sarah rubbed her ear. "What are you gonna do when it rains?"

"Wear a coat?"

"What about when it gets cold?"

"Wear a *big* coat." Ben pointed at the Cadillac. "No Jake?"

"You…create a lot of paperwork," Sarah said, choosing her words carefully. "Especially last time. He's taking tonight off."

Ben nodded. "Are we going in the woods? Can I bring the moped?"

"Absolutely not."

犬

The forest was dark at night. The lights of the city faded behind the trees, and the constant drone of traffic was muffled to a soft hum. Toby zigzagged from tree to tree along the trail, sniffing each with great interest. Sarah clicked her flashlight on periodically. Ben poked a few suspicious branches with the Onislayer, but none of them caught fire.

"What are we looking for?" Ben said.

"The locals over in Sauganash are reporting missing pets and tipped-over garbage cans." Sarah lifted up a log with her boot. "It could be a coyote, but Animal Control thought the numbers were suspicious."

"Animal Control knows about us?"

"They know to call me when there's weird stuff." Sarah shrugged. "You remain strictly off the record, dog walker."

"Well, if it's a yōkai problem, we'll solve it, right, Tobe? Oh, sorry."

Ben turned away. Toby grunted at him, then lifted his leg again. Unlike most dogs, Toby refused to pee if someone was looking at him. Inugami were special dogs. Inugami knew shame. A branch cracked under Ben's foot, and he jumped.

"Are you okay?" Sarah said.

"Yeah." Ben shivered. "I used to ride bikes through here when I was a kid. My mom always said I had to be out of the forest preserve the moment it got dark, cause that's when the pervs come out and run around naked."

Sarah laughed. "What, like witches?"

"That's not a real thing?" Ben smiled. "Naked forest pervs?"

"I mean…depends on how your mom defines 'perv.'" Sarah paused long enough that Ben stopped smiling. "No. That's not a thing. You shouldn't be going into the forest at night, though. That's how every fairy tale starts. Big Bad Wolf's gonna get you."

"There's no wolves in Illinois."

Something rustled in the woods. Ben, Sarah, and Toby all froze.

Ten feet into the forest, a deer stepped into a beam of moonlight, sniffing at a big pile of mud and leaves. It was a male deer, a stag, antlers and everything. Ben had never seen one with antlers in the forest preserve.

TOBY EAT, Toby thought.

"No," Ben whispered.

"Is that a, uhm…a demon deer?" Sarah said.

The deer stopped sniffing and raised its head. Its ears darted around. The rest of it was completely still.

"There is one deer yōkai. The…*kirin*?" Ben said. "It appears when great rulers and heroes die. But I think it has scales."

"Well, maybe this one—"

The pile of leaves and mud exploded upward and engulfed the deer. The animal cried out briefly, a soft bleat, before its head was submerged. The leaves rustled, the mud undulated, and wet, slurping sounds echoed into the forest, broken sporadically by the crunching of bones. The muddy leaf pile flopped back to the ground, one deer bigger than before.

A beat passed.

"I don't think it's the deer," Ben said.

The leafy blob rushed toward them. Sarah and Toby dove to either side, and Ben raised the Onislayer defensively.

Slooch! Ben's weapon sank partway into the creature. The mud around it sizzled, but the cool wetness seemed to absorb most of the effects. It continued oozing around the Onislayer, then onto Ben's hands. The leaves quivered, vibrating audibly like a rattlesnake's rattle. Ben could smell rot and waste and deer flesh in the mud.

"Toby…" he whined. "Any day now…"

The Shiba Inu sprang forward and bit at the mud, then hacked out what was in his mouth, disgusted.

STINK MUD, Toby thought. *YUCK MUD.*

"Just kill it!" Ben shouted. The mud was up to his forearms.

A monstrous shadow emerged around Toby. Sharp tendrils of translucent black fur whipped up from his back. The tendrils all pointed at the mud pile, and he unleashed a flurry of quick stabs into the mud's surface. *Thip thip thip thip thip thip!* Leaves tore and broke away, fluttering to the ground. The mud rippled.

The creature retreated enough that Ben could free the Onislayer, then it began encroaching again. Toby took a step back, continuing his barrage of shadow spikes. He growled. Sarah didn't have a magic weapon, so she picked up a large branch and swung it at the thing. The mud pile absorbed the branch and grew slightly larger.

"We need room to maneuver," Sarah said, taking off into the forest.

Ben took a deep breath and chased after her. "Toby, come!"

Toby held out until the mud pile was almost upon him then zoomed after the humans. The moment he left, the mud rushed in and filled his space.

Ben looked back. The creature was following them. The way it moved was vaguely animalistic, but it wasn't so much running as lurching. It was like a walrus on land. Branches crunched, and the smaller trees fell in its path. Ben turned to watch where he was going just in time to see the tree he ran into.

He rolled out into the grassy field head first, pain throbbing in his chest and shoulder. A full moon glowed in the night sky, reflecting off the grass and the asphalt of the parking lot. It was almost like daytime. Sarah unclipped her gun from its holster and watched the trees. Toby stopped next to her, snorted, and re-extended his shadow form.

Nothing happened.

Ben sat up, spitting out grass and dirt. He reached around for the Onislayer and found it flat on the ground next to him. He turned to Sarah.

"Guess we must've scared it off."

Mud and leaves surged upward on either side of him and smashed together.

The dog walker was buried alive in thick, wet darkness.

FOUR.

An ear-splitting howl rang out through the field, rattling the trees. The blob creature shuddered, and a crack opened at its center. Ben's arm wriggled free from the mud, grasping desperately for anything to hold on to. Sarah holstered her gun, dropped to her knees, and grabbed Ben's hand. Toby's ears rotated this way and that, searching for the origin of the sound. He squinted.

Two more howls came, overlapping the first, vibrating at a dissonant frequency. It made Sarah feel queasy. She could feel it in her teeth. Toby growled. The blob retreated back into the trees as Sarah yanked Ben free.

The mud clung to Ben's clothes, hair, and skin. He spat out a soggy clump of gray before trying to stand, and then he dropped, crying out. His left tibia was poking out of his shin and his foot was facing the wrong direction. More howls.

Sarah let go of him and covered her ears. "What *is* that?" she shouted.

The howling stopped. Ben turned to Toby, who looked as confused as he and Sarah were.

NOT TOBY, Toby thought.

Out in the field, a tall man stepped up onto a grassy knoll, revealing himself. He wore a brown leather duster with beige fur on the collar and cuffs. He had a big black beard and longish hair flopping to one side. The sides of his head were shaved.

"Your mom was right," Sarah said. "Here come the pervs."

The man put two fingers to his lips. *Fweep!*

Three huge dogs trotted up next to him. They were gray, darker on their backs and lighter on their paws, like huskies. Their eyes glowed red. Shadow tentacles whipped around on their backs.

"Oh shit," Ben muttered. Toby's tail wagged briefly.

Fweep fweep! the man whistled.

The dogs bolted out across the field toward Ben and Sarah. The man followed casually with his hands in his pockets. Two of the dogs rushed past Ben and Sarah, straight into the woods. The third, the smallest one, stopped next to the humans. Upon closer inspection, this was no husky. It was the biggest dog Ben had ever seen, with jagged claws, long whiskers, piercing red eyes, and curved fangs poking out of its mouth.

"Wait. Is that a wolf?" Ben said. Sarah reached for her gun again.

Suddenly, the blob of mud and leaves burst from the trees, slithering across the grass and recoiling when it got close to the wolf. Shadow tentacles rose like cobras off the wolf's back and began stabbing at the blob in quick, staccato bursts, just like Toby had done earlier. The other two wolves emerged from the trees and did the same. *Thip thip thip thip thip!*

The creature was surrounded. Each time it chose a direction to flee in, it was met with snarling wolf jaws. The flurry of tentacles chipped away at the mud and leaves, and the blob began to shrink.

TOBY KILL, Toby thought, hobbling over on three legs. His left hind leg, like Ben's, was twisted 180 degrees. A shadow emerged from his fur, and he stabbed at the blob along with the wolves. *TOBY KILL. TOBY EAT.*

Sarah gripped Ben under the armpits and dragged him from the action. The man in the fur coat stopped next to them. He winked at Sarah.

"Keep it in the circle!" He gave three quick whistles. "Come on, now!"

The blob creature was shrinking. Most of the leaves were gone, and a bit of gray flesh had been exposed beneath the mud. Toby and the wolves advanced on it, increasing the pace of their attack. The shadow around Toby grew more opaque. Glowing red eyes opened on the shadow's head.

TOBY KILL. STINK MUD. TOBY KILL.

More and more mud flaked away. The creature thrashed and rolled. The skull of the deer it had eaten, one antler still attached, popped out and rolled up to Ben. He kicked it away with his good foot.

The blob flipped onto its back, revealing a flat gray fleshy surface like uncooked liver and a round mouth encircled with pointy teeth. From below, the creature looked like a leech, except four feet long and covered in foliage. The mouth hissed.

Fweep! the man whistled, and the wolves dove in, chowing down on the giant leech. The creature made one final lurch toward the trees, toward freedom, then went limp. The wolves ripped its flesh away in thick chunks, chewing, swallowing, their faces drenched in purple-black goo. Toby glanced at Ben, gauging his reaction, then also dug in. Ben could feel the leech's life force flowing into him, fixing his broken leg. A twinge of pain hit him in his shin.

"Sarah!" he said. "You gotta set my bone! It's healing wrong!"

Sarah nodded. She knelt down by his leg and held his shin with both hands.

"Hey, what's that?" She pointed off in the distance with her nose. The moment Ben looked, Sarah cracked his bone into place.

Ben screamed and fell back. He lay there, whimpering, and listened to the gruesome sounds of the wolves eating the big leech. He watched the leaves flutter in the trees above him. The pain faded. He sat up and wiggled his toes. All better. Toby put his back leg down. He was all healed up too.

"Your superpowers are disgusting," Sarah said.

She stood and helped him up. He instinctively went easy on his left leg, but it didn't really hurt. They both remembered the weird guy standing next to them. The man stroked his beard as he watched the wolves eat.

"Umm, excuse me." Sarah got into his line of sight. "Hi there. Who are you?"

The man reached into his coat and handed her a business card. "That your inugami?" He gestured to Toby, who was up on his hind paws, his entire head deep inside the leech carcass.

"Toby's with me." Ben picked up the Onislayer and brushed grass off of it. "Are those wolves?"

"As much as that's a dog." The man smiled. "Toby. Cool. May I?"

Before Ben could respond, the man approached the wolves feasting on the demon leech. Generally, when people asked Ben about the inugami, they tried to murder him soon after, so he followed close behind, Onislayer at the ready.

The man tore a piece of meat off the leech and held it in front of Toby, leading him away from the carcass. He put his hand up and whistled. Toby sat.

The man paused, then chucked the hunk of flesh straight up in the air. He clapped his hands together.

Voosh! A tentacle shot off Toby's back, spearing the piece of meat like a shish kebab. Toby guided it into his mouth and chewed.

"Good boy! You trained him well." The guy kneeled and pet Toby behind the ears. He offered his hand. "Lucas Alcindor."

"Ben Carter," Ben said, shaking it.

"That's Taka, Toshi, and Miya." Lucas pointed to the three wolves, one by one, ending on the largest. Toshi kept nudging Taka with his shoulder so he could get all the good meat. Miya looked up, burped, then continued gnawing on a hunk of fatty leech flesh. Two of the wolves swapped places, and Ben immediately lost track of which was which.

"I didn't know there were inugami wolves. Actually, I didn't know there were any other inugamis." Ben paused. "I have a lot of questions for you."

Sarah squinted at Lucas's business card one last time before handing it to Ben. "This says you're a professional demon hunter."

"That's right." Two of the wolves snarled at each other, fighting over a piece of skin. Lucas walked over and smacked one on the snout, getting between the two beasts. "Farmer hired me to find out what was picking away at his livestock. Thought his dead brother was haunting him, killing his cows as revenge for something they did as kids. You believe that?"

"I'm watching four immortal dogs eat a giant slug," Sarah said. "I believe lots of things."

Lucas smiled. "Doesn't mean *ghosts* are real. Anyway, I tracked this sucker all the way down here from McHenry. It's been feeding its way along the Metra tracks. Left behind a lot of animal bones. What's your story?"

"Pretty much the same thing," Ben said. "Well, kind of. Sarah's a cop. I'm, uhh, I help out for free. I'm pro bono."

He went to lean on the Onislayer in a cool, casual way and stumbled.

"Pro bono…" Lucas shrugged. "Your loss."

Toby and the wolves had more or less picked the dead leech clean. Toby walked in circles to keep the wolves from sniffing his butt. Apparently not taking part in your standard canine butt-sniffing was a Toby thing, not an inugami thing.

The wind picked up. Lucas looked in the direction of it. Sniffed. "Well, now you know me. You've got my card. Call next time you need help."

"We'll see," Sarah said with a tone that suggested they wouldn't.

"Yeah, man," Ben said with the opposite tone. "We can always use more people."

A pocket of air escaped from the dead leech with an audible fart sound, and the carcass deflated.

"Some kids are gonna step in that," Sarah said. "If you really want to help us, Mr. Alcindor, give Ben a hand with the—"

Lucas and the wolves were gone. Sarah sighed. Toby looked around, confused. Their exit had escaped even his notice.

"Nice." Ben laughed. "I do that too."

犬

Sunlight beamed in through the glass block windows and straight onto Ashley Ocampo's face. She groaned and turned away, opening her eyes. What time was it? She found her phone face down on the floor, barely within reach. Ten a.m. She didn't remember going to bed last night. Last thing she remembered, she was sitting at her desk, doing her homework, and then—

"Ten a.m.?!" Ash shot out of the bed, pulled on pants, and grabbed her backpack. She was late for school! She hopped around, pulling on a sock as she opened the door.

Cartoons blared on the TV across the hall. Taylor was sprawled out on the couch in the same spot she'd been last night.

"Why aren't you at school?" Ash said.

Taylor snorted. "It's Saturday, dingus."

"Saturday?" Ash tried to think. That couldn't be right.

"Nice job on my homework, by the way. The teacher said I'm showing a lot of improvement."

Ash rooted through her backpack and pulled out her math workbook. Everything was done, but the last few answers seemed…off. The handwriting was all scratchy.

"We've got a big essay due next week, so keep it up!" Taylor laughed, one loud honk, like a goose.

"Taylor, sweetie," Mrs. Greco said, storming into the room all frazzled. "I'll be home in forty minutes, there's Hot Pockets in the freezer if you're hungry. Ashley! God damn it! Are you even ready?"

Ash shivered. She felt like she was still asleep.

"Was I…" She had a throbbing pain in the back of her head, right where her skull met her neck. "Did I go out yesterday?"

"You went to school, you came home, you did your homework, and you went to bed. Barely said a word. I wish there were more days like that," Mrs. Greco muttered. "You wanna go to your class or not? Get your shit!"

Right! Lucha class. Ash had private lessons with Tatsuya-sensei on Saturday mornings. She turned to go back in her room and change into her—

The pain in Ash's head increased tenfold, and she clenched her teeth as she leaned against the doorframe. The throbbing turned to burning. Burning from the inside. Her brain felt like it was on fire. Ash whimpered, eyes shut, tears running down her face.

And just like that, it was over. The fire was gone. Ash opened her eyes. Taylor was staring at her.

"What's wrong with you?" the girl said.

Ash slammed her door.

犬

"Moonsault Double Foot Stomp!" Tatsuya-sensei shouted.

Ash did a backflip off the top rope, landing with her feet together on the mats. There wasn't enough room for an entire wrestling ring in Lucha Dojo, but Tatsuya had put together one corner so the kids could practice aerial moves.

"*Yosh!* Good! Keep your feet straight. You do not want to twist an ankle on the landing."

Ash smiled, bowed, and climbed back to the top of the corner piece.

"Let me think...Shooting Star Elbow Drop!"

Ash leapt off the rope, did a backflip in midair, and landed elbow-first on the mats. Had an opponent been lying where she landed, they would not have gotten up after that.

"Aha! Good! You are improving each day, niña!" He helped her to her feet. "I have seen professionals struggle to do these moves! Keep it up and you will be a real *luchadora!*"

"Sensei..." Ash said. She took a breath. "If Mrs. Greco said I couldn't come here anymore, would you still let me? Even if I had to sneak out to do it?"

Tatsuya grunted. "Have you done something wrong?"

"I didn't do anything! Mrs. Greco is..." Ash ran through a list of words in her head that weren't swear words. "She's just *mean*. Her real daughter doesn't have to do anything but sit on her fat butt and watch TV. I do all her homework and all the chores. And every time I have lucha training, Mrs. Greco acts like she's doing me a big favor. 'Oh you're so lucky I'm taking you to your class.' And every time she wants me to do something, she's like 'If you don't do this, you can't go to your class anymore.' Good parents don't do that. My parents didn't do that."

She perched herself on the ropes and looked down at her feet as she kicked the mat. "She doesn't care about me. I'm only there so she can have money."

Tatsuya nodded. He walked over to the mini fridge behind the counter. "When I was very young, I was forbidden from becoming a luchador."

He tossed Ash a Pocari Sweat. She caught it.

"My father did not approve. He was a serious man, and he thought wrestling was *kudaranai*. A waste of time. He wanted me to focus entirely on the family business."

Ash set her Sweat on the counter, unopened. "What was the family business?"

"Er…" Tatsuya glanced at Toby's empty dog bed. "Dog breeding. The local lucha league held a tournament. The men they had were getting old. They needed fresh blood. I had never fought, but I was big. I was always big. But I was a minor, and I knew my father would never sign off on it. I was a good man. I could not disobey him, unless…I became *more* than a man."

Ash's eyes lit up. "A samurai."

"No." Tatsuya clicked on the light above the glass case containing his luchador mask. The smoke from the burning incense around it glowed in the lamp light. "A dragon."

He cracked open another Sweat and chugged it in one go. He tossed the bottle into the garbage, then leapt over the counter and onto the mat, right in front of Ash.

"*Mascara de Dragón contra, El Diablo Guapo! Duk duk duk!*" The sensei punched the air in rapid succession, making punching sounds with his mouth. "*K.O.! Fuera de combate!*"

He spun, bowing and accepting praise from an invisible crowd. "*Mascara de Dragón contra Super Juan!*"

Tatsuya grabbed his own bicep and struggled against it as though he were wrestling himself. Ash snorted.

"*El Oso Grande! Mil Mendosa! Angelo Atomico!*" Tatsuya rolled, kicked the air, and flipped to his feet, fighting a mock battle against multiple opponents.

"Did you win the tournament?" Ash said.

"Ha!" Tatsuya took his hands off his neck and stopped choking himself. "No. I had never wrestled. I lost my only match very badly. And then, I went to the next event three months later. I had the warrior's spirit, niña. You have it too. You will fight. Regardless of where you are and who you are with. No one could stop you. Not your foster mother. Not me. You *will* fight. What matters is what you are fighting for. The way of the warrior."

"Bushidō," Ash said quietly.

"That said..." Tatsuya knelt in front of Ash and put his hand on her shoulder. "You are always welcome in my dojo. Always."

Ash nodded. She pointed at the clock. "Two thirty. Big Ben coming soon?"

"Big Ben canceled his lessons for today. He has a date."

Ash made a face. "Gross."

"Yes," Tatsuya said solemnly. "It is gross."

FIVE.

Waves lapped the shore next to the beachfront restaurant patio where Ben and Kaylee sat. Theirs was the only occupied table. Kaylee was talking, but Ben wasn't really listening. He tugged at the collar of his shirt. He didn't wear shirts with collars that often, didn't need to, and it was rubbing against his freshly shaved neck something awful. He was deeply uncomfortable, partially because he was on a date for the first time in months, but mostly because of the three-story chicken carcass rotting half submerged in the lake behind him.

A hunk of spoiled meat the size of a small horse peeled away from the bone and plunged into the sea. Ben winced as cold water—invisible to Kaylee—splashed him in the back and ran down his shirt.

"Are you okay?" Kaylee asked. She'd ditched her dog walking gear and gotten dressed up too—short floral-print dress, makeup. She looked good.

"Yeah, I, uhh...." Ben dried his back on the back of his chair as casually as possible. "Sorry. I'm sorry. You were talking about stand-up?"

The stench of the giant chicken carcass stretched a couple miles past its actual location, blanketing most of the northeast side of the city—and parts of the suburbs—in a distinct funk that only a select few could smell. Sarah called it the Poultry Zone. Ben tried to stay out of it when he could, but when Kaylee had suggested a restaurant twenty feet from ground zero, he had struggled to come up with rational excuses. So he got there early, acclimated himself as best he could, and threw up into the lake before his date arrived.

"The stand-up scene in Chicago isn't what I thought it would be. It's an improv town, you know?" Kaylee paused. Ben nodded. "You can only do the same three or four open mics so many times before it starts to feel like you're spinning your wheels. I'm thinking of moving to LA? I have a friend who hosts this show in the back of a diner. The podcast got up to number ten on iTunes. I should get in on that."

"I always wanted to do that." Ben took a quick, filtered breath through his shirt and forced himself to act like a normal person for thirty goddamn seconds. "Move to LA, I mean. Not podcast."

"You're like a screenwriter, right? That was the only thing you ever talked about when I first started."

"Yeah. No," Ben said. "Not really. I don't know. I haven't written anything since college, and everything I wrote then was just combinations of other movies. Nerd shit mixed with other nerd shit."

Kaylee shrugged. "I like nerd shit."

"Yeah, but I didn't have anything to *say*, you know? Every time I sat down to write after graduation I just...blanked. Nothing. For years. I think maybe I like the idea of being *A Writer* more than I like writing." Another smaller piece of meat splashed down into the water. "Anyway, I'm busy."

"There's this thing in stand-up..." Kaylee unconsciously wiped water off the table with her hand. "...where when you first start out, you go up there and bomb, night after night, every single time you do it, and you don't even realize it because you're new and you're oblivious. But eventually, with enough practice, you hit a point where you're smart enough that you know you're terrible, but you're still not smart enough to fix it. And that's when most people quit."

"What about the people who don't quit?"

"They're not quitters, Ben."

Ben looked at her, forgetting for the first time about the rotting chicken. She smiled. She had a terrific smile. He'd never noticed.

"This is a great first date," Ben said. Kaylee laughed. "Exposing all my anxieties and such. You wanna get together next weekend, really dig into each other's physical flaws?"

"I don't have any physical flaws," she said. "Your nose is a little crooked."

"I get hit in the face a lot."

"I'm not surprised. What do you *do* at night?"

"What do you mean?"

"Well, you said you're not writing." Kaylee leaned in closer to Ben. "And every time we meet up to exchange keys, you act all tired and surly. And it turns out you get hit in the face a lot, which is a thing you just said out loud that we haven't actually addressed yet."

Ben was never sure how much he should tell people. His work was mostly off the record, and "I kill demons for the police" was more of a third-date revelation.

"Wait, so you think I'm kind of a jerk…"

"That's accurate," Kaylee said, nodding.

"But you asked me out."

"I guess I like jerks." She thought about that for a moment. "*That* doesn't bode well for the future."

"This is going in your stand-up set, isn't it?"

"I barely have to change anything. Have we ordered drinks?"

"I'm not even sure this place is open." Ben leaned back to peer into the window. It was dark inside the restaurant. "Are you super into seafood?"

"It just seemed like a date place. I'm gonna go investigate the situation and also pee. Try not to get hit in the face while I'm gone."

She smiled as she left. Ben sighed, unbuttoning the top button on his shirt. Kaylee was very cool, and he was totally blowing this. He glanced up at the gargantuan pile of decomposing meat and bones half drowned in Lake Michigan…

犬

The dog walker clawed his way up from one three-foot feather to the next, finally reaching a point on the enormous, rampaging chicken where he could stand upright. Apartment buildings and the tops of trees whooshed past on either side of him. Ahead, a spinning pillar of flame, a fire tornado, swirled around the spot where the chicken's head ought to be.

Ben took a breath and closed his eyes. An image formed in his mind of the streets below, black and white with a green tint, blurry, always moving. The chicken's taloned foot smashed into the asphalt, crushing a newspaper box and a stop sign in the process. The inugami, in its full monster form, dodged the wreckage and continued its chase. Rough panting echoed around Ben's head. The inugami's thoughts were simple, primal. *EAT BIRD. EAT BIRD.*

Backlit by the pillar of fire, facing away from Ben, a nude humanlike creature crouched in the plumage. Ben drew the Onislayer, which he had tucked painfully between his shirt and his back, and trudged carefully toward the figure. The giant chicken swayed with each step. Wind rushed all around. Ben clutched a handful of feathers with his free hand at all times. He was close now. He could feel the heat from the chicken's flaming head.

The creature before him was a butt-centric mockery of a human. Every part of its body above the waist was tiny, shriveled up like a raisin, and drooping limply to one side. The creature's legs were bent the wrong way at the knees, and it was searching the distance intently with the single eye at the center of its anus. It hadn't seen him. Ben raised his weapon, ready to strike.

Fire whipped through the air, and Ben staggered back. The eyebutt had a burning feather clutched like a sword in its tiny, atrophied hand.

"*Baka na gaijin!*" the shirime said. "Stab me in the back? Humans are truly shameful!"

It speared its feathersword at Ben, who barely blocked the attack. The feather was grown by a demon, and it burned brighter on contact with the Onislayer. Something crunched beneath them, and the two warriors separated, stumbling back to regain their footing. The chicken must've stepped on a car or something.

"Send this thing back to hell before anyone else gets hurt!" Ben shouted.

The mouthless creature laughed somehow. "This is only the beginning, inugami boy! You brought back the dog! You have defied fate! The door has been opened, and it will not easily be closed!"

The shirime lunged for Ben, its large glistening eye squinting in anger. Ben dove to the side, almost losing his balance and rolling right off the chicken. The feathersword was already coming at him again. Ben blocked it, shoved it away, and swung the Onislayer, which the creature dodged with ease. It was a butt with legs, but it knew how to swordfight. Ben had never touched a sword before yesterday.

"A price must be paid!" said the eyebutt, swinging wildly. Ben blocked as best he could. "I will be free when I take it from your flesh!"

The butt creature did a quick thrust forward and dodged Ben's weak counterattack. It hooked one of the spikes on the Onislayer with its blade and whipped the weapon out of Ben's hand. The Onislayer tumbled through the air before landing in a tree, which quickly vanished into the distance behind them.

The tip of the feathersword poked at Ben's chest. The eye at the center of that butt seemed to smile.

"You can't kill me," Ben said.

Pain speared through Ben's ribs. His shirt was on fire, but he felt cold and wet. He tried to breathe, but he could only drool out the blood that had filled his mouth.

"Even the kakawari has limits, gaijin," said the talking butt, removing its sword from Ben's torso. The dog walker fell to his knees, and the eyebutt placed the burning feather against his neck. "That dog can protect you from much, but I doubt it can grow you a new—"

The giant chicken stopped suddenly and swayed forward. The eyebutt tumbled over Ben's shoulders and into the swirling pillar of fire. The creature screamed, rolling in the feathers to douse the flames. Beyond the screams, Ben heard waves. He tried to mentally contact Toby, but he always found it hard to concentrate while dying.

"*Baka na niwatori!*" the eyebutt shouted, half of its buttface smoking. "The lake! Be careful! If you fall in the water—!"

In Ben's mind, he had a vision of sharp black claws slashing at the chicken's leg. He heard a deep, sinister howl in the distance. The inugami had done its part. The avian leviathan tipped forward.

As he fell with the chicken, Ben started losing consciousness, but he had enough time to see the inugami leap off the side of an office building. Cool black tentacles of fur wrapped around Ben's torso and yanked him away just as he was about to roll into the fire.

The giant chicken plunged into the drink, its flaming head steaming like an underwater volcano. Moments later, Ben and Toby followed it.

"Hey! Space case!"

Kaylee snapped her fingers. Ben blinked.

"Is that your moped in the lot?" Kaylee grabbed her sweater off the back of her chair. "I've always wanted to ride one of those."

Ben smiled.

犬

They sat in the grass together, leaning against the side of the moped, eating takeout burritos. The Blues Brothers danced on a big projection screen at the other end of the public park. It was after ten and getting cooler out. Most of the people who'd come out for the movie had gone home. Beans and rice spilled out from Kaylee's burrito and onto her lap.

"Ugh," she muttered. "Get it together, Kaylee."

Ben laughed. "Do you talk to yourself a lot?"

Kaylee pulled a spare poop bag from her sweater pocket and used it to pick the beans off her dress. "I never used to."

"I think it's from being alone with dogs all day. You get in the habit of saying whatever pops in your head and not expecting a response."

"Oh God, yeah. You should hear some of the things I say to those dogs. Do you ever sing to them?"

Ben took a suspiciously long time to respond. "I do not."

She put the rest of her burrito in the poop bag, tied it shut, and tossed it underhand toward a nearby trash can, missing it completely. Ben smooshed his garbage into a ball, lobbed it, and also missed.

"I like you back," Ben said. "For the record."

Kaylee scooched down and rested her head on his shoulder.

"Good," she said.

犬

Ashley Ocampo stood at the bathroom sink, brushing her teeth. The dull, painful itch at the back of her head refused to go away, but something kept her from scratching it. She couldn't explain it. Something deep inside wouldn't let her touch her head. Every time she started to, the pain would fade and her mind would wander. Even now as she stood there, alone, her brain kept blinking to other topics.

Her hair moved.

She raised her hand, then stopped. It was getting pretty late. She should finish brushing her teeth before—

"No," Ash said. She thought of her Bushidō. *Self-control.* She had to control herself. She had to focus.

She raised her hand to the back of her head and ran it upward along her neck. Every instinct urged her to stop, to do anything else, but she pressed on. She had to know. She reached her hairline, went a little further, then...

The toothbrush dropped from her mouth and clinked into the sink.

She felt lips.

She felt teeth.

Ash's own hair whipped forward and wrapped around her face, holding her jaw shut and stifling her scream.

"Shh..." said the mouth in the back of Ash's head. "All is as it should be."

SIX.

Detectives Bolland and Martinez waited outside of the St. Roch's Catholic School gymnasium. It was Sunday afternoon. The last of the elderly parishioners was chatting up the priest outside the church across the street. The priest had his keys out, ready to lock the doors the moment the old lady finally went home.

"All these stupid missions..." Jake bounced a stray dodgeball off the brick wall. "It took me eight years to make detective. All I ever wanted to do when I was a kid, you know? Solve crimes, bust crooks, keep the streets safe."

"Me too," Sarah said, half listening while deleting emails on her phone.

"This is a waste of our time. I became a detective to do detective work."

"We're helping people."

"Are we? Martinez, look"—Jake caught the ball and walked over to Sarah—"you're a good cop. You're my partner. Our dads worked together back in the day. I try to give you the benefit of the doubt."

Sarah looked up from her phone. "What're you getting at?"

Jake sighed, trying to think of the right way to put it. "Every time you bring in your friend to fight invisible demons with his magic dog, I respect your judgment a little less."

A moped buzzed across the school parking lot, wobbling unsteadily around parked cars. Ben waved to them. Sarah waved back.

"They're only invisible to you, Jake," she said.

A big brown van right out of the 1970s followed Ben around the corner. The van had an elaborate mural painted across the right side, depicting three wolves running through snow under a full moon. It was really ugly. Sarah frowned.

Ben rolled up to the curb and kicked out his kickstand, and the van slid up behind him. Lucas stepped out, and his fur-lined leather duster swayed dramatically. He strutted to the back of the van and popped the rear door open. Three wolves—identical to the ones painted on the van—lined up along the sidewalk in front of their portraits.

"Officers." Lucas greeted the two cops with a slight bow.

"This is...different," Jake said.

Lucas palmed a few treats and popped one into each of the wolves' mouths. Jake went over to him, keeping his distance from the wolves, who watched him with dark eyes as they chewed.

Ben hoisted Toby out of his basket and onto the concrete. The dog shook and stretched. Sarah grabbed Ben by the shirt and pulled him in close.

"You brought the *wolf guy*?" she whispered.

"Lucas is cool," Ben said. "We've been texting back and forth. He knows a lot about yōkai. He can help us."

"We can't trust him."

"Why not? If he wanted to kill me, he had a pretty good opportunity at the forest preserve."

"Yeah, that's not what I meant, Ben." Sarah rolled her eyes. "There's a wide range between best friend and murderer, and I think he's—"

"Hey, Sarah?" Jake backed away from the wolves as they stood and approached him. "Can I, uhh, can I talk to you for a second?"

"Go get coffee," Ben said. "We'll get rid of the thing before you guys get back. What is it, anyway?"

Lucas sniffed the air, just like he did at the forest preserve. He plucked the dodgeball out of Jake's hands and held it in front of the wolves, who sniffed it intently. The priest walked past, did a double take when he saw the wolves, then kept walking a little more quickly.

"It's a foot with a face," Sarah said. She didn't look happy about it.

"Roger that."

Ben jerked the Onislayer free from the moped's frame with a loud screech.

犬

It took the two inugami owners a minute to find the light switches in the dark gymnasium. Ben slid his hand along the wall. He'd hated gym class as a kid—he hadn't been inside a gym in years—and being in one that was essentially *haunted* was doubly unsettling. His fingers brushed across a few bits of plastic. There were six switches, and Ben didn't know which was which, so he just flipped them all. The lights all clicked on.

Something gasped.

All the way on the far side of the room, atop a pile of ripped-up gym mats, stood a severed human leg. A tuft of light-brown hair grew from the top, where the knee would be. On the front of the shin, a humanoid face with a single large eye and a bulbous nose. The leg flared its nostrils. Gym mat stuffing dribbled from its mouth.

The creature shrieked and bolted. Lucas whistled, and the wolves chased after it. Toby ran with them. Ben went to follow, Onislayer held above his head, but Lucas stopped him.

"Let 'em run," the man said. "The dogs need the exercise."

The sentient foot hopped like a bunny around the edge of the gym, circling it. The wolves and Toby trailed behind. Toby raced out ahead of the wolves, his tongue bobbing out the side of his mouth. The foot bounced past the humans and briefly made eye contact with Ben.

"*Tasukete!*" said the foot. "Aieee!"

It tried to hop out the door, but the wolves boxed it in and herded it along the wall, back toward the mats.

"I hate the ones that look like rearranged human body parts," Ben said, lowering his weapon. "It's an uncanny valley thing. I don't like looking at them."

Lucas grunted. "You ever meet an old man with an eyeball in his ass?"

"A *shirime*? Yeah, dude, he's basically my arch nemesis. This one time—"

Toby barked. The windows rattled. A shadow started to form around him, tentacles whipping off his back. The foot with a face squealed in terror.

"*Ie!*" said the foot. "*W-Warui inu!*"

"Toby!" Ben closed his eyes and held his pointer fingers to his temples. Toby slowed down a bit, and the shadow around him faded.

"You in his head right now?" Lucas rubbed his chin. "That kakawari shit is insane. I don't do it like that."

"You're not bonded to them?"

"Only the old-fashioned way. I tried with the first one, Miya, but neither of us took to it. You actually can't do it with three inugami at once. That much conflicting sensory information would blow your brains out."

Ben nodded. "Where'd you get three inugamis, anyway?"

"Back in the day, I was teaching English in Japan, down in Kunisaki." Lucas made a Japan shape with his hand and pointed at the bottom of his palm. "I was hiking up near Futagoji Temple, alone, and I slipped on some loose rubble and broke my ankle. Miya found me and led me to safety. If it wasn't for that wolf, I would've died up in those mountains."

The wolves and Toby had their fur tentacles out, poking at the terrified foot sporadically but not hurting it, just taunting it. There was a cruelty to the act that Ben didn't like, regardless of how the foot creature looked.

"A couple years later, an old Buddhist monk saw me in town with Miya and offered his wolf to me. He wanted to make sure someone could take care of Taka when he died. Toshi, I didn't get until I was back in the states. Dental hygienist in Ohio found me on the internet. She wanted to go straight and get married. There aren't shelters for inugami, you know? If you ever want to give them up, you have to find someone. What about you? How'd you and Toby get hooked up?"

Ben went through the basics. Tatsuya's family had watched over the inugami for several generations, until the night when Emily Gritz's Tengu cult tried to sacrifice Toby. The old luchador was unavailable due to a decades-long drunken stupor, which led the inugami to bond himself to his dog walker, Ben, for protection. The cult chased them around for a while until Gritz finally managed to sever the kakawari and kill the dog. Ben then entered the Land of the Dead to bring Toby back, and succeeded, freeing a whole bunch of yōkai from Hell in the process. Ben skipped that last part in his recap.

"Now we fight yōkai crime," he said. "Kind of like Sherlock Holmes but mostly like Batman."

"Here's what I don't get," Lucas said, lighting a cigarette. "The cops find the yōkai, the old wrestler man tells you everything you need to know about the yōkai, and then Toby eats the yōkai. Right?"

"Right."

"So what do you do?"

"Me? Lots of things. I've got the Onislayer. Demons burn at its touch." Ben held up his weapon. "And with the kakawari, Toby can't be hurt unless *I'm* hurt, so I make him virtually indestructible. Also I drive him around." He coughed. "You shouldn't smoke in here. This is a grade school."

Lucas took a long drag. Smoke poured from his nose. "So, you're in there swinging the magic paddle around..."

"It's really more of a sword," Ben said.

"Aren't you getting injured a lot?"

"Yeah, constantly. I got my hand cut off a few days ago."

"And those wounds transfer to Toby. So how is it better to have you in there, actively involved, than if you stayed out of it? You have a mental link with him. You could do your whole part from the parking lot, and he wouldn't be virtually indestructible, he'd be *completely* indestructible."

"I..." Ben didn't have an answer. He put the Onislayer down.

The foot was slowing down. The face on its shin was panting. The wolves weren't playing with it anymore and were actually hanging back, trotting along, looking kind of bored. Toby, on the other hand, was in full beast mode, big and black and bear-shaped, his eyes glowing red. He didn't cut loose very often. The chase had riled him up.

"Toby!" Ben shouted. "Cool your jets!"

Lucas whistled. One of the wolves separated from the pack and trotted over to the two men. A shadow tentacle emerged from its back, swung over to a nearby window, and slid it open. Lucas flicked his cigarette butt outside, and the wolf closed the window and rejoined the others.

"I wouldn't normally do this, but…I can train you and Toby," Lucas said. "I can make you integral to the operation."

"Uhh…" Ben laughed nervously. "No thanks. Tatsuya's already training me."

"I'm sure Tatsuya's great, but he's had one inugami. I have three. I know how to handle an inugami. You've gotta be the alpha dog."

"Alpha dog. With him?" Ben pointed at Toby, who was currently five feet tall and twice as long, his long white fangs curving out of his jaws.

"Show the animal its place. You are the leader of his pack. You can't be in there swinging your paddle around. You have to stand back and supervise. Watch."

Lucas whistled again. The three wolves sped up, zooming past Toby and pouncing on the foot. The foot made one last futile hop toward the door, but strong lupine paws pulled the creature back into the pile. The sentient appendage screamed.

"These are killing machines," Lucas said. "They are literally *made* for murder. You shouldn't need your own weapon."

Toby charged past the foot and the wolves. His eyes were blank. He wasn't focused on the foot anymore. The rage had taken him. The door opened behind Ben and Lucas, and Jake stepped into the gym holding a large coffee.

"Are you weirdos almost d—"

Toby leapt on him, claws out, snarling. Jake's coffee exploded onto his shirt as he fell back.

"No! Toby! No!" Ben stepped toward them but was swatted away by flailing tentacles.

"Jesus!" Jake shouted. The inugami roared in his face, teeth bared. Jake tried to crawl backward, but the beast kept him pinned. "Get him off of me!"

Lucas stepped forward, dodging tentacles, and pulled a small metal tube from the inside pocket of his duster. He placed it to his lips and blew. There was no sound, but the wolves all looked up. The foot, still alive, whimpered. Lucas reached down and grabbed the raging inugami by the scruff of his neck, giving him a quick tug. Toby blinked and backed away from Jake, shaking his head.

The cop scrambled to his feet, dripping with coffee. He pointed at Ben. "Control your mutt, Carter!"

Sarah entered, carrying three coffees, just as Jake stormed out. To him, it had simply been a small orange dog jumping on him. As angry as he was, he had no idea how much danger he had been in.

The beast sat, staring at Lucas and his dog whistle, head tilted to the side. Lucas stepped toward him and gently placed his hand in front of the beast's face, an inch from his snout. The giant black inugami form slowly faded until only the Shiba Inu remained.

"What the hell just happened?" Sarah looked past Toby and saw the wolves tearing the foot to shreds. It let out one final pained shriek. Both she and Ben winced at this. Lucas did not.

"This one mine?" He took one of the coffees from Sarah and sipped it as he pulled out his phone. "Tomorrow morning. Meet me at this address."

He sent a text. Ben's phone buzzed.

"I'll teach you the most important lesson you'll ever learn."

犬

Ash sat at her desk, trying to focus on her spelling homework. She had a mouth on the back of her head. A *talking* mouth. Last night, when she'd tried to show Mrs. Greco, her foster mother had been unable to see it, and Ash had been unable to describe it. When she tried, her thoughts got all jumbled and her words came out slurred. Her foster mother assumed she was faking sick to get out of school, something Ash had never even considered.

Tatsuya-sensei could help her. He would know what to do. She just had to make it to tomorrow night.

"I will free you," said the mouth on the back of Ash's head.

Ash stopped writing. She closed her eyes. "You're not real."

"All I need is your permission. Can't you see, young samurai? You are changed. You have power now. You don't need to stay here."

"You're. Not. Real," Ash said, continuing to write in her notebook. A strand of her hair reached down and plucked the pencil from her hand.

"You keep saying that," said the mouth. "You are wasting time."

Just then, Mrs. Greco burst in the door holding a history textbook and a laptop. She dropped them both on Ash's desk. The picture of Ash's parents wobbled, and the girl reached out and caught it right before it fell.

"Taylor's got an essay due tomorrow," Mrs. Greco said, yawning. "Three pages. Civil War or something. It'll say in the book."

"What?" Ash noticed the pencil in her hair and grabbed it, brushing her hair down as casually as possible. "No."

"Ashley, I can either stand over her all night while we stare at a blank screen, or you can bang it out in an hour, and we can all move on with our lives."

"No, I'm not..." Ash's head burned. "I already do her math homework. I make her breakfast. I do her laundry. I'm sick of this shit."

Mrs. Greco raised an eyebrow. "What did you just say?"

"You're not my mom!" Ash stood up. "And I'm not writing Taylor's fucking essay!"

A beat passed. Mrs. Greco squinted at her. In the other room, the TV blared. Taylor laughed at a commercial.

"I feed you," Mrs. Greco said. She took a step toward Ash, who took a step back. "I clothe you. I let you live in my home. All out of the kindness of my heart. And this is how you thank me?"

"Y-you can't make me—"

"I can make you do anything!" Mrs. Greco shouted. "I own this house. You belong to me. You think your life is so hard? I could make it *so* much worse."

Ash tried to rush past her, out of the room. Mrs. Greco grabbed her by the shoulders and slammed her back into her chair.

"I've been too easy on you. That's the problem here." The woman took a breath and then nodded. "You're spoiled. No more phone. No more TV. No more wrestling class."

"No!" Ash said.

"You are grounded indefinitely. You go to school, you come home, you do homework, and you go to bed," Mrs. Greco said. "Or, I can call the city and tell them you're acting out. I think you might be dangerous! Do you know how she *spoke* to me? They'll put you back in that group home. Do you really want that?"

Ash stayed silent. The blood rushed to her ears. She felt hot. Her head buzzed.

"Good. Essay." Mrs. Greco pointed at the laptop and walked toward the door. "Let me know when you're done."

She stepped out into the hall and slammed the door behind her. The picture of Ash's parents slapped down onto her desk, louder than usual. Ash picked it up. Broken glass spilled out of the frame. Her mom's face had a big scratch in it.

"I can end this," said the mouth.

"Do it," said Ash.

Her neck cracked, and her head tilted at an odd angle, facing her left shoulder. Another crack, and her head twisted all the way around, a full 180 degrees. The mouth, now in front, smiled. Several strands of Ash's hair stretched out and gripped different parts of the room.

Ash's body rose off the floor.

The door to Ash's room tore from its hinges and crashed into the TV room, landing mere inches from Taylor, who was sprawled out across the couch. The girl yawned.

The creature that once was Ashley Ocampo emerged from the dark bedroom, its hair propping it up like spider legs, its small human body dangling limply at the center. Two cats bolted from the room, howling.

"Mo-ooom..." Taylor said without looking up from her phone, "Ash left her room."

Mrs. Greco stepped out of the bathroom, her hair wet, her makeup smeared. One of the prehensile hair strands shot forward and wrapped around her wrist.

"Damn it, Ashley!" Mrs. Greco said, unsure why she couldn't

move her arm. She saw Ash standing in the TV room, looking normal, if a bit creepy. "What did I just—"

The creature darted forward and wrapped all of its hair limbs around the woman. The girl's hair spiraled and tightened like an anaconda around the woman's neck, torso, and limbs. Taylor looked up from her phone for the first time and saw Ash standing near Mrs. Greco, arms outstretched.

"Dork." She rolled her eyes and changed the channel on the TV.

The tendrils of hair squeezed around the woman, ever tightening. Mrs. Greco gasped. Blood dripped from her lips.

"A...Ashley..." she gurgled. Dark red pooled in the whites of her eyes as they grew wide in horror. "Ash...ley..."

The mouth smiled.

SEVEN.

The sun was beginning to rise as Ben pulled to a stop outside the dilapidated old barn. Purple and orange light cascaded out over cornfields that stretched to the horizon in either direction. Ben checked his phone again to make sure this was the right place.

"Hello?" he said.

No one answered. Ben yawned and helped Toby out of his basket. He cracked open the Red Bull he'd bought at the last gas station. Toby sniffed around on the grass.

There was a *thunk* inside the barn, and the big wooden door swung open. Three wolves pranced out, followed by Lucas Alcindor. He nodded to Ben.

"Little early for you?"

"So early that I just stayed up all night."

Ben chugged his energy drink in one go. The wolves circled Toby, and he wagged his tail, letting the bigger animals sniff his butt, then he sniffed theirs. He was getting more comfortable around them.

"There's too much nature out here," he said. "Are we still in Illinois?"

Ben's moped had a top speed of about forty-five miles per hour—forty if he had Toby in the back—and it had taken him three hours to drive out to Lucas's barn, hugging the shoulder the whole way as cars and trucks flew past. He'd had to stop for gas four times. A mosquito buzzed near Ben's ear. He swatted at it.

"Stay right there," Lucas said. "I wanna show you something."

Lucas whistled, and the wolves came running. They headed back into the barn.

Ben leaned against his moped, pulled out a Slim Jim, and took a bite. Toby trotted over and sat in front of him, so Ben ripped off a small piece and tossed it. Toby caught it in his mouth.

"Hey." Ben knelt and pet the dog. "You haven't said anything in my head in a while. Are we cool?"

The inugami did not respond, in either body language or mental link. Ben ripped off another piece of Slim Jim. Maybe some old-fashioned bribery would change his attitude.

Something mooed. Ben and Toby looked at each other.

"Did you just moo?" Ben said.

Lucas stomped out of the barn, dragging a dairy cow into the light. The animal was mostly white, splattered with a few big brown splotches, including one over its left eye. The wolves circled it, nipping at its heels, herding it out of the barn toward Ben and Toby. The cow seemed understandably nervous about that.

"Is that a cow?" Ben had never seen one up close like this. They looked a lot smaller from the highway. "Where'd you get a cow?"

"I bought it." Lucas stopped about ten feet from Ben and Toby. He pulled a pile of leather and steel from the inside pocket of his coat and tossed it to Ben.

"You can buy cows?"

"Have you *ever* left the city? Put that on Toby."

Ben unfolded the device in his hands. It was a dog harness, but the kind you'd see on a one-eyed pit bull in a *Mad Max* movie. The leather straps were chained and bolted together. The leash was a metal chain. Ben fastened it all onto Toby, much to the inugami's chagrin.

"All right. This"—Lucas held up a small metal bottle with a spray nozzle on top—"is the poison from a *nigawarai*'s claws. Inugami can't get enough of the stuff. It's inugami catnip. When Toby smells it, he's gonna lose his mind, but you're going to keep him from eating this cow. Okay?"

"Sure, but he won't do that," Ben said. "Toby's not just gonna go rip into a live animal. He's a city inugami. He eats hot dogs and stuff. See?"

Ben held the piece of Slim Jim next to Toby's snout. The dog ignored it and stepped closer to the cow. There was a red glow in Toby's eyes.

MEAT, Toby thought.

"What do you think a hot dog is, Ben?" Lucas said, patting the side of the cow. The cow mooed again. "Pure beef franks! You ready?"

"Uhh..." Ben dropped the Slim Jim and gripped the leash with both hands. He planted his feet in a good, stable luchador stance. "What about the wolves?"

"They know who the alpha is." Lucas smiled. "It's him I'm worried about. You gotta show him who's the leader of your pack. Be calm. Be strong. Use that mental link. He goes for the cow, you give him a yank on that collar."

"Okay. You know that when he gets mad, he turns into a giant wolf-bear with tentacles for fur, right?"

Lucas let go of the cow's rope, and the wolves circled the animal, keeping it where it was as the man paced over to Toby. He covered his face with his sleeve, took a deep breath, and spritzed the catnip onto Toby's snout. In an instant, the dog shifted into its full inugami form, jet black and monstrous, fangs bared, snarling. The beast barked at the cow, which backed away. The wolves circled it, emotionless.

"Talk him down," Lucas said.

"Toby! Stop! Come on!" Ben said. He switched to thinking. *Toby! Stay calm!*

KILL, thought the inugami.

The inugami stepped forward, and Ben slid along with it. He slammed his heels into the dirt and pulled on the leash with all his might. The inugami took another step. And another. Ben was having less than no effect. Ben looked at the cow, and it stared back with its big empty brown eyes.

"No! Stop!"

The beast bounded the last bit of distance between it and its prey, throwing Ben to the ground as it pounced upon the cow and tore a chunk of meat from its neck. Hot, fresh blood splashed onto Ben's face.

Lucas grunted, barely audible over the cow's bleating. "I thought you'd last longer than *that*."

He whistled, and the wolves dove in, pinning the cow to the ground and joining in on the feast. Lucas helped Ben up and wiped his blood-drenched hand on Ben's shirt.

"You know why you can't control him?" He pointed at the demon that was Toby. "That is not a dog. You don't play frisbee with him, you don't take him out for walkies, and you sure as hell don't feed him Slim Jims. That is a predator. He needs to hunt. He's a demon bred for murder with a thousand years of pent-up aggression, and all you ever do is whine at him. Of course he doesn't listen to you. I wouldn't listen to you, either."

Lucas took Toby's leash and gave it a quick, violent yank. The inugami looked back, its snout and teeth dripping with cow blood.

"Sit," Lucas said.

The inugami growled. Lucas took a step forward.

"Sit," he said, louder. Ben wiped the cow blood from his eyes.

The inugami snorted, glanced back at the wriggling, wounded cow, then sat. Lucas handed the leash back to Ben.

"How did you do that?" Ben said.

"Three days a week. Early morning. Right here. I'll get you going well enough that you don't need me."

The moment the inugami saw that Ben had the leash, it spun around and attacked the cow again. The helpless bovine let out a bellowing noise of pain and horror before gurgling and falling silent as the four inugami ripped into its flesh. Ben would never forget that sound.

It was almost human.

犬

Several cats, newly loosed upon the world, scattered across the lawn as Sarah and Jake approached Maureen Greco's house. Three squad cars were already parked out front, lights flashing. The front door hung loose and diagonal. The bottom hinge was broken. One of the guys from Forensics fiddled with the door, his hand resting directly on a splash of dried blood. He nodded to Sarah as they passed.

A blonde girl, about thirteen years old, sat on the living room couch, answering a beat cop's questions. She stared at her shoes, hands in her sweatshirt pockets, eyes hidden behind her bangs. Sarah recognized the cop as the one Ben had freed from a spider sac back in the video store. The cop patted the girl on the shoulder and went over to the detectives.

"Chris, right?" Sarah said. The cop smiled sadly. "What've we got?"

"Not much." He flipped through his notes. "One adult and one child missing. She says her mom and her foster sister were fighting, shouting at each other, and then they hugged and made up and left the building together."

Jake looked at the girl, who was still staring at her shoes. "They hugged and made up? How did the door get broken?"

"She doesn't know. Her story's vague and inconsistent, and it doesn't match the evidence, but I don't think she knows she's lying. She might be in shock."

"Okay. We'll talk after the EMTs take a look at her," Jake said, heading for the bedrooms. Chris rubbed the back of his neck, staring at the blood on the doorframe.

Sarah waited until Jake was out of earshot. "You can see the blood."

Relief washed over Chris's face. He gestured for her to come in close. He spoke quietly, deliberately. "I thought I was going crazy. Why can't anyone else see it?"

"Every day of your life, you see something impossible, and your brain erases it to protect your sanity. But one day, you see something so weird, so incompatible with your sense of reality, that you can't filter things out anymore. Everybody's got a different threshold." Sarah snatched his notepad out of his hand. "You been getting headaches?"

The cop nodded. "I've been seeing lots of things since the spider. Weird animals. Talking plants. Hands reaching for me out of the shadows. Faces in the trees. I'm not crazy?"

"You're definitely crazy, but you're not alone." Sarah handed the notepad back with her phone number on it. "There's a few of us on the force. We meet up from time to time to touch base. If you see anything that looks like it might hurt somebody, you call me."

The girl on the couch screamed. The cops ran over. A small brown arachnid—a common house spider—was crawling across the carpet near her foot. The girl cowered in the corner of the couch, pointing at it, hiding her face. Sarah turned and stormed toward the bedrooms as Chris comforted the girl. She found Jake standing in the hallway, meticulously scanning a frame full of family photos.

"You didn't think the witness screaming was worthy of your attention?" Sarah said.

"I'm sure you handled it. There's no pictures of the foster daughter anywhere. The file said she's been here over a year, but looking at the place, you'd think she didn't exist. So why did Maureen Greco run off with her and not her own kid?"

Sarah noticed the bedroom door leaning against the wall. Something ripped that one from the frame, too.

"I don't think she ran off. We need to—"

"We're not calling Ben."

"Jake, trust me on this."

"No." He turned toward her, eyes full of anger. "This isn't a noise complaint. It's a missing persons case, maybe a kidnapping, worst-case scenario, a murder. There's nothing going on here that can't be explained by human beings acting like humans."

"I can name a few things," Sarah said, pointing to the other room. "Two doors are knocked down. And the girl's story—"

"She's lying to protect her mom, she's lying to protect the other kid, she's lying to protect herself, or she's blocking it out because she is a *child* and she saw something horrible. It's not mystical! Not everything is little demons! I'm not going to—" Jake took a breath, collecting himself. "Can we *please* just do our jobs and solve one damn case like regular cops?"

Sarah started to argue, then didn't. "Okay."

"I'll get some straight answers from the kid. Check the bedrooms."

Jake headed back into the living room. Sarah looked at the door leaning on the wall, checked the broken hinges, and found the room it belonged to. It was a child's room, mostly empty, very spartan. Blank gray walls, painted brick, a small desk, a twin bed. There was a pile of clothes on the floor next to the bed.

One of the shirts looked familiar. Sarah picked it up, flattened it out. Screen-printed on the back was a white luchador mask surrounded by the words "Dragon Mask Lucha Dojo."

"Like regular cops," Sarah said.

犬

Ash drifted in and out of consciousness as the wind rushed by and the buildings slid past. The world was a blur. She had a sense of moving upward and a feeling in her stomach, a dizzy feeling, like when you go upside down on a swing set. She felt fear, she felt anger, but none of it truly mattered because it was all so far away.

Ash opened her eyes. Cars zoomed along the highway many stories below. The girl shrieked, grasping around desperately for something to grab on to.

"You should rest, young samurai," said the mouth on the back of her head. "You've had a very busy day."

Ash's hand brushed something sticky. She was dangling between two tall buildings, suspended at the center of a massive spiderweb. Her hair, impossibly long, was shaped into eight spider legs, each delicately clutching a strand of webbing. Ash ripped her hand away, and the whole web wobbled. The city lights around her drifted back and forth.

"Ahh! Take me down!" Ash said.

"We are safer up here."

"Take me down!" Ash repeated. "Down! Down! Down!"

The mouth sighed. The hair legs carefully stepped from web to web, onto the side of one of the buildings, and began silently skittering from window ledge to window ledge to drainpipe, down toward the ground. Ash's body dangled helplessly. She tried to move her hand and couldn't. She was no longer in control.

They touched down in the middle of a dark alley, in front of a red door and a big metal dumpster, which was locked shut with a chain.

Rock music played quietly, muffled through the door. Ash scratched her face. She could move again. She reached for the mouth on the back of her head. Her own hair swatted her hand away.

"You killed Mrs. Greco," Ash said, rubbing her hand.

"I gave you exactly what you wanted," the voice said. "There is no need to thank me."

"No! I'm not! I wasn't..." Ash rubbed her eyes. They felt dry and gritty. When she pulled her hands away they were covered in green dust. "Why are you doing this?"

"We're going to help each other. We're going to make this whole city, the whole *world* better. Together. You and me, samurai."

The music suddenly blared as the red door opened. A busboy—under twenty, white apron, wispy facial hair—stepped out into the alley carrying a full trash bag in each hand. He and Ash made eye contact.

"H-Help me!" Ash said. "Help!"

Before the boy could respond, the girl's neck cracked, and her head spun around 180 degrees. Ash found herself staring at a brick wall. She felt her hair rush away from her body. There was some soft scuffling and what sounded like a body hitting the ground. The busboy didn't even have time to scream.

"Don't hurt him," Ash whimpered.

"Weakness doesn't suit you. Come," the mouth said, extending its hair legs and lifting Ash back off the ground. "There is work to be done."

EIGHT.

Sarah lobbed a tennis ball to the opposite end of the dog park. A cluster of smaller dogs scattered as Sarah's boxer, Magnum, charged after the ball.

"You went on a date in the Poultry Zone?" she asked incredulously.

"I didn't know what to tell her!" Ben watched as Toby worked the perimeter along the chain-link fence, peeing at strategic locations only when he knew no one was looking. Ben brought the inugami here to socialize, but Toby never really mingled. He was, admittedly, eighty or so generations older than these dogs. "What am I gonna say? 'Hey, can you pick a different restaurant? That one's got an invisible carcass the size of a house rotting behind it.' I didn't want to spook her. She already thinks I'm kinda sketchy."

"You *are* sketchy," Sarah said. "Did you eat food there?"

"No, we, uhh, left before that." Ben shrugged. "I thought you'd be impressed! It was like twenty feet from me, and I held it together enough that we've gone out again since then. Actually, do you want to go to her open mic tonight? I'm supposed to invite people. The show is free, but there's a two-drink minimum."

"Hmm." Sarah rubbed her chin, thinking. "Do I want to watch your co-worker do stand-up at an overpriced open mic…?"

"Well, when you say it like *that*."

Magnum brought the ball back, wet with slobber. Sarah wiped her hand on her pants as she threw the ball again.

"She's not just my co-worker," Ben said.

"You really like this girl, huh?"

"Yeah." Ben smiled and looked away. "We've been hanging out a lot since Saturday. It's nice to have someone outside of all of our paranormal shit. We talk about old movies and go to trivia nights at bars. Nobody gets their limbs cut off. Nobody gets eaten."

Magnum nudged the ball into Sarah's hand. She tossed it. "Well, sure, that's what dating is, but do you *like her* like her?"

The tennis ball bounced and hit Toby in the leg. He spun around, eyes red, fangs bared, shadow wolf encasing his body. Magnum dropped onto her belly and then scampered away, whimpering. The three or four other dogs near them also scattered, much to the confusion of their owners, who saw nothing unusual.

Ben thought calming thoughts in Toby's direction, but they were muddled and mixed with fear and embarrassment. His mental connection with Toby was more emotional than logical, and the quality of their communication depended largely on Ben's feelings, which was not an area in which he excelled. The inugami growled, then went back to sullenly circling the park. It was impossible to tell if Ben had gotten through.

"Sorry," he said. "Toby's been acting weird lately. Even for him. Lucas says it's cause I'm not the alpha dog."

"Lucas would say that, wouldn't he?" Sarah muttered. Magnum was leaning against her legs, demanding comfort pets.

"He won't sleep in my apartment. Toby, I mean. The old lady down the hall gives him bacon and sausages and lets him come and go as he pleases. She doesn't even question it. We still have the kakawari. The mental link is technically there, but I think I'm losing him on a personal level, you know? I'm still the dog walker. I take him out three times a day to eat demons."

"Well, Tatsuya said Toby never stayed with him either, right? He likes being spoiled by old women all day—which is surprisingly sexist for a dog—but that doesn't mean he doesn't like you."

"Yeah..." Ben said, unconvinced. "I just thought we were going to be closer than that."

Sarah nodded. "Hey, before you spend forty dollars on amateur stand-up, can you come look at a crime scene with me?"

"Sure," Ben said.

"No wolf guy. No Jake. This is, uhh…just don't tell anybody."

"Okay," Ben said. "I trust you."

Sarah looked at him. She threw the tennis ball. "Just like that?"

"Yeah." Ben smiled. "Just like that."

A shadow tentacle whipped through the air and cleaved the tennis ball in half. The two ball slices landed on either side of Magnum's head. The dog sniffed one, confused.

"That's enough dog park for today," Ben said.

犬

The moped swerved to a stop across the street from Maureen Greco's house. Sarah stumbled off the back, and Ben went to help Toby down, but the inugami brushed him aside, using shadow tentacles to lower himself onto the pavement.

"Ugh," Sarah said, wiping a dead bug off her cheek. "*Please* buy a normal form of transportation."

She looked up at the house and immediately yanked Ben back behind the parked car next to them.

"The kid's in there with the social worker. Probably picking up her stuff."

"The missing kid?"

"No, doofus, the other one. Shit. We'll have to come back later."

Ben peeked around the bumper. Inside the house, a middle-aged woman in a skirt suit led a teenage girl around the living room. Ben glanced down at Toby, who was chewing on something crunchy he'd found in the grass.

"Run around to the back," Ben said. "I'll meet you there."

Sarah nodded, heading around the other side of the car. She ducked behind a tree and then crouched her way past a set of bushes. Once she was out of view from the front window, she walked as casually as she could into the backyard. She wanted to look official if any of the neighbors saw her.

A few minutes passed as she waited at the back door. A caterpillar with a human face slowly worked its way across the lawn, grunting with each forward wiggle. It gasped when it realized Sarah could see it. She pointed at her eyes with two fingers, and then at the caterpillar. She was watching him.

The door opened. Ben was alone.

"What'd you do?" Sarah asked.

"I told them Toby was a comfort dog, donated by the church down the block." Ben opened the door a little further. Down the hall, the teenage girl, Taylor, was kneeling on the floor petting Toby with both hands. The social worker was standing over them on her phone, asking her superiors about church-donated comfort dogs.

"Toby!" Taylor said. "Good boy! He's a good dog!"

"Is that, uhh..." Sarah searched for the right word. "Safe?"

The girl threw her arms around the inugami, hugging him. Toby glared at Ben.

KILL YOU, he thought.

"It's fine," Ben said.

He closed his eyes, touching his forehead. Down the hall, Toby rolled onto his back and exposed his belly. Taylor and the social worker both *Awwl*ed at the sight, and Sarah used the opportunity to take Ben into the bedroom with the broken door.

"We've got some evidence the normies can't see," Sarah said. "Blood on the doorframe. A couple of slash marks on the walls. And this..."

She gestured to the heating vent, where a faint green stain dusted the grate. Ben went in for a closer look. He scratched at the green with his fingers and sniffed them.

"It's the stuff that Toby breathes out when he bonds with humans," Ben said. "Me, specifically. I don't know if there's a word for it. Kakawari juice?"

Sarah scowled at the sheer grossness of that phrase. "You think this kid has an inugami?"

Ben shook his head. "Dunno. There's other yōkai that bond with humans. Offhand, there's a rat one and like three different catfish that I can't keep straight. There's also a sentient dishrag that slaps onto people's faces and controls their brains. Draws a new face on itself with mud. Tatsuya will know what to look for. I'll ask him."

"Tatsuya. Yeah. Ben, listen…" Sarah bent down and picked up a T-shirt. "I was going to ease into this…"

She held the shirt so Ben could see the lucha dojo logo. All of the color drained from his face.

"What's the kid's name?"

"Ashley Ocampo. Do you know her?"

Ben nodded slowly. "She beats me up five times a week."

"God. I'm sorry. What are the odds of—" Sarah stopped. "He still makes you fight the kids?"

犬

The entire time the spider was in control, Ash's head was pointed in the wrong direction. She had a hard time keeping track of where she was. When her parents were still alive, she would sit in the way, way back of their station wagon and watch gas stations and fast food places go by in reverse. She used to perch her feet on the door and pretend she was in an out-of-control spaceship or on the back of a dragon.

These types of thoughts helped to distract her from the fact that a spider was controlling her body and murdering people. A little, anyway. She was clutching desperately to any sanity she could.

The spider brought her indoors. They were in some sort of small church. Or was it a temple? There was a lot of gold glinting in the darkness, a smell of incense burning in the air.

"Where are we?" Ash said.

"Quiet," said the mouth on the back of her head. "*Mikoshi nyūdō! Konbanwa!*"

"*Futakuchi-Jorōgumo,*" a male voice responded. It was a deep voice, and old. "I had heard you were back in Yomi, but this is a surprise. I was deeply saddened to hear about your young."

The spider bowed, and for a moment, Ash was staring at the ceiling. Beyond the rafters, the streetlights gleamed in through cracks in the roof.

"They will not have died in vain," the spider said.

"You seek revenge on the inugami and his boy."

"I seek revenge on all of them. It is becoming difficult for yōkai in the land of the living. More and more humans can see us. These people carry infinite libraries in their pockets. They have instruments of death beyond imagining. We have teeth and claws and parlor tricks. We are relics of a prior age, and we are running out of darkness in which to hide. Alone, we are easily dispatched. Together, we can take power back from the humans. We were here before them. This world should be ours."

Ash didn't like the direction this conversation was going at all, but she wasn't really listening. If she concentrated hard enough, she could wiggle her toes while the spider was ranting. When the spider wasn't paying attention to her, she had more control.

"Why is your rage my concern?" said the male voice.

"*Mikoshi*," said the spider, "the other yōkai won't listen to the spider. They think I'm mad. Everyone listens to the Tall Priest. I want a meeting with the leaders of every clan in this city. *Obake, Yurei, Oni*, even the *Tsukumogami*."

Ash's toes stopped. She felt the spider's focus slip back to her. She took a deep breath. *Wait for it.*

"And what do I tell them we are meeting for?" said the voice.

"*Niku no gisei*. At a scale that this continent, this civilization has never seen."

Now! Ash turned her head. She saw old hairy feet in wooden sandals, dusty, faded blue robes, and an elderly man's face. He had black hair, a long mustache, and was bald on top. He had thick, bushy eyebrows, like twin black caterpillars above his eyes. As Ash's gaze moved upward to look at them, his eyes kept rising to meet hers. She found that she couldn't stop—looking up, meeting the man's gaze, looking up, meeting his gaze. Soon she was leaning so far that she fell onto her back.

The Tall Priest pounced on her, digging his long, pointed nails into her arms. His neck had stretched to be at least twenty feet long, and it curved down to his shoulders like the body of a snake. He smiled, baring dozens of pointy teeth.

"Go back to sleep, child," the Tall Priest snarled. "The adults are talking."

Ash's neck twisted around with an audible snap, and all she could see were floorboards.

"I apologize," said the spider as it hoisted Ash's helpless body back upright with its hair. "This host is strong-willed. In the end, it will be better, but the early stages can be difficult. If she had been any older, I never could have bonded to her."

The Tall Priest grunted amiably. "Be here tomorrow night, spider. I will get you your meeting."

Ash heard footsteps. A door closed. She tried to wiggle her toes, but they stayed frozen still, dangling an inch above the dirty wooden floor.

"You'll regret that," whispered the spider.

NINE.

Ben yawned as he ascended the steps to Bailey's house. He and Toby had gone out last night to try and track down Ash, mopeding around the neighborhood, but the trail had gone irretrievably cold less than a block from her house. Whatever it was that took her, it could fly or teleport or something. Ben stopped at the door. He didn't have Bailey's key on the ring he kept attached to his belt, and for a moment he panicked before he noticed the welcome mat was missing, and it all came flooding back. He looked in the window. No furniture. The house was an empty shell.

Bailey was gone.

After a quick scooter ride, he was huffing and puffing his way up the stairs to the greyhounds' apartment. The dogs lived up on the third floor. It was a lot of stairs.

He would have to tell Tatsuya about Ash, whether he wanted to or not. The old man would take it hard. Tatsuya had recruited Ash himself and molded her into his top student. She took his half-assed Americanized Bushidō code seriously. He still called Ben "gringo". They had a real connection that he and Tatsuya had never really had. Still, Ben thought with no small amount of guilt, it would be nice to have Dragon Mask back in action. It was great that he got sober and all, but deep down Ben missed the old dynamic. There was something important missing when it was just him and Toby and Sarah out there. He reached the door and went inside.

The front hallway of the greyhounds' apartment was lined with portraits of dogs—photos, paintings, and sketches, along with little inspirational sayings in needlepoint. *A house is not a home without a greyhound. Love is a warm greyhound. Any woman can be a mother, but it takes someone special to be a Greyhound Mom.* That sort of thing. The lady who lived here—who Ben had never met—had been adopting former race dogs for decades, and she kept a portrait of each one. There were at least a dozen.

"Fergie! Stoney!" he shouted. "It's walkin' time!"

The dogs stood in the kitchen, wagging at him, pressing their noses against the baby gate that kept them confined to that room. Sunlight glinted off a spot on the floor. Ben sighed. Fergie, ever nervous, had a history of getting scared and peeing right through her doggie diaper. Ben checked her. All clear.

He looked up at Stoney, who was now hiding his face behind a potted plant.

"There's a first," Ben said.

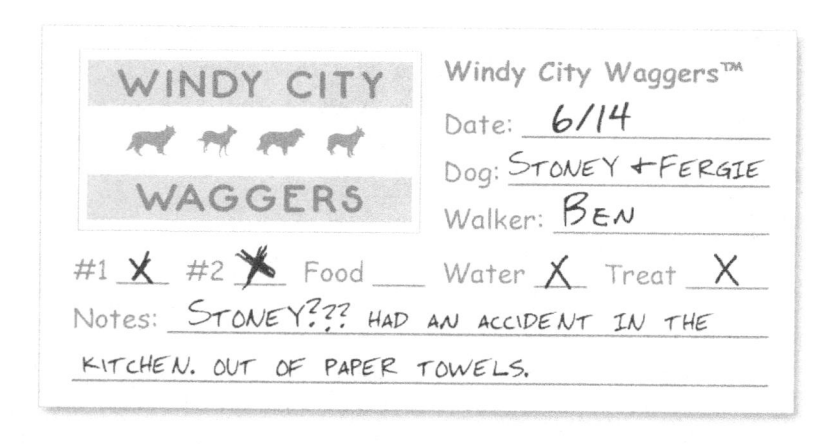

WINDY CITY WAGGERS

Windy City Waggers™
Date: 6/14
Dog: STONEY + FERGIE
Walker: BEN

#1 X #2 ✗ Food ___ Water X Treat X
Notes: STONEY??? HAD AN ACCIDENT IN THE KITCHEN. OUT OF PAPER TOWELS.

"I mean, it's cool that you trained her and all..." Kaylee watched Libby trot along. The dog's brown undercoat swooshed along the sidewalk like a broom. "I just can't believe it took you that long."

Ten minutes ago, Ben had been excited to introduce Kaylee to Libby. One major sticking point in their relationship thus far was Ben's flakiness, and Libby was living proof that he could, if pushed, be responsible. If he knew women, there was nothing they found more attractive than basic competence at a minimum-wage job.

"Dachshunds are notoriously hard to train," Ben said.

They stopped at the corner. Kaylee looked both ways before crossing. "Did you look that up?"

Ben laughed. "I did! All these little tiny dogs, man. They're stubborn. They're all bred to catch rats in barns and stuff."

"You *actually* used to just carry her outside and hold her above the grass while she peed?"

Ben shook his head. "She really didn't like walking."

"Well, you wouldn't know it now." They'd been moving along at a good pace for twenty minutes. The dog barely stopped to sniff anything.

"Yeah, she's walking good today. A little...*too* good." Ben squinted at the dog as though she were up to something sinister. Libby looked back at him, her tail wagging. "It's probably cause you're here."

"I'm a calming presence. I have the magic touch." Kaylee handed the leash back to Ben as Libby finally stopped to pee. "Hey, so, uhh, I want to write a pilot script."

"Did those commercial people call you?"

"Not yet, but when they *do*, and this commercial goes national, a big-shot executive is going to check out my set and then offer me a deal for my own prestige cable show about how hard it is to be a struggling female comedian in the big city."

"Yep, that all tracks," Ben said.

"Do you want to write it with me?" Kaylee asked.

"Well—"

"And before you're like 'Oh, but I'm one of those self-hating artsy people who's all cynical and broken'..."

Ben shut his mouth.

"A: You took a bunch of screenwriting classes I didn't. I mostly need you for structure and formatting. B: It's a Kaylee vehicle starring Kaylee, so it won't be your self-indulgent bullshit; it'll be mine. And C: we need something to do together besides watch movies and eat burritos."

Ben gritted his teeth, turning away. "I *like* movies and burritos."

"Ben, come on," Kaylee said. "Let's make a thing. Let's do something creative. Do you really want to be a dog walker forever?"

There was a yank on the leash. Libby was standing at the very end of it, facing home.

Ben shrugged. "End of the line."

> **Windy City Waggers™**
> Date: 6/14
> Dog: LIBBY
> Walker: BEN
> #1 X #2 X Food ___ Water X Treat X
> Notes: LIBBY WOULD WALK ALL DAY IF I LET HER!

Tatsuya and Sarah stood to the side, arms folded, as the line of eight-to-twelve-year-olds pushed sponges back and forth across the mats in the ancient lucha dojo tradition, which Tatsuya had partially stolen from karate but mostly made up. Tatsuya was very interested in preserving traditions where the kids did his chores.

"I can't tell Jake all of his theories are wrong, you know? He's been looking into the foster mom's past. He wants to talk to the ex-husband that this woman hadn't spoken to in twelve years. We spent all day yesterday at the horse track looking for the guy." Sarah sighed. "I know it's a yōkai. All signs point to yōkai. It's frustrating, you know? He's so dead set on doing the work *correctly* that I have to dork around pretending to do my job instead of actually doing my job."

Tatsuya grunted to show that he was listening. He adjusted one of the mats with his foot just as a girl sponged past.

"There's a beat cop in Norwood Park who can see everything after one experience. Jake's been around enough yōkai at this point. How can they still be invisible to him?"

"I spent years training to see *los demonios*," Tatsuya said. "It does not come easily to everyone. I seem to remember you getting into multiple fights with them before you could see them."

"That was what, a week?" Sarah smiled. "I worked it out. I was ready for it."

Tatsuya nodded. "You were always ready. Samurai! Your dojo is clean and your class has ended! Go and serve your neighbors! Do nothing which is of no use."

The kids all filed into the changing rooms. The bell above the door clinked, and Toby trotted in. He sniffed a backpack that was sitting next to the door then hopped up into his dog bed.

Ben followed the dog in, looking serious. "Did you tell him?"

"I was waiting for you," Sarah said.

Tatsuya looked from one to the other. "Tell me what?"

犬

The old luchador wailed on the training dummy he kept in the corner of the dojo. Ben had always assumed it was decorative, since they never used it in class, but as Tatsuya unleashed a flurry of punches and kicks and elbows and knees, Ben understood exactly what it was for.

"She came to me!" Tatsuya whacked the dummy across the face with his forearm. "She told me she was having problems at home, and I let her walk out the door! I should have done something! I should have stopped her! *Baka na jiji!*"

"You had no way of knowing she was—" Sarah said.

"Who better than me?" he cried. "I protected the inugami for decades! I have fought more demons than anyone on this continent! And for what? What good have I done?" He punched the dummy one last time and turned to face Ben and Sarah. He looked past them at the Dragon Mask shrine behind the counter. "What do you know?"

"Invisible scratch marks. Invisible blood. Kakawari residue on a vent in her room. About…" Ben made a square with his hands. "Too small for Toby, but I guess it could be a chihuahua or something."

Tatsuya shook his head. "That is not enough. It could be anything.

A cat, or a snake, or—"

"It's a spider."

Everyone turned. Lucas Alcindor stood in the doorway. His wolf-themed van was idling in the parking lot behind him. His wolf-themed wolves were watching through the windshield. Sarah noticed—and Ben did not—that the man must have walked in very slowly and carefully not to jingle the bells on the door, just so he could make a dramatic entrance.

"*Nan da yo,*" Tatsuya muttered. "Who is this?"

"I've checked with a few contacts," Lucas said. "There's word on the street of a spider woman bonded with a little girl, one who's gathering up yōkai for some kind of big meeting. I don't know where. But it is a lead."

"A spider," Sarah said. She and Tatsuya both turned and glared at Ben.

Tatsuya pointed at him. "You said you killed it!"

"We did!" Ben looked at Toby. "Most of it! The head might've gotten away. The building was burning down, and we had an injured guy to pull out. We couldn't exactly double-check!"

"Every time!" Tatsuya kicked the dummy in the stomach to punctuate his point. "You screw it up and make excuses, and everyone suffers but you!"

"We saved a man's life!"

"And now more people are dead! And you!"

Tatsuya pointed at Toby. The inugami growled, standing up in his bed. Tatsuya put his hand down, frowning.

"He has never growled at me before."

"With all due respect, Sensei, that's no way to handle an aggressive inugami. Now, as you can see"—Lucas gestured to the wolves observing them all from his van—"I have three of the beasts myself, which I politely left outside so as to not spook the karate kids. I would be happy to teach you a few tricks."

Tatsuya charged forward. "Get the hell out of my dojo, you strange fur-coat-wearing man!"

"Whoa, whoa, whoa!" Ben got between them. "This is Lucas! This is the inugami trainer I was telling you about! He can help us! Lucas,

Tatsuya. Tatsuya, Lucas. See? We're all friends!"

Tatsuya stopped but did not visibly relax. Lucas inhaled, flaring his nostrils.

"We're...we're friendly." Ben turned to Lucas. "What can we do?"

"There's one more person I want to talk to," Lucas said. "Figured you might want to come with for this one, get some hands-on experience."

"Yes! Great. Good." Ben clapped his hands. "That's perfect. Sarah, you can drive this time so we don't have to—"

"Er..." Lucas gritted his teeth. He pulled Ben into a football huddle, facing away from everyone else. "The place we're going...you don't want to walk in with a cop."

"She's not in uniform."

Sarah was wearing a tucked-in collared shirt with slacks and a sport coat. She put her hands on her hips when Lucas looked at her.

"They'll know," Lucas said.

Ben nodded in agreement.

Lucas patted his own leg, heading for the exit. "Toby, c'mon, let's go see your friends."

Toby tentacle-launched himself off the counter and followed Lucas out the door. Ben paused before leaving.

"I, uhh..." Ben rubbed the back of his neck. "I'll call you guys after. Tatsuya, we're gonna find Ash. I promise."

"Ben," Sarah said, "where are you going?"

Lucas opened the back of his van, and Toby jumped in. The wolves ducked away from the windshield to greet Toby. The van shook.

"I'll call you," Ben said, and he slipped out the door before Sarah could respond.

Ben climbed into the passenger seat, and Sarah watched as, for a brief moment, the rakish grin dropped from Lucas's face, before returning once Ben was looking. Sarah knew Lucas. She'd known so many Lucases. Much of her time as a beat cop was spent dealing with the wreckage left by Lucases.

"I don't like this," Sarah said as she watched them drive off.

Tatsuya just scowled.

犬

The spider, the Tall Priest, and several other atypical creatures all sat in a circle at the center of the priest's dilapidated Buddhist temple. Their conversation was mostly in Japanese, which Ash didn't speak, so she had some time to think. Her head was still twisted around, but there was a small dusty round mirror on a table in the corner, angled so that she could see some of what was happening.

The Tall Priest sat cross-legged directly to her right, running a set of prayer beads through his long, clawed fingers as he spoke. Next to him, a red-furred creature caked in dust and dirt knelt on all fours, sporadically licking the floor with its long, prehensile tongue. To Ash, it looked like a combination between Elmo from S*esame Street* and an iguana. Dirtier, though. An Iguana Elmo that had fallen on hard times.

Next to that thing, a thin, pale woman hovered a foot above the floor. She wore a dark-red kimono with the sleeves torn away. Her exposed arms were far too long for her body and covered in little human eyes. At any given moment, a few of the eyes glanced in the mirror. Ash wasn't sure if the others knew she was watching, but this woman definitely did.

There was also a sky-blue anteater/elephant-type beast with a glowing orange mane, a full-sized ox with a human face, and a vaguely person-shaped pile of blankets with an ukulele for a head. A few days ago, any one of these would've been the weirdest thing Ash had ever seen. Now, it was just another Wednesday.

"I, for one, think it's a terrible idea," said the mouthless ukulele somehow, in English. "We *tsukumogami* are fallen objects, human tools given life with age. We require humankind to exist, and we hope to gain nothing from open war with them."

"Biwa, you're a lute," the spider hissed. "When was the last time you saw another lute?"

Since last night, when Ash had turned her head of her own accord, the spider had kept a much tighter mental grip on her. Still, whenever the creature spoke, that grip lessened almost imperceptibly.

Ash would have another moment. She just had to be ready when it came. She mentally repeated her Bushidō code. *Righteousness. Courage. Compassion. Respect. Honesty. Honor. Loyalty.*

Self-control.

"I need everyone united on this. We are not going to kill all the humans." The spider stood and paced through the room, taking Ash with her. "We are merely changing the dynamic. A sacrifice of a significant scale will blend the worlds of the living and the dead."

"That won't come without a price," the Tall Priest said.

"We can come out of the shadows. We outnumber them. We can consolidate our might in the world of the living. All we need is meat."

The ox with a human face gulped at the word "meat." The geisha with the seeing arms gave him a gentle pat. A peal of laughter escaped from the shadows in a spot Ash couldn't see. She hadn't known someone was there.

"You want meat?" the voice crackled with energy. "Meat! I can get you meat. More meat than you can imagine."

"You have been mostly silent," the Tall Priest said. "What do you want in return, shirime?"

The spider twisted to look, and Ash got a full view of the voice's owner in the mirror. It looked like a naked old man, facing away, leaning down with his butt up in the air. He stepped backward into the light.

Ash gasped.

The old man's legs were bent backward at the knee. A thick, gnarly scar ran diagonally across his butt, and at the center, a large brown eye blinked. The eye seemed to smile.

"I want..." growled the creature, "the dog walker."

TEN.

The three inugami wolves swept into the alley, nudging trash bags with their paws and sniffing around under the dumpsters. The shadow tentacles extending from their backs flailed above them and flicked at loose bricks and cobwebs. Once they had thoroughly cased the joint, lead wolf Miya let out a quick bark, and Lucas strolled in from the street, flanked by Toby and Ben. Ben had the Onislayer on his back in what could charitably be called a "sheath" but would more accurately be called a "cricket bat cover he bought on eBay."

"Where we going?" Ben asked. Techno music thrummed through the brick wall next to him.

"A club," Lucas said.

"Like a...like a neon-lights-and-dancing club?" Ben's closest friends were a homebody cop, an elderly luchador, and a magic dog. He'd never been to a club. "Should I have changed my shirt?"

Lucas didn't answer. He scanned the brick wall, his face inches from it, his eyes moving from brick to brick.

"Are they gonna let us in with three wolves and a dog?"

"They wouldn't let us in without 'em." Lucas sniffed the brick in front of him, then reached up and poked it with his finger.

The wall shuddered. A human eye at the center of each and every brick on the wall opened. Dozens of eyes simultaneously locked onto Lucas.

"THE FOUR INUGAMI MAY ENTER," a deep voice boomed.

The bricks in front of Lucas, from the ground to his waist, slid and parted into a dark rectangular opening. It was just large enough for a wolf. "HUMANS WAIT OUTSIDE."

Toby brushed past Ben, tail wagging, and trotted toward the doorway.

"Hey!" Ben said.

"We're not here to party," Lucas said, stopping Toby with his leg. He shifted his focus constantly from brick eye to brick eye. Behind him, the wolves were doing the same. "We're not even going in the club. I just wanna talk to one of the staff."

"HUMANS WAIT OUTSIDE."

"We'll be in and out." Lucas rooted around inside his coat pocket and pulled out a fifty-dollar bill. He stuck it in one of the eyes, between the bottom lid and the eyeball. "No one will even know we were there."

The eyes blinked in a wave, rippling out in a ring as they all pointed at the money. Ben turned away and rubbed the bridge of his nose. He found it disorienting to try and focus on an entire talking wall as if it were a person.

The cash sucked into the eye socket with a wet slurp. Brick grinded on brick as the doorway raised up. It was now an inch or so above Lucas's head.

"YOU HAVE FIVE MINUTES," the wall said.

Lucas slapped Ben on the chest and went inside. The wolves followed.

"How does a wall with eyes spend cash? What does it even buy?" Ben muttered. He looked down. Toby was already inside.

Ben rushed in after the rest of them, and the wall closed behind him. He ran his finger along the wall. The seal was seamless. Ben wondered what the plan was for when they decided to leave.

A pulsing beat throbbed inside his chest. The techno music was much louder inside. They were in a dark hallway lit with one flickering fluorescent light. The walls were painted black. There was one door at the end of the hall, closed, and another one to Ben's right, open. He peeked inside.

A strobe light jittered to the beat of the music. Ben caught a glimpse of a tentacle. A beak. A claw. Something wet. Ivory horns.

Teeth? Lucas yanked Ben back into the hallway.

"You don't want to go in there," he said.

"How do you know about this place?" Ben said. "I thought you lived out in the suburbs."

"I come in for work. There was plenty of yōkai business before you came along," Lucas said. "C'mon. I need you to be the nice guy in there."

"Why?"

"Joey's afraid of me. He'll open up to you. Your inugami is cuter."

They continued on to the end of the hall. The kitchen they entered had once been white, but with age and neglect it had faded to a sickly yellow. Mold grew in patches in the corners. The oven had no door, and the empty fridge was hanging open. A second door to their right led into the club proper. If it wasn't for the music, this place would seem long abandoned.

"Kitchen's closed," Ben said.

"Yeah, they don't serve food here," Lucas said. "The yōkai definition of 'food' is pretty loose, anyway."

Ben heard tiny footsteps on the tile floor. A young boy leaned around the corner of the counter. He had one eye at the center of his face, blinking above an overly large mouth.

"G-greetings, human sirs!" said the little cyclops. He stepped out so Ben could get a look at him. He was wearing a kimono, and he was holding a dinner plate with a wiggly beige block on it. "W-Would you like to lick my tofu?"

A pink tongue, far bigger than it should have been, slid out of the boy's mouth and brushed against the side of the tofu. Ben could see individual taste buds rubbing on there. Lucas nudged Ben and shook his head.

"I wasn't that tempted," Ben said quietly. Toby sniffed in the tofu's direction, licked his chops, and sat, begging.

"We've got some questions, Joey," Lucas said. "We're looking for a little girl."

"N-No, thir!" Joey said, his tongue still on the tofu. He sucked it back in. "I'm not t-telling *you* anything, Lucas!"

"Joey…" Lucas pointed at him. "You owe me. I spared you when the wolves and I were cleaning out that grocery store."

"I owe you f-for not killing me." Joey backed up against the counter. "Some debt. It's too dangerous! If the g-guys knew that I—"

Lucas whistled. In an instant, the three wolves surrounded Joey, growling, teeth bared.

"Ahh!" the boy screeched. "No! I can't!"

"Hey!" Ben said, hands up. He walked past the wolves and knelt in front of Joey. The wolves backed up and looked at Lucas, waiting for his command. The tiny cyclops's single eye blinked up at Ben. "That's not necessary. You all right? Here, pet the doggie. Toby!"

Toby trotted forward, face blank. Ben gestured toward the boy. Toby squinted at him. Ben gestured again, more firmly. Toby exhaled and sat down in front of Joey.

"I-is he a real dog?" Joey reluctantly stroked Toby's fur.

"No, don't worry. He's a terrifying monster in disguise like yourself."

The boy nodded, petting the inugami more easily.

"A girl is missing. Long black hair, about yay tall." Ben held his hand a few inches above Joey's head. "She's, uhh…how old are you?"

"Three hundred and seven."

"Right. So she's a little older than you look," Ben said, smiling. "Do you know who I'm talking about?"

The boy looked away, nervous. "My friends will hurt me if I talk to you."

"Well, I'm Ben, this is Toby. We're your friends now, too. And you know what? Real friends don't hurt each other like that. Friends help each other. And if those guys try to hurt you, I'll protect you. Okay?"

There was a noise in the hallway. Another yōkai had arrived at the club, a big one from the sound of it. Lucas and the wolves turned to guard the door to the kitchen. The boy watched them.

"Don't worry about him, either," Ben said. "You and me and Toby. We're good guys. We help people. The girl is my friend, too. She's been missing for a few days. She might be in trouble. Can you help me find her?"

The boy thought, stroking Toby's fur. He held his plate of tofu up to the dog's face. Toby's eyes flashed red, and he licked the side of the wobbling cube. Ben got a hint of a dusty cardboard taste in his mouth. He coughed. Toby's tail wagged.

"The spider's host," the boy said. "I don't know where she is."

Host? That sounded bad. Ben's heart sank. "Is she alive?"

"I don't know what that means."

Several dozen eyeballs opened on the yellow tiles to Ben's left.

"FIVE MINUTES ARE UP," said the wall.

"Damn it! The leaders of the yōkai clans are organizing!" Lucas said. The three wolves turned, growling, matching his energy. "This spider is at the center of it! *Where?*"

"I don't know!" the boy said. "Biwa Bokuboku! The lute! He can tell you. He's the leader of the Tsukumogami. He will know!"

"He'd better," Lucas said. He turned and walked out. The wolves followed. Ben and Toby stood.

"Being a spider's host," Ben said. "Is that...reversible?"

The boy held up his tofu. "Would you like a lick for the road, new friend?"

Ben frowned. "Maybe next time."

He sprinted back through the creepy hallway as quickly as possible, carefully not making eye contact with any of the creatures in the club and sliding sideways through the self-sealing exit. Ben found Lucas and the wolves waiting for him in the alley. The wolves were all prancing around, play fighting, hopped up on adrenaline. Toby ran past Ben and joined in.

"Tsukumogami are human objects," Lucas said. "Lawn chairs and hammers and stuff. They come to life when you leave them unattended for a hundred years. I know a few, so we got what we need here." He patted Ben on the shoulder. "You did great. You make a very convincing sensitive wuss."

"Thank you. Now what?" Ben said.

"Now..." Lucas smiled. "We hunt."

ELEVEN.

The paper umbrella hopped across the rooftop on its foot-shaped handle, the human face etched onto its wooden shaft twisted into a mask of terror. Toby the inugami was quickly gaining on it. The umbrella only had one shot at this. As it reached the edge of the roof, it leapt and flipped open its canopy.

"Ha-ha!" the umbrella laughed, gliding gracefully across the empty lot toward the next roof.

"Yeowch!" it wailed as Toby's jaws latched on to it, the weight of the demon dog dragging it downward.

It flapped its canopy, briefly hovering in place, but it wasn't enough to stay aloft. The umbrella looked down. Three wolves were sitting in the yard below, gazing up at the umbrella hungrily.

A winding tangle of tentacles spiraled upward toward the whimpering yōkai.

犬

A beautiful woman took off the expensive Japanese sandals she'd bought on her vacation to Tokyo. She dropped her robe onto the deck and dove into her swimming pool, enjoying the flow of the cool water across her body. When she surfaced, she saw a man in a long leather coat standing at the edge of the pool. He pointed at her shoes.

"*Bakezōri!*" he shouted.

The sandals shrieked and hopped of their own accord back toward the house. Three wolves and a dog burst out from the bushes and into the pool, kicking and splashing and snarling their way to the other side, where they chased after the sentient sandals. The man in the coat followed.

The woman barely had time to process these events before a younger man carrying a cricket paddle squeezed through the bushes and stopped himself from falling in the pool. He saw the woman and blushed, embarrassed, trying not to look at her.

"Sorry, lady," Ben said. "We need to talk to your shoes."

His phone buzzed. He had a text from Sarah:

Any progress?

犬

Sarah looked up from her phone. Jake was still questioning Mr. Greco. The two of them were standing outside the man's trailer, arguing loudly. The man, mid-fifties and overweight, hadn't seemed particularly upset that his ex-wife was missing, but he also hadn't seemed suspiciously unsurprised. This was all irrelevant, and Sarah knew it. She should be out there searching for the spider yōkai with Ben. Her phone buzzed.

Ben: *Working on it. Have you seen any sentient objects?*

She texted back. *You mean like people?*

He responded with a gif of the singing candlestick from *Beauty and the Beast*.

Ben: *Like that*

There was an empty beer bottle in the dirt in front of her. She nudged it with her foot, and it didn't talk to her. She knelt down and flicked it with her finger. The bottle rolled in a semicircle and continued not being alive. Sarah looked up.

Both Jake and the suspect were staring at her.

犬

The dark inugami pounced, chomping down into the cow's neck and tearing out its jugular. The pitiful creature mooed briefly before falling silent. Ben turned and hid his face in the hood of his rain poncho seconds before he was splattered with blood.

Lucas clicked the stopper on his stopwatch. The three wolves prowling around his waist joined in on the bovine feast.

"Eleven seconds." He looked at Ben. "You've done worse."

The blood on Ben's poncho dripped onto his shoes.

犬

"I don't think Kaylee would do this," said Kaylee. "The whole plot is built around her taking this restaurant job and then ducking out in the middle of it to go do a stand-up gig, but why would she take a job knowing she already had plans for that night?"

She and Ben were sitting outside at Pelican Coffee, as they were most days when the dog walks were done. Kaylee was at her MacBook, typing and pausing and typing more. Ben was lying across two chairs, watching the clouds drift and the airplanes form a line in the sky as they prepared to land at O'Hare. He'd been up late the past few nights chasing down yōkai, most recently a set of old church keys. The keys spoke Greek, and they whirled through the air like a ninja star when threatened. Toby caught them like a frisbee around three a.m., and they'd subsequently given Ben and Lucas no valuable information whatsoever.

"I mean, you wouldn't. She might. She's not you, right?" Ben yawned and tried to hide it. "Pilot-script Kaylee is like a dumber version of you that learns valuable lessons every twenty-two minutes."

"She's not *dumb*," Kaylee said. "She's young and naive. Are you still mad that you're not a character in this? Do you really want to see my sitcom version of you?"

Ben sat up. "Ben Carter, twenty-four, looks up from his arm-wrestling match and smiles as Kaylee walks in the room."

"Oh, Christ," Kaylee muttered.

"Ben: 'We'll have to cut this short, Dwayne "The Rock" Johnson.' His arm muscles bulge as he casually slams the Rock's hand onto the counter. The crowd around him is cheering, but he doesn't hear it.

The only thing he cares about right now is her."

Kaylee mock-barfed. Ben stood and walked around the table to look at her script.

"She is extremely into it; everyone in the crowd can tell. As Ben approaches her, he wipes sweat from his brow with his too-small T-shirt. His exposed abs glisten under the bar lights like…"

"Like what?" She jabbed him in the gut with her elbow. "What do your stupid abs glisten like?"

"Like…uh…like…overripe…" Ben trailed off as he focused on the screen, scrolling down. "You just need to motivate it more. The setup has to be more dramatic. Have her get kicked out of her apartment because she runs out of money. And set up the day job versus dream job thing harder. The person who runs the open mic tells her she has one more chance before she's out of the show."

"That's not really how that works."

"She's at her lowest point, she's about to quit the whole comedy thing. She doubts she even wants to *do* this anymore. So—"

"So when she gets fired from the restaurant and nails her stand-up set, she knows what she wants. She is all about the dream job. Yeah. That's good, actually. You're good at this. Maybe I'll use you for more than formatting." Kaylee glanced down, then did a double take. "You have blood stains on your shoes."

Ben stepped back, hiding his feet behind her chair. "I mean, if you wanna do this right, I still have the student version of Final Draft on my computer." His phone buzzed. He looked at it. "I have to go."

"Right now?"

"Lucha class." He leaned down and kissed her on the cheek. "Tatsuya wants me to come early and help him set up."

"All right. Same time tomorrow? I think we could finish this thing this week."

"Wouldn't miss it."

Kaylee watched as Ben walked away. The stains on his shoes traveled up his socks. Whatever bled on him did it this morning. There was something very wrong in his life, and Kaylee was tired of pretending not to notice.

犬

An exhausted father of four leaned back into the couch he'd bought at the flea market. He patted the armrest. It was a good couch with a lot of life left in it, and he'd gotten it for practically nothing. The rest of his family would love it once they got used to it. He sighed as he stood, then turned off the lights and headed upstairs to bed.

The couch shifted, the back pillows tilting toward the stairs, watching the man leave. The moment the stairway light turned off, the couch waddled over to the big-screen TV and plopped the appliance facedown onto its cushions.

Soon the couch was out on the front porch, covered in fine china, jewelry, and various other valuables. The upholstered burglar chuckled to itself as it gently pulled the door closed with its wooden leg. As it turned to leave, it heard growling from every direction.

犬

"So, you've been doing this for a while." Ben balanced the Onislayer vertically on his palm. He and Lucas stood near a bus stop down the block, using the bus shelter to keep out of the rain. The buses had stopped running an hour ago. Pedestrians were minimal. The rain was light but cold.

"You've been around."

"I have been around." Lucas was mostly listening to something else beyond Ben.

"Is there an FBI-type government agency that keeps track of yōkai and prevents the general public from finding out about their existence?"

Lucas looked at Ben. "Like *Men in Black*?"

"Yes. Exactly. Is there a yōkai *Men in Black*?"

"Why?" Lucas smiled. "Are you afraid that they're coming for you, or are you looking for a job?"

"I don't know. Neither?" The Onislayer dipped toward Ben's face, and he caught it by the handle just before it would've stabbed him in the eye. "I think it would legitimize this whole thing if there was someone above our level. You know? It's more of a real thing we're doing if there are big leagues to graduate into."

Lucas thought. "Most of what I know is off the internet. There's a guy with an occult bookstore in St. Louis who mods most of the forums. He's got a group of people that go out on yōkai hunts on weekends. New York's got a whole underground community, but it's a different sort of thing. They're pretty aggro about it, and I say that as someone with three wolves." He started counting on his fingers. "San Francisco. LA. Two women in Texas—"

"There's no big leagues."

"Government's never gotten involved. Everyone I've ever met is a regular person." Lucas shrugged. "We *are* the big leagues."

Ben put the Onislayer down and let that sink in. "I think I respect this job less now that I know I'm good at it. Is that weird?"

"Good's a strong word. Here they come! Act casual. On three…"

A beat-up orange couch came galloping of its own accord down the sidewalk, trailed by three wolves and a Shiba Inu. Lucas put his hands in his pockets and whistled softly. Ben hid the Onislayer behind his leg and pulled out his phone, pretending to look at it.

The couch approached them, bobbing along on four stubby wooden legs. As soon as it was directly behind them, Lucas shouted, "Three!"

The two men hopped back and smashed the wet, filthy furniture to the ground with their butts. The couch groaned. One of its wooden legs rolled into the gutter.

"Biwa Bokuboku!" Lucas said. "The—"

"The lute," the couch said, the words oozing up from between the cushions. "I know who you seek. I know who you are."

"Where is he?" Ben said, holding the Onislayer up to the couch's skirt. The fabric began to smoke.

The wolves encircled them. Toby hopped up onto Ben's lap. He was on the job, but that dog could never resist a chance to sit on people furniture.

"T-There's a meeting tomorrow afternoon," the couch stammered. "All of the leaders. Please, if you let me go, I will—"

"Where?" Lucas shouted.

"The temple!" the couch cried. "They meet at the temple!"

Ben grinned. *Got 'em.* "Which temple?"

犬

Sarah sat on the counter in Maureen Greco's kitchen, kicking her feet as she absentmindedly flipped through tax records from 2009. Jake had hundreds of pages spread out on the dining room table, and he carefully combed through each one, looking for evidence of wrongdoing, searching for any reason, logical or otherwise, that the woman might've run off with Ashley Ocampo. The front door was still broken, and the cold night air drifted in whenever the breeze kicked up, scattering the papers Jake hadn't weighed down.

"Hm," he said, chewing on the end of a pen. "Ten years ago, she and the husband sold a summer home up in Delavan that he never mentioned. Worth a call? Maybe she took the kid there."

"I need a smoke," Sarah said, heading for the door.

Jake looked up. "I thought you quit."

犬

Three family-size bags of chips hit the counter at the 7-Eleven, along with two packs of Twinkies and jar of ranch dip. The clerk put down a mop and started ringing Sarah up.

"Big Tuesday night party?" he said.

"Something like that. Oh." Sarah took the straw out of her mouth and held out her Slurpee so he could scan it. "Hey, have you seen anything out of the ordinary in the last month or so?"

"Like what?"

"Like—"

Bzzakt! The lights in the store flickered, and a shower of sparks rained down into the parking lot.

"Sorry," the clerk said. "It's the sign. It's been doing that for a week. I called corporate. They're supposed to send a repairman out, but…"

He shrugged. Sarah went to the window. It was a tall sign, meant to be seen from the Kennedy Expressway, which sliced its way through the city a few stories up and a couple blocks down. Sarah had to press her ear against the glass to see it.

Sarah squinted. "Did your sign always bulge out at the bottom like that?"

"Bulge?" The clerk looked confused.

Sarah reached in her coat and held up her badge.

"You got a ladder?"

犬

The sign shook as Sarah ascended, carefully climbing from metal rung to metal rung. The clerk's ladder had only gotten her about fifteen feet before she'd had to switch to the built-in pegs, which were, as Ben would say, "rickety as balls." The clerk had rushed inside and watched from the window the moment he and his ladder were unnecessary, partially because the sign was still barfing out sparks, but mostly because he didn't want to be standing there when Sarah fell and died.

As she got closer to the top, Sarah noticed something sticking on her hands. There was a film on the sign, like tree sap or...

"Spiderwebs," she said.

The air around her grew hot and wet. There was a scent of rotting leaves or an ant burning under a magnifying glass. The sign flickered, and Sarah clung closer to the ladder, hiding her face, waiting for sparks. The light just turned off.

She ascended the last few feet until she was at the base of the actual sign, directly beneath the bulge. There were webs flowing out from a crack in the sign. The plastic around it had stretched and broken. Sarah rifled through her jacket pocket and pulled out her flashlight. She pointed it up and shrieked.

She gripped the metal ladder tight and then cursed herself for getting startled. She was a police officer. She was better than that. She pointed the flashlight up again.

Maureen Greco's face, bloated, eyes bulging, stared down at her from the crack on the sign. Thick webs covered the woman's mouth and forehead.

"Jesus Christ. *Madre de dios.* Son of a… Okay," Sarah said, taking a breath. "Okay. Get it together. You need to call Jake, get him over here, call the city and get a…crane."

And then the dead woman blinked.

TWELVE.

Ben tugged lightly on Fergie's leash, urging the dog along. He let Stoney keep doing what he was doing. The owner had left a note stuck between the leash hooks, saying that Stoney was on a "low liquid diet" to keep him from peeing inside the house. He was trailing a few paces behind Ben, panting hoarsely. Ben reached back and scratched the dog's head.

"Ben?" Sarah said. "You there?"

"Sorry." Ben switched his phone to the other ear and held it there with his shoulder as he untangled the leashes. "One of the dogs I walk is...he was old when I started, but now he's like, *old*. I think he's really sick. That hasn't happened to me. I don't know what to do about it."

"I thought you'd have more of a reaction to me finding a living person crammed inside of a 7-Eleven sign."

"Right. You're a great detective."

"It was a very tall sign, Ben. I had to climb it in the dark."

"You're a great, brave, athletic detective. What does this mean for us?"

"Well," Sarah said, sighing, "it means your friend from school isn't a murderer, as far as we know. But we don't know anything else, because this woman is in a coma."

"Does she look like she's going to..." Ben phrased it as gently as he could. "Explode with spider babies?"

"I assigned Chris to stand guard at the hospital. He's gonna watch her for signs of spiders and keep the normies away. Not sure what else we can do. We can't exactly set up a quarantine for that."

Fergie spun in a circle several times before squatting to pee, as was her way, and Ben twirled the leash with her.

"Who's Chris?"

"He's the guy whose life you saved in the video store. He's nice. He can see yōkai now, so he came to the last meeting. You should actually go to one of those. It helps to talk about this stuff."

"Yeah, maybe. Hey, actually, I have a lead too." Ben paused. Lucas had told him not to do this. *Cops bring trouble,* he'd said, but…

"The leaders of the different yōkai clans are meeting at an abandoned Buddhist temple at two this afternoon," he said. "A talking couch said the spider would probably be there. Do you want to meet us?"

"A talking couch?"

"He was also a burglar."

"Sounds promising, but uhh…" Sarah looked over the top of her monitor. Jake motioned to her, car keys in his hand. "We're heading out to the 'burbs to talk to Mr. Greco one last time. Ask him about stuffing his ex-wife inside a sign."

"Really? You're *still* working the boring regular case?"

"I'm doing my job, Ben. You do yours. Keep me posted."

Sarah hung up, and Ben put his phone back in his pocket. He reached down and rubbed his shin. It was especially hot today, and Ben had worn shorts for the first time on the moped, never considering the tiny pebbles that would be flying up and thwacking him on his naked legs the whole time.

Fergie growled. Ben looked up.

The nervous dog was pointed directly at a goose statue in a yellow raincoat, the same goose that had upset her a few days ago. Her ears were back, her fangs were out, her tail straight down.

"Fergie, c'mon…" Ben wiped sweat from his brow. He glanced at the goose again and froze. The statue was looking directly at him.

Fergie kept growling. Stoney stood on the sidewalk, panting, oblivious to the drama. Ben stared at the goose. He could swear it had been facing left a moment ago. Goose statues didn't move. That was ridiculous and impossible. But the dog walker had seen a lot of ridiculous, impossible things. Sometimes talking couches were burglars.

"All right, Ferg," Ben said, a little louder than necessary. He knelt down in front of the female greyhound and fiddled with her collar. "I'm gonna let you off the leash for a second, and you can show me what's bugging you. Are you ready?"

He checked the goose. It was still facing him. "Go!"

The dog bounded across the lawn and pounced, stopping a mere inch from the goose. The leash Ben hadn't actually unhooked went taut. Fergie barked.

The stone goose hissed, shifting between forms. A lawn jockey. A lawn gnome. An iguana. After mere moments, it settled on what appeared to be a raccoon. The shapeshifting animal took a step back, away from the snarling greyhound. It was still wearing a little yellow raincoat and hat.

"Holy shit," Ben muttered. "She was right!"

The raccoon bolted, leaving its little rain outfit in a pile on the grass. Fergie chased it, and so did Ben. Stoney did not.

"Stoney!" Ben stumbled back. "C'mon! Let's get 'em!"

The old dog whimpered, glaring side-eyed at Ben. He peed while standing there, without lifting his leg. Most of it hit his front legs.

"Oh," Ben said. He petted Stoney's back. The dog was shaking. "Okay. I thought…okay. We don't have to chase it. I'm sorry. Sorry."

Stoney leaned against Ben, still shaking. Ben looked up. The tiny rain gear was still there, but no signs of raccoons or geese. Fergie sniffed the hat.

"We'll go home," Ben said, petting Stoney. "We'll just go home."

DOG WALKER II: SHADOW PACK

> **WINDY CITY WAGGERS**
>
> Windy City Waggers™
> Date: **6/22**
> Dog: **STONEY + FERGIE**
> Walker: **BEN**
> #1 **X**   #2 **X**   Food ___   Water **FERG ONLY**   Treat **FERG ONLY**
> Notes: **STONEY'S REAL SICK**

Libby led Ben up the sidewalk as he pondered the situation. He'd been in this boat before. As if he didn't have enough going on in his life, someone, *something* was tailing him. Another death cult wanting to sacrifice Toby? Had the spider sent someone after him? Ben hadn't exactly kept a low profile as of late. He wasn't sure what that raccoon creature was, but this probably wouldn't be the last he saw of it. He needed to talk to Lucas or Tatsuya, someone with a more encyclopedic knowledge of yōkai at the ready.

Ben looked around. They were three blocks from Libby's house. He had trained her pretty well, if he did say so himself. She'd been walking far from home lately. If he didn't know any better, Ben would think…

He stopped. The dog glanced up at him. Her ears raised up, listening.

"Libby, sit."

The mini dachshund sat.

Ben's blood ran cold. Sweat gathered under his shirt. Toby was back at home, eating all the bacon he could handle with Ben's elderly neighbor. The Onislayer was secure in its case on Ben's moped, two blocks from here. It was the middle of the day on a weekday on a side street. There were no pedestrians and no moving cars in sight. Ben was alone and unarmed. He double-wrapped the leash around his palm. He swallowed.

"Libby's never done a trick in her life," Ben said.

A moment passed. Ben and The Thing That Wasn't Libby each waited for the other to make the first move. Ben blinked.

Libby snarled. The dachshund's head morphed into that of a raccoon, round brown eyes within black circles, pointy yellow teeth, thick whiskers. The rest of its body soon followed. Stripes formed on the creature's tail as it poofed up from a dog's to a raccoon's.

The critter pounced at Ben, who dodged left and yanked hard on the leash. The sinister raccoon gagged, flopping neck first onto the sidewalk. Its tongue lolled out and its back leg twitched. It looked a lot like how an animal would die in a cartoon, and it gave Ben a brief flash of guilt.

"W-What are you?" Ben said. "Why are you following me?"

The raccoon scurried to its feet and leapt at Ben again, this time at an angle where the leash would be no help. Ben blocked it with his forearm. The creature dug into Ben's exposed flesh with its terrible claws and then thrust its face at Ben's, biting him in the cheek. The dog walker screamed and fell backward onto the sidewalk, barely holding the raccoon back as it chomped and scratched at him.

Ben rolled and pinned the animal down in the grass. He grabbed it by the collar.

Bam! Ben punched the raccoon in the face. It squeaked, stunned, then attempted to wriggle free. Ben punched it again. *Bam! Bam!* The raccoon grabbed his fist with its little people hands and bit his knuckle. Ben loosened his grip.

The raccoon bolted across the grass, leash unspooling behind it. Ben caught the end with the tips of his fingers. The animal froze mid-stride like it hit a brick wall, then clawed at its collar. Ben stood. He grabbed the leash with both hands. The creature tugged, tugged again, then turned and bounded toward Ben, teeth bared.

Just as it pounced at him, Ben spun, swinging the leash like a mace.

Wham! The raccoon's body slammed into the side of a tree. It shifted forms as it slid downward—a branch, a possum, a mailbox, the stone goose, Libby—before returning to its raccoon form. It slumped into a ball amidst the roots of the tree, unmoving.

Ben stepped forward. The creature rippled like water, then

became a snake, slithering out of Libby's collar and across the grass. Ben dropped the leash and jogged after it, but it was halfway down a storm drain before he reached the curb.

"Yeah, you better run!" Ben said. He kicked a rock in after it.

Blood had soaked into most of his shirt. His face must've been bleeding pretty bad. He wished Toby was here so he could toss the dog a Snausage and fix his face. What was the point of a mutant healing factor if he couldn't use it? He picked up the empty collar, and a realization dawned on him.

"Libby!"

犬

The dog walker burst into Libby's apartment and dove forward, lying on the floor on his belly and scanning the space underneath the dining room table. He checked the kitchen cabinets, inside the oven, behind the fridge. He peeked up above the cabinets, in the garbage can, inside the fridge. He looked under the couch, behind the couch, under the cushions. Finally, he heard a soft whimper in the coat closet. He hustled over and swung the door open.

"Oh, thank God."

Libby the mini dachshund trotted out from beneath the coats, tail wagging furiously. Ben lay down on the floor on his back, completely exhausted. Libby climbed up on top of him and sniffed his face.

"You ever have one of those days where nothing makes sense, Libby?"

The dog licked his bloody cheek wound.

"Gross." Ben sighed. "What time is it?"

```
┌─────────────────────────────────────────────────┐
│  ┌─────────────────────┐  Windy City Waggers™   │
│  │    WINDY CITY       │  Date: _____ │
│  │   🐕 🐕 🐕 🐕        │                        │
│  │                     │  Dog: _____ │
│  │     WAGGERS         │  Walker: _____ │
│  └─────────────────────┘                        │
│   #1 ___  #2 ___  Food ___  Water ___  Treat ___│
│   Notes: _____│
│   _____│
└─────────────────────────────────────────────────┘
```

Ben held a wet paper towel against his face as he walked down Libby's front steps. His cheek stung as the cold water seeped into the wound. Had he filled out the poop sheet? If the owners came home and the sheet wasn't filled out, they would assume he hadn't walked their dog. Which was technically true. *Notes: Great walk! Not Libby, though. She was in a closet. I walked a demon raccoon.* Ben was so lost in thought that he almost missed Kaylee standing on the sidewalk, waiting for him.

"Hey," Ben said. "What're you doing here?"

"You were supposed to meet me half an hour ago, so I figured you were still here." She looked him up and down. "What happened to you?"

Ben examined the scratches on his arms and the blood on his shirt. He put the paper towel behind his back. "It's nothing."

"You have an open wound on your face, Ben!"

"I do! I do have that. That is a thing I have. Look, I, uhh, there was, I was out walking Libby and—"

"No! Don't even start! Do *not* lie to me!" She stepped toward him. "You always lie to me!"

"I didn't say anything yet!" His phone was buzzing. It was Lucas. Kaylee knocked the phone out of his hand and onto the grass. "Hey!"

"This is not normal!" she shouted. "People don't get their faces sliced up and act like it's nothing! What are you hiding from me?

Where do you go all the time?"

Ben ran over various lies in his head, and they all sounded cheap and stupid. The silence lasted for several days.

"I was giving you time," Kaylee said. "I thought, 'Maybe he's got a rough home life. He's a good guy. He'll get to it on his own. He'll tell me when he's ready. He's a little weird, so what? Everyone's a little weird.' But you are a lot weird, Ben. You are extremely weird, and there's this, like, violent edge to it. You are serial-killer weird, Ben."

"I got attacked by a raccoon," Ben said.

"Shut up," Kaylee said, rolling her eyes. "It's been weeks. This is not fair to me. Are you a drunk? Are you on drugs? Are you a drug dealer? Are you in a gang? A fight club? Dog fights? Are you a hit man?"

Ben picked up his phone. He had a missed call and a text from Lucas:

Meeting starting. Get your ass over here.

"Ben," Kaylee said. Her expression softened. "Talk to me."

"You're right."

"Which part?"

"It's not fair to you." Ben wiped a drop of blood from his chin. He turned toward the moped. "I gotta go."

"Ben," Kaylee said. "You're not my problem anymore. Don't call me. Don't text me. You understand?"

Ben started the engine. The moped buzzed like an angry bee. He pulled away from the curb and down the street.

"You psychopath!" Kaylee shouted. "We're done! You hear me?"

Ben didn't look back. It seemed important not to look back.

"You are not my problem!"

THIRTEEN.

Ben pulled up outside a dilapidated, crumbling Buddhist temple. He had Toby in his crate and a plastic grocery bag dangling from the handlebars. He looked around. Two boarded-up storefronts rotted on either side of the temple. There was an alley across the street, between a bar and a burnt-down shoe store. Nude mannequins, limbs missing, leaned in piles amongst charred shoes. Rough neighborhood. Ben wished he had a way to secure his moped beyond it being heavy and kind of shitty.

A whistle echoed through the intersection. Lucas leaned out of the dark alley, and three wolf heads leaned out with him. He beckoned Ben over. The dog walker scooted across the street and parked behind a dumpster. He hoped the garbage men wouldn't collect his ride home.

"A floorlicker and a *baku* just went in." Lucas pointed to the temple. "Definitely a yōkai meetup."

"What's a baku?" Ben said. Toby trotted over to the wolves, who greeted him with wagging tails.

"It's like a sky-blue anteater. They eat dreams."

"Oh yeah." Ben nodded. "Tatsuya calls them 'dream eaters.' No sign of Ash?"

"No girl, no spider, no lute. Once we see the lute, we'll head in. We know he's working with the spider."

"Okay. Listen." Ben leaned in close, almost whispering. "There's something tailing me. It's like a raccoon, but it can change into other things."

"Tanuki," Lucas said, his eyes not leaving the temple. "They're not raccoons; it's a different species. The real non-magic ones, I mean. The yōkai are their own thing."

"There's one following me. It was in disguise as one of the dogs I walk."

"Sounds right. They can also blow up their scrotum like a balloon and float around on it."

"Fun," Ben muttered. He untied the handles of the plastic bag. Toby stopped playing with the wolves and watched it with great interest.

"How do you not know what a tanuki is?" Lucas said. "There's a whole Ghibli movie."

"I don't know, man. I broke up with my girlfriend twenty minutes ago." Ben pulled a raw steak out of the bag and tore it from the packaging. "I'm having a hard time focusing. Why is one spying on me?"

Lucas shrugged. "We're into a lot of shit lately."

Ben tossed the steak onto the pavement in front of Toby, who immediately dug in. The tanuki wounds on Ben's face, hands, and arms started to heal. He sighed, closing his eyes. "I just need a minute here."

"You know, if you're feeling overwhelmed by all this, I can find a good home for Toby."

Ben opened his eyes. "What do you mean?"

"There're channels for this sort of thing. I got Toshi off the internet." Lucas held out his hand, and the wolves went to him, rubbing their noses on his palm. "I'm sure we could find somebody decent to take Toby. After we rescue the kid, I mean."

"I can't just...I promised Tatsuya," Ben said. "It's his family legacy."

"There's more than one inugami in the world, and none of the other ones have an unbroken line of samurai watching over them. Toby's not a birthright. You're not his chosen protector. He's an exotic pet. People give up pets they can't take care of all the time."

Toby finished the steak and started licking the pavement.

"I'm not saying you *have* to give him up. I'm just saying. If you ever—" Lucas stopped, peering over Ben's shoulder. Ben turned to see what he was looking at.

A bundle of cloth with a lute for a head ducked from the shadow of a mailbox to an abandoned newspaper dispenser and, once it thought the coast was clear, slid past the solid wood door of the temple. Ben, Toby, and all three wolves turned to Lucas, waiting for his command.

"Showtime," he said.

犬

Inside the temple, the yōkai were sitting in a circle, deep in conversation. The spider, the Tall Priest, Iguana Elmo, the ten-foot woman with the eyes on her arms, the blue anteater, and the ox with a human face all hovered over scrolls with various scrawlings and diagrams. The Tall Priest was holding court, but the spider did most of the talking.

"We must act soon," the spider said. In the time since she'd bonded with Ash, a cluster of black asymmetrical eyes had grown above her mouth. Her human fingers were twitching. "The meat is sufficient for the ceremony, but it is quickly rotting."

The Tall Priest nodded. "We can begin tonight, if we are all in agreement."

"We must kill the dog walker first!" squealed the battle-scarred eyebutt, who was pacing behind them. The scar running across the expanse of its buttface pulsed as the creature raged. "We know where he is! We must strike now while he is unsuspecting!"

Ash was only half listening. After several days of focus and practice, she'd gotten her fingers and toes mostly under her own control. She tapped her toes against the floor. If the movement was subtle and rhythmic, the spider didn't notice. Soon, the demon's concentration would slip, and Ash could get herself out of here, away from this monster uprising.

"I have reservations."

All of the yōkai turned and looked at the ox with a human face.

Ash listened, too.

"The humans can be wicked," the ox said. "These modern ones, especially. I am a living metaphor for the cruelty of eating meat. I know this better than anyone. But if we bridge the worlds and reveal ourselves, the death toll could be catastrophic."

Ash gasped, and she felt the spider take full control of her face in response. Her toes stopped tapping. *Oh no.* Was the spider on to her? Maybe she'd better—

Just then the doors swung open, and the lute-headed bundle of cloth slithered in.

"Sorry I'm late, everybody!" Biwa said. "I had to get my face tuned."

The eyeballs on the tall woman's arms shifted their gaze from the lute to the doorway behind him. The eyes bulged. The woman screamed.

Three wolves swept into the room, with three-dimensional shadows of larger, more feral wolves emerging from their fur. Two of the animals pounced on the lute, and the sentient instrument howled as its cloth body was ripped to shreds. The third wolf leapt between them and rushed toward the woman with the eyes on her arms.

The sky-blue anteater raised its trunk. *Honk!*

In an instant, the temple was flooded with a blast of white light. The wolf rolled to a stop, rubbing its eyes with its paws. When its vision cleared, the yōkai were all fleeing in different directions.

The Tall Priest stretched up toward the rafters, carrying the blue anteater and the eyeball woman under his arms like sacks of flour. The spider scurried up the Tall Priest's back with her hair-tendril limbs. There was a skylight toward the back of the building leading out to the alley, and all of the yōkai leaders were converging on it.

Ben, Toby, and Lucas all entered at the same time. A blue ox with a face like a man charged at them. Ben swung the Onislayer blindly and lopped off one of the anthropomorphic beast's horns. The ox kept running, heading out the door and down the street. It wasn't trying to gore anyone. It was just escaping.

STEAK. Toby turned to chase the great beast. *EAT STEAK.*

"No!" Ben shouted. "Later! We're here to find—" A small girl dangled from the ceiling by her hair. Her head was twisted the wrong way, but Ben recognized the face. "Ash!"

A brief expression of recognition flashed in the girl's eyes before a wooden support beam hid her from Ben's view. The spider cursed in Japanese as it scurried out the open skylight. The Tall Priest was right behind them, tossing his companions out first and then clutching the sides of the window. He grunted as his legs lifted off the floor, retracting up toward his body. Soon, he was out too.

Lucas hung back by the exit as Ben hustled toward the skylight, scanning the room for a way up. He whistled, and two wolves rushed to Ben's side on the front lines. The third stayed with the lute, keeping it pinned while gnawing at the instrument's handle.

Toby barked. The two wolves growled. There was a shape hiding behind a dilapidated shōji screen. Ben did a double take as a very familiar figure stepped into view.

The eyebutt was nude. His wrinkled legs bent backward at the knee, and his tiny shriveled upper body was caked in dirt and grime. A pale jagged scar ran diagonally across his buttface. His single eye squinted in a way that resembled a smile.

"Dog walker," he said, relishing every syllable.

"You look terrible," Ben said. "Even for a talking butt."

"Hey!" Lucas shouted from across the room. "Is that your arch nemesis?"

Ben blushed, embarrassed.

"You were a fool to come here," said the shirime. "My final revenge is at hand!"

"Still talking out of your ass, I see." Ben wished Lucas was close enough to hear him say that. He raised the Onislayer. "Your last final revenge didn't work out so well."

"Your threats are worthless, gaijin! I see through you! You are a child with a toy!"

"You don't even have a giant chicken this time."

"I still have some tricks! *Hibagon ni natte!*"

A fist the size of an armchair—white furry palm with black fingers—burst from the floor to the eyebutt's left. A second fist smashed upward to the eyebutt's right, this one black with white fingers. The shirime cackled as two identical creatures climbed up from the dust, the wood, and the rubble. The demons had black-and-white fur, large hands and feet, and wrinkled humanoid faces. One looked like a gorilla that dressed like a panda bear for Halloween. The other looked like someone had taken a picture of the first one and inverted the colors: white fur with black highlights.

The two wolves at Ben's side lowered their fronts and raised their rears, ready for action. Toby did the same.

"Ben!" Lucas shouted. "Those are—"

"Hibagon," Ben said. "The Japanese Bigfoot. I know! Can you get over here?"

"No I cannot. You know what a hibagon is, but you don't know a tanuki?!"

"*Osotte!*" shouted the eyebutt.

The panda-patterned sasquatches roared.

Lucas whistled. The two wolves at Ben's side threw themselves into the space between Ben and the White Hibagon. Twin tentacles of darkness blasted off their backs and wrapped around the ape's wrist.

Ben swung the Onislayer at the other one. The panda sasquatch caught the blade in its palm, and its entire hand burst into flames. The hibagon stumbled back and fell halfway into the hole it had just climbed out of.

"All right, Tobe!" Ben said. Toby stood next to him, still in regular dog mode. He gave Ben the side eye. "Hurry up! I did the hard part, you just have to—"

A massive flaming fist smashed into the little dog, who flew across the room and through a wall, out onto the street outside.

"Welp," Ben said.

The hibagon grabbed him and lifted him off the ground.

"Your inugami won't save you, human!" The eyebutt danced around victoriously, his shriveled upper body flopping against his butt like a dead fish.

The White Hibagon struggled against the wolves' shadowy grasp. It yanked its arm back. Both wolves were hoisted up in the air by the fur tentacles. The great ape swung the wolves over its head and loosed them across the room. One smashed into and through a wooden pillar. The other soared straight into Lucas, who fell backward under the weight of his pet, cussing like a sailor. The third wolf was curled up on the floor, chewing on the handle of the lute. It looked up, sensing its brothers' pain.

Ben tried to swing the Onislayer, but his arms were pinned by the Black Hibagon's enormous fingers. The wooden blade wobbled helplessly at Ben's waist. The sasquatch held Ben up to its face, close enough that he could smell its rancid breath. It looked at its other hand, still burning from the touch of the Onislayer. Comprehension flashed in its eyes as it connected the dots between Ben and the fire on its hand. This was not a smart demon.

"Let...me...go!" Ben said.

The hibagon squeezed, and Ben felt a bone in his left arm snap. His mouth filled up with blood. Several ribs cracked inside his chest. His vision blurred, but not before he saw the eyebutt climb up onto the ape's shoulder.

"You have always been weak, *gaijin*," the eyebutt said. "You were also lucky but, alas, your luck has run out."

Lucas shoved the wolf off of himself, swearing. He got to his feet and brushed off his coat. The other two wolves rushed across the room and launched themselves at the White Hibagon. One went for the leg and was kicked away. The other went for the jugular and was punched.

"Work together, damn it!" Lucas shouted as he stomped down the aisle. He stopped just out of reach of the apes. "Come on!"

He pulled out his dog whistle and blew into it. The wolves all stopped what they were doing and sat down in front of him, tails wagging. The white ape roared and beat its chest.

"You can't...really hurt me," Ben gurgled, his mouth full of blood.

The eyebutt patted Ben on the head with its foot. "We'll find out together!"

The Black Hibagon wrapped its other still-smoldering hand around Ben's head. The dog walker closed his eyes.

Whoom! The full monstrous form of the inugami charged through the outside wall, smashing a much larger hole out of the regular-sized Shiba Inu one it had flown through earlier. Jet-black whips of fur flailed on the beast's back. Its claws dug deep into the floor. Its eyes glowed. Its fangs glistened.

The inugami barked, piercing and shrill. The panda sasquatch dropped Ben to clutch its ears, and the eyebutt and dog walker both tumbled onto the floor. The Black Hibagon raised its fists to attack and took a swing at the inugami. Toby dodged with ease and pounced, sinking his teeth into the demon's neck.

Lucas whistled and pointed. The first wolf ran forward and dodged the White Hibagon's grasp. A tentacle shot forth from his back and wrapped around the ape's wrist. Lucas whistled again. The second wolf expelled a tentacle, which wrapped around the other wrist. The third wolf glanced at Lucas, and the man nodded. The wolf wrapped several tentacles around the White Hibagon's neck and yanked the creature onto the floor, face down.

"You hit *me!*" Lucas kicked the creature in the head. "Nobody hits *me!*"

Ben sat up, feeling his arm and several ribs click back into place as the inugami took a big bite out of the hibagon's shoulder. He spat out the last of the blood in his mouth and took a deep breath as his lungs healed. He wiped his mouth with his shirt.

Several feet away, the eyebutt was also recovering. Between them, the Onislayer was lying flat on the floor.

The Black Hibagon flailed its oversized arms and moaned in terror as the inugami mauled it mercilessly. Green blood splattered the walls and ceiling around it. The inugami shook like a wet dog, and a warm spray of green blood misted off its fur. It reared back and howled.

As the eyebutt was watching this, Ben dove forward and grabbed the Onislayer.

"All right, you leathery old perv!" Ben said, pointing the Onislayer at the demon. "Show's over, let's—"

He dropped his weapon and ran.

"He's got a gun!"

Blam! Ben dove behind a wooden pillar as a bullet ricocheted next to him. The eyebutt laughed, a smoking Ruger Mark III clutched in his tiny, shriveled hand. Where he'd been keeping that gun prior to this moment was an unsolvable mystery.

Lucas frowned and ducked behind the altar cabinet. Each of the three wolves had a shadow tentacle around their hibagon's neck. The tentacles twisted, and the sasquatch's head popped off with a wet *slurp*.

Blam blam! Two more bullets ricocheted off the pillar. The wolves scurried behind the cabinet with Lucas.

"Since when do you guys use guns?" Ben shouted.

"*Baka na gaijin!* All I wanted was to show my beautiful eye to unsuspecting mortals! And you ruined it!"

Blam! Debris rained down in Ben's hair. He looked around. There was nowhere he could go that wasn't in the eyebutt's line of sight.

Glowing red eyes emerged from the carcass of the Black Hibagon. Toby growled.

"You killed my chicken!" said the shirime.

Blam!

"You scarred my glorious flesh!"

Blam blam!

"You've sent all of my friends back to the Land of the Dead! You've stolen everything!"

In an instant, the inugami was upon him. The eyebutt screamed, firing a single final shot into the ceiling. Ben, Lucas, and his wolves all popped up from their hiding places.

"Yeah!" Ben said.

"Eyugh…" he added a moment later as the eyebutt's screams turned to gurgles, which were soon drowned out by the sounds of flesh being ripped from bone. Toby made snorting sounds and light growls as he ate. Lucas frowned. Ben went pale. The whole experience was more visceral than either human in the room was quite ready for.

"Well," Lucas said, putting his hand on Ben's shoulder, "you defeated your arch nemesis pretty, uhm, decisively. That's nice, right?"

Toby burped, which made Ben burp at the same time.

"I feel sick," he said.

犬

The fleeing yōkai—the spider, the Tall Priest, the others—settled onto a baseball field a block away from the temple. Everyone but the spider and the priest continued on into the night. The priest scanned the skyline back toward his temple. Their attackers were not following.

"This is a minor setback," the Tall Priest said. "We already have what the shirime had to give. Our goal remains the same."

"Tomorrow we will…" The spider moaned, holding her head. "Tomorrow…"

The Tall Priest squinted at her. "Are you well?"

"I'm fine. Go. Gather our yōkai."

The Tall Priest nodded, stretching his body to the next rooftop over and hoisting himself up. The spider was alone.

"Mendokusai shōjo!" the spider snarled. "Idiot girl! This body is mine!"

"Nnnno!" Ash said, struggling to control her face enough to get the word out. "Someone in there said my name! They're looking for me! They're here!"

"No one is coming for you! I am your only friend!"

Ash grabbed her head with both hands. Several tendrils of hair wrapped around her arms and pulled them away. She screamed, throwing herself into the chain-link fence separating the baseball diamond from the bleachers.

She grasped for her head again, and the tendrils caught her hands. She reached harder, managing to touch her head with her palms. She was growing stronger.

The spider's mouth bit her finger. Ash shrieked, letting go and rolling into the dirt. The hair tendrils lifted her off the ground and slammed her into the fence again, and then again, and again, until Ash stopped struggling. It laid her down on the ground.

"There," the spider said softly. "Feel better now?"

Ash jammed a fistful of dirt into the spider's mouth. The spider wheezed, coughing. Ash clutched her head.

"You're not killing any more people!" she shouted. She twisted her neck with her hands. It crunched audibly and stopped partway, so that Ash was looking at her shoulder.

The spider shrieked. Hair tendrils flailed all around Ash's head and began whipping her, hard enough to break her skin. She fell to her knees but kept her hands on her skull. She had to remain calm. If she got scared, the spider would take control. She had to remember her Bushidō.

Righteousness. A samurai knows when to strike.

The hair tendrils lifted her off the ground, then dropped her.

Courage. Courage without honor is stupidity. True courage is doing what is right.

The tendrils hoisted her up and smashed her into the fence, this time hard enough to knock it over. She collapsed into the dugout, two feet underground, surrounded on three sides by wooden walls, with a corrugated metal roof overhead.

Compassion. My fists are weapons. This power should be used for good.

Ash punched the back of her head, right in the cluster of spider eyes. The tendrils wrapped around her wrist and forced her to punch her own nose.

Respect. That one is for my parents, who are not here.

"You are nothing without me!" the spider said.

Ash grabbed her skull and held it tight. *Honesty. Honor. Loyalty.*

"You need me!" shouted the spider.

"I don't need you!"

With all of her strength, Ash wrenched her head fully in the right direction, wincing as her spine clicked into place. The tendrils of hair flailing violently around her dropped to the ground, limp, then shriveled and collapsed into dust. She let go of her head slowly, waiting for her own hair to attack her. Nothing. She looked around.

She was in a baseball field, in a sketchy part of the city she had never been to. There was a basketball court with no nets on the rims and a playground with no swings on the swing set. She was in her pajamas, the same ones she'd put on weeks ago, and she was barefoot. Ash felt the back of her head. No mouth. No eyes. She patted her body and closed her eyes, thinking around inside her brain for any sign of the spider. It seemed to be gone. A police siren echoed in the distance.

"Okay," Ash said. "Now what?"

FOURTEEN.

Tatsuya stepped to the center of the dojo, fresh Pocari Sweat in his hands. Condensation dripped off the bottle from the heat. A line of fifteen kids jogged in a circle around the old luchador.

"Quickly, children! Pump those legs! ¡Ándale!" He twisted the cap and started chugging.

Ding! The door opened, just barely enough for a small girl to slide in. She was wearing dirty blue pajama pants and a T-shirt. She had no shoes.

"Sensei?"

The boy at the front of the jogging line stopped and stared. "Ash is back!"

All of the other kids stumbled into him, each knocking the next one over. Tatsuya dumped his drink onto his shirt in surprise and dropped the bottle.

"Ashley!" he said.

The students swarmed in a cluster around Ash, asking her questions and tugging at her filthy clothes. She took a step back toward the exit and glanced at Tatsuya, fear in her eyes.

"Niños! Give her space!" Tatsuya waded through the crowd and knelt down in front of Ash.

"I need help," she said.

犬

Ben and Lucas raised their glasses and downed their shots of whiskey. Ben coughed, spit half the whiskey back into the glass, and slid it down the bar a couple of feet so Lucas wouldn't see.

"What's our next move?" Ben leaned against the counter extremely casually to block Lucas's view of the glass.

"Well, the yōkai scattered to the winds." Lucas flipped his glass and set it upside down on the counter. "Taka ate the only one we were tracking. Sorry about that. He's got this thing with wood. See?"

One of the wolves was lying on the brick patio, gnawing on a branch. The other two were chasing Toby up and down the alley. Lucas had taken Ben to the only outdoor bar in the city where they could show up with three wolves and a dog and no one would bat an eye. It was that kind of place. But unlike the last one they'd gone to, this one was mostly humans.

"Maybe we can track that bull," Lucas said. "Did you get a good look at him?"

"He was blue with a people face." Ben's phone buzzed.

"Well, that's a start. There's a whole section of the south side that used to be slaughterhouses. Maybe—"

"Toby!" Ben stood, showing Lucas his phone. "We're leaving!"

犬

Jake and Sarah's Cadillac idled in rush hour traffic on the southbound Tollway. Anthony Greco, the ex-husband, hadn't been there when they'd arrived. Jake saw this as a further sign of guilt. Sarah thought otherwise. It was going to be at least another hour before they were back in the city. The sun had mostly set beyond the horizon, and Jake flipped the headlights on. Sarah gasped at her phone.

"We need to go to Tatsuya's." Sarah rooted around under her seat for the detachable siren lights. "Right now."

"What?"

"Dragon Mask Lucha Dojo! It's on Milwaukee, in Niles! Used to be a Pizza Hut."

She clicked on the hidden lights and siren. Jake pulled around the car in front of him and accelerated along the left shoulder of the highway.

"Why?" he shouted. "What? *Why?*"

"Jake!" Sarah said. "Tatsuya found the kid!"

犬

Ash sat in the beat-up office chair Tatsuya kept behind the counter, hugging her arms and pushing herself from side to side with her foot. After the other kids had gone home, she'd cleaned up in the sink in the bathroom and changed into a spare uniform. She examined her reflection in the glass case containing Dragon Mask's dragon mask. The dark circles under her eyes had dark circles of their own. She tilted her head from side to side, and her hair didn't move of its own accord, which seemed like a good sign. Tatsuya-sensei set a mug full of green tea on the counter, pulled up a folding chair, and sat down in front of Ash.

"Do you want to talk?" he said.

"I can't explain it." Ash looked down at the floor. "It's too weird. You won't believe me."

"I will," he said.

Ash took a deep breath. She made eye contact. "I have a demon in me."

"I understand." Tatsuya nodded. "We both have demons."

"You don't drink anymore, though."

"I know. That was...not a metaphor."

"There's a spider inside my head," Ash said. "It talks to me. It takes control of my body and makes me do things."

"What things?"

"Hurt people. She's been plotting with a bunch of other demons to blow up the city and overthrow the government. Or something. I don't really understand it because they mostly speak Japanese. They said something about a 'neeko no-gi-say,' bridging the two worlds."

Tatsuya said, "A...sacrifice of meat? Which meat?"

"See? You don't believe me." Ash turned away. "You think I'm lying."

Tatsuya stood. He paced around to the other side of the counter, rapping his knuckles on the wood as he thought.

"I've never told anyone this. Years ago," he said, "I had moved from Guadalajara to Mexico City and started fighting in Arena Mexico. And I was good! I headlined my first match—twelve-minute fight with Johnny Crossbones. Sayonara Slam from the top rope! *¡Pataplum!*"

He slapped his elbow. Ash laughed.

"My manager tells me, 'Dragon Mask, do not miss next Friday's event, there will be an NWA scout in the front row.' Arena Mexico is good, top tier in Mexico, but NWA is America, with American money. I can be on TV! Dragon Mask in prime time! Dragon Mask the movie star! Then I get a phone call. My, uhh, my father was sick."

He inhaled, scanning the empty parking lot. "We had not spoken in a long time. He was not happy with his luchador son. I decide I will go home, talk quickly, and come back before Friday. So I go home." Tatsuya made a wide gesture with his hands. "Dogs. Dogs everywhere. He was a dog breeder. We always had dogs. But this was, ehh, *muchos perros. Un mar de perros.* I find him lying in bed with a Shiba Inu. He asks me, have I noticed he always has one Shiba Inu. Even before I was born, one Shiba Inu. There was Aki, Hiro, Good Tatsuya, and now this one. So—"

"Wait," Ash said. "He named a dog 'Good Tatsuya'?"

Her sensei frowned. "He was a bad parent. I ask him, Shiba Inus, so what? He says, 'Tatsuya, it is the same Shiba Inu.'"

"So the dog was like…" Ash sat up. "Twenty?"

Tatsuya shook his head. "The dog was five hundred years old. Centuries before, in Japan, a man used dark magic to create an inugami, a demon dog, to kill the cruel father of the woman he loved. The inugami was successful in its task, but the woman poisoned the man before the dog could kill its master and free its soul from his service. The inugami was doomed to walk the earth for all eternity. Soon after, it was found by a masterless samurai, a *ronin*, who cared for the demon dog until he passed it on to his son, on and on to my father, and then to me. This is the future he had planned for me.

Cleaning up after an immortal dog. He asked that I swear to carry on our family legacy."

"And you said yes," Ash said, tapping the glass luchador mask case. "So that's why you're not famous."

Tatsuya shook his head. "I said no. I said he was a crazy person, I wanted no part of his madness, and I left. I am not famous because I am not famous. I wrestled okay at that match, but the scout was not looking for me."

"So..." Ash squinted. "Wait. I don't get it."

"I went home again a month later. My father was long gone. The other dogs had left, but the inugami had been there for weeks, alone with my father's remains. Watching over him. Starving. Waiting for me. Toby never forgave me for that. I never forgave *myself* for that."

"Toby." Ash leaned up and looked at the dog bed on the counter, finally making the connection. The back of her head itched. *Oh no.*

Tatsuya put his hand on hers.

"You are not lying," he said.

"Toby's immortal?"

Inugami! a voice shouted inside her head, distant but clear. *Satsujinsha! Kodomogoroshi!*

"He is very old."

Ash nodded. "Does Ben know?"

Ding! The door opened, and two adults that Ash didn't know entered the dojo. The woman smiled at Ash. The man goggled at the room like he'd never seen a lucha dojo before.

"Ashley?" the woman said. "I'm Sarah, this is Jake, we're—"

"You called the *cops*?" Ash stood and backed into the corner.

"*Oi oi!* Ash!" Tatsuya said. "These are my friends. Talk to Sarah. She can help you."

"It's okay," Sarah said. She nudged Jake, who put the handcuffs away. "We're the good guys."

"We're not gonna hurt you, kid," Jake said.

"I'm not going with you! You're not putting me in another home! I'm not going back to that!"

The hairs on the back of Ash's neck stood up. Her head buzzed.

The hair dangling on either side of her face converged into leglike strands and shifted of its own accord. The voice inside her brain growled.

"That's not why we're here," Sarah said. "Did anyone hurt you? Are you in danger right now?"

"I didn't kill anybody!"

Jake squinted at her. "Nobody said anything about that."

"We found your foster mom," Sarah said. Her partner did a double take. Telling the girl *that* right now was way out of line.

"Y-You did?" Ash said.

Lies! thought the spider.

"She's alive."

Ash's hair settled. She stumbled forward a few steps and slumped back down into the office chair.

Jake leaned over to Sarah and whispered, "What are you doing?"

"Are you hungry?" Sarah pulled out her wallet. "Do you want a burger or something?"

Ash nodded. "Chicken nuggets. And a vanilla shake. And cheese fries."

"Cool, that's...specific." Sarah handed Jake a twenty. "Jake's going to get you some food, we're gonna talk, and then you can stay here with your sensei until we figure this out. Okay?"

Jake put the money in his pocket somewhat reluctantly and turned toward the door, which swung open inches from his face. Ben Carter stopped, startled.

"Carter?" Jake put his hand on Ben's chest and pushed him back out the door. "Oh no. No, no, no. This isn't your goofy shit. This is an active investigation, and we don't need you—"

"Big Ben!" Ash said. The voice inside her head, a little louder now, shrieked.

"It's all right." Ben brushed past Jake. "We know each other. How you holding up, Ash?"

"I'm okay," Ash said. The hum inside her head grew louder. She rubbed her eyes and tried to ignore the voice in her brain and the itchy tingle in her scalp. "I'm fine."

"You wanna go a few rounds?" Ben put his dukes up. "I've been practicing."

Ash smiled, but she didn't laugh.

Kodomogoroshi! screamed the spider. *Kumogoroshi! Kodomogoroshi!*

"Ashley?" Tatsuya could tell something was wrong.

"Sorry. She... She hates Ben." Ash gritted her teeth and took a deep breath.

Ben took a step back. Toby was still out in the parking lot with Lucas and the wolves, sniffing around and eating weeds. He called for the dog mentally.

"Who does?" Sarah said. "The spider?"

Ash nodded. Sweat ran down her neck. "He killed her babies. They died in flames, and he doesn't..." She looked at Sarah. "How do you know about the spider?"

They know too much! They lie to you! thought the spider. *You are not safe here! Run! Run!*

Ding! Lucas walked in, holding the door open. He noticed Jake. "Hey, man."

"No!" Jake said, pointing at him. "I'm done. Carter! This guy with the coat! Out! Someone is going to tell me what the hell is going on here!"

Toby trotted into the dojo, stopping briefly to sniff Jake's leg.

"Inugami!" shouted the mouth on the back of Ash's head. "*Kodomogoroshi!* Child killer!"

Jake frowned. "Who said that?"

Ash's hair whipped around her head in a flurry of tendrils, growing in length as they spread throughout the room. The storefront windows cracked, then shattered. The mirrors along the back wall did the same. Tatsuya grabbed Sarah by the arms and yanked her behind the counter. The tendrils slashed open Ben's face, then his shoulder. Matching wounds formed on Toby. The dog's eyes flashed red.

The remaining fluorescent lights flickered. The girl's head twisted forcefully and her neck snapped. She rose above the office chair, held aloft by thin hair legs. Eight black eyes glared down at Ben.

"Oh boy," he said.

The spider snarled, flashing its yellowing fangs. Several hair strands wrapped around the office chair and hurled it at Ben. He ducked, and the chair hit Jake hard enough to knock him across the room. Jake crashed into the rack of training pads and broke clear through the wooden shelves.

The spider swooped out through the broken window, and Ash's body drifted across the parking lot, gliding along on legs of hair.

"She's on the move!" Ben said.

He slid sideways through the broken door and darted toward Lucas's van. Toby and Lucas followed.

Sarah stood up from behind the counter. Jake was sprawled out on the floor, not moving. The training dummy fell on him.

"Damn it!" Sarah hurried out the door too.

犬

The girl with the spider hair swung from streetlight to streetlight, dodging branches and power lines as she went. Lucas's brown seventies van spun out onto the road behind her, narrowly dodging a slow-moving postal truck. Three wolves rolled around in the back seat, loose amongst dog toys and bones and trash. Ben held Toby a little tighter in his lap.

"You oughta get them seatbelts," he said. "Can't you go any faster?"

Lucas honked the horn and swerved around a white sedan. "This van's forty-four years old. It's kind of a novelty vehicle."

Ben glanced in the rearview mirror and saw Sarah's Cadillac gaining on them. The siren flicked on. She was probably enjoying this, he thought. Sarah had a thing for bad action movies, and she always seemed to miss out on the real-life car chases.

The spider turned back and saw that she was being followed. It growled.

A tendril of hair plucked a trash bin off the curb and hurled it into the street. Lucas winced as the van smashed into the bin, then wobbled over it. The bin got caught under the van for a moment, scraping loudly along the road before snapping free and rolling out in front of the Cadillac. Sarah swerved to avoid it.

"Damn it!" Lucas said. "That better not have broke anything!"

The wolves had all rolled into the front of the van with the humans and Toby. Ben took a wolf's paw out of his mouth.

"*See?*" Ben shouted. "Seatbelts!"

They started losing the spider in the dense line of trees along the street as they entered the city limits. Ben scanned the leaves, squinting as they passed streetlights. He made eye contact with Ash, the human face on the back of the spider's head. She mouthed something to him. It looked like *Go away.*

"She's still in there," Ben said. "We gotta help her."

The spider abruptly shot to the right, up in the air, and over the roof of an apartment building.

"Take the alley!" Ben shouted.

Lucas spun the wheel, and the van veered right into the next alleyway. The Cadillac followed close behind. Ben caught a glimpse of Ash up in the trees, beyond the power lines.

"She's right there! Go left!"

"Do you wanna drive?" Lucas shouted.

"Can I?"

"No!"

At the end of the alley, the van turned left, narrowly avoiding a couple parked cars as it zoomed down a side street. Lucas gulped audibly. Sarah was right behind them. It was a one-lane street—if another car came from the other direction, they'd have to pull over.

Both cars blew through a stop sign, and two cars at the opposite ends of the intersection skidded to a stop. The spider hopped off a loose branch, which came crashing down into the road. The van crunched right over it. The Cadillac scattered the splinters.

"We're losing her!" Ben said.

The spider swung left, again over the rooftops. There was no left turn, so Lucas drove straight at the next intersection, then slammed on the brakes as a blue SUV pulled halfway out of a driveway. Sarah swerved around the van, straight through a fence and into a backyard.

The woman in the SUV gasped, dropping her coffee. She leaned out her window. "Are you out of your mind?!"

Three wolves matching the ones painted on the van barked at her from the passenger's seat. The woman sat back, inhaled, then climbed out of her car and ran screaming into her house.

"Ash is getting away," Ben said.

Lucas switched gears and started backing up.

"What're you doing?" Ben said. "Just go straight."

"SUV's sticking out." Lucas reversed into the intersection and turned, heading around the block. "I'll scrape the paint."

"'Scrape the paint'?" Ben said. "It's Ash!"

"I don't even know Ash!" Lucas said. "I just got this van detailed."

Ben looked at him, a little disgusted. "Are you serious?"

"You're the one with the hero complex, not me. I'm doing all of this as a favor to you. So don't act like I'm obliged to wreck my shit just because you—"

"All right, all right!" Ben threw his hands up. "Just gently coast toward the spider girl!"

犬

The spider swooped out of the residential area and perched itself in a tree above the next busy street over, getting her bearings. The Tall Priest's temple was southeast. The meat was due east. Either way, deeper into the city. It would be easier to lose the humans there anyway.

"Please," Ash said. "Just let me go. Find a new host."

"It's too late for that," said the spider.

The wolf van zoomed onto the street, and the spider saw Ben inside, pointing at her. She sneered back. Suddenly, a wooden fence smashed to pieces as the brown Cadillac burst onto the road and overtook the van, tires screeching, police siren wailing.

The spider cast out its hair to the next streetlight and swung, continuing the chase. The cars blew through a red light, first the Cadillac, then the van. There was a double flash of white light.

"Ah, shit!" Lucas said. "Did the red light camera get us?"

The spider propelled itself from streetlight to apartment building to power line to streetlight, putting more and more distance between it and the cars. The van, especially, was falling behind.

"Are you *slowing down?*" Ben said.

Lucas tapped the brake. "God damn it! I told you! This van's not designed for—"

Ding ding ding ding! Up ahead, red lights flashed as the railroad gates began to lower. The Metra train was coming. Ben glanced at Toby, and he and the dog ducked into the back of the van.

The spider hopped off the lowering gate and onto the other side of the tracks, continuing down the street. Sarah's Cadillac zipped under the gates before they were fully down. The second gate bumped against her trunk. The train's whistle blared. It was close.

Lucas flared his nostrils. He took a moment to decide what to do.

Train whistle again.

He saw the engine. It was right there. There was no way.

He banked right, and the van rolled to a stop among the rocks at the sides of the tracks. The were no airbags, so he smacked his nose into the steering wheel. Three wolves all tumbled into the front seat.

"Sorry, kid," Lucas said, wiping the blood from his mouth. "Looks like we'll have to find her later."

The back doors of the van burst open, and a rusty green moped zipped out, Ben in the seat, Toby in his basket. The three wolves went to the back of the van and watched the boy and his dog go.

Ben skidded along the side of the train tracks, wobbling on loose rocks. The train roared past in the opposite direction. When he got to the end of it, he hopped the moped over the rails and back toward the street.

Sarah swerved around a car and got within shouting distance of the spider. She clicked the siren off and leaned out the window.

"Ashley!" she yelled. "Stop running! We can help you!"

"Leave me alone!" Ash shouted.

The spider hurled itself to the right and up the side of a four-story condo building. Sarah braked, skidded up onto the curb, and stopped inches from a group of diners, who were sitting in the curbside patio of a sports bar. The man closest to the curb silently moved his tray of nachos away from the Cadillac's engine.

Sarah got out of her car and watched as the spider crawled farther and farther up the building. A small engine puttered up from the street. Ben's moped teetered to a stop next to her.

"She's gone," Sarah said. "Sorry, Ben."

Ben smiled and leaned back, speaking directly to Toby. "Time for that thing we've been practicing."

HATE THING, Toby thought.

Ben sighed. "I'll buy you a steak."

PIG, Toby thought. *WHOLE PIG*.

"I'll buy you a ham."

"What're you gonna do?" Sarah said.

Toby snorted and closed his eyes. Darkness formed around him— this time engulfing not just Toby, but also Ben and his moped. Shadow tentacles emerged from the darkness above the dog, behind Ben's head. Two shot upward and grasped the ledge of the building. Ben revved the engine.

"Here we g— *Uhck!*"

His stomach dropped into his pants as Toby's tendrils hoisted him upward, moped and all. The man with the nachos did a double take, noticing Ben was gone.

Sarah took one of his chips and ate it.

犬

The spider stumbled on Ash's human legs as it came to a rest on the wide flat roof, smiling at the view of the skyline from up here. The lights of the city reflected off the spider's eyes.

"We're free," the spider said. "Freedom. Isn't that nice?"

"It sucks and I hate it and I hate you," Ash said.

The spider *tsked*. "Child, it will be easier if you just accept it. The humans have failed. No one is coming for you."

A shape rose into the air over the spider. The dog walker, clinging to a moped with all four limbs, collapsed as the inugami's tentacles dropped him onto the roof. He screamed as the moped landed on his ankle, snapping the bones in two places.

"Mother fu—" Ben rooted around in his pockets until he pulled out a foot-long Slim Jim folded in three places. He ripped open the wrapper and passed the salted meat back to Toby, who gobbled it up in one bite. Ben twisted his ankle around until it popped back into place, ready to go. The wounds on his face healed up, too. He looked up. A cluster of black eyes blinked at him.

"Hi," Ben said.

"Ben!" Ash gasped at the sound of his voice.

The spider shrieked. She threw several hair tendrils upward, which wrapped around the power line above Ben's head and wrenched it down. The cables tore from their poles with a metallic screech.

Vrrr! Ben hit the gas and the moped zipped forward. Sparks showered from the broken lines behind him. The spider turned, her hair swooped out, and she swung to the next building.

"Toby!" Ben shouted.

The dog closed his eyes. The vaguely blurry shadow surrounding the moped expanded. A wolf's head made from darkness emerged above the handlebars, with glowing red eyes and liquid black fangs. Two front paws coalesced to the size of a lion's, followed by strong front legs. They were fast approaching the edge of the roof.

"Toby!" Ben repeated.

The shadow paws gripped the rubber tiles of the rooftop, and just as the moped was about to slam into the edge, they threw the vehicle and its riders upward. Ben gulped as he rose into the air.

The bottom of the moped scraped against shingles as it bounced onto the next roof. A piece of metal clanked off the engine and rolled away behind Ben. He hoped that wasn't important.

The spider was already leaping to the next building. The dog walker hit the gas and picked up a little speed. At the edge of the roof, the shadow wolf threw itself skyward again.

Zoom! They flew between the buildings and touched down on the other side, smoother this time. Ben smiled. He was getting the hang of this!

The spider glanced back, enraged. The dog walker was gaining on her. She jumped to the next roof. Ben hit the gas. The shadow paws launched the moped, harder this time.

Vroom! The front wheel of the moped wobbled loosely in the night air. Ben saw the spider beyond it. The inugami had overshot, and they were in danger of flying right over the spider, over the building, and four stories down onto the street below.

A half dozen shadow tentacles latched on to the roof and yanked them back down to it. The moped and its passengers touched down directly in the spider's path, stopping it in its tracks. The arachnid demon snarled.

Ben drew the Onislayer from its spot behind the engine. "Let Ash go!"

Prehensile hair whipped across the roof and ensnared a dusty brick chimney, which was soon hurtling toward Ben. His first impulse was to block it with the Onislayer, but while demons burned at the Onislayer's touch, Ben was more likely to hurt himself than a chimney. Instead he ducked, and the chimney sailed over Ben's head and directly into Toby's. The inugami rolled out of his basket and onto the roof, surrounded by rubble and bricks and mortar.

"Oof. Sorry, dog," Ben said. The lupine shadow around him faded.

The spider was already on its way down the side of the building. Ben watched as it swung off a flagpole and skittered across four lanes of traffic, heading toward the half-empty parking lot across the street. Beyond the parking lot was a twisting series of alleys and side streets. Ben would never get down there in time. He was about to lose her. Unless...

This roof curved up at the edge. The moped's engine was still running.

He *could* jump it.

If anything went wrong, he would plummet four floors and flatten like a pancake, but as long as Toby ate something before Ben died, he would be fine. He looked back. Toby was still buried under a chimney.

This was a stupid plan.

"Toby," Ben said, "you're gonna earn the crap out of that ham."

He held his weapon in front of him and gunned it for the ramp. Fear washed over him and beads of sweat slid back across his head in the wind. This was a lot scarier without the inugami supporting him. He hit the edge.

Time seemed to slow as the dog walker flew his moped across the street, multiple stories off the ground. He felt weightless and sleepy. He had a sense that this wasn't real, that none of this was truly happening. The cars and the people in the street down below grew larger and larger as Ben careened toward them.

This was an extremely stupid plan.

犬

The spider was delicately raising Ash's motionless body over the barbed-wire fence surrounding the parking lot when it heard screaming.

Ben launched himself off the moped and tackled the spider into the lot, moments before his scooter smashed into the fence and the whole damn thing came crashing down.

The two bodies tumbled through the air before the spider caught herself with her hair and cushioned their landing, inadvertently saving Ben's life in the process. He let go of her and rolled into a parked car, fast enough to dent the door but not fast enough to die.

The spider cast out its hair tendrils toward Ben. He swung his blade. *Voosh!* The spider recoiled as its singed hair retracted to its head. Severed tendrils burned away as they cascaded around the dog walker. He stood firm.

"Yeah, remember that?" Ben shouted. "Let Ash go!"

Another hair tendril shot around Ben's wrist. The hair squeezed and twisted, and he cried out as he dropped his weapon. More tendrils shot out. His other wrist. His arms. His legs. His neck. The hair forced him onto his back, and the spider rose up from the ground, hovering over Ben on thin arachnid legs.

"Die!" the spider hissed.

The tendrils around Ben's neck twisted, tightened. He couldn't breathe. He struggled, but the spider held him down. The Onislayer was inches from his hand. If he could just reach it...

The hair around his neck constricted. His eyes bulged and his face turned red. His legs stopped kicking. His arms went limp.

"No!" The spider's head twisted 180 degrees. Ash was back in control. "Don't kill him!"

The hair around Ben loosened. He gasped, coughing. The tendrils dissolved as Ash was slowly lowered to the ground.

Ben rubbed his neck and took a few breaths. He sat up.

Ash had her eyes closed. She was standing completely still, hands at her sides.

"Ash?"

"You have to go." Ash looked at him, unblinking. Her voice was quavering. "I'm not...I'm holding her in, but I'm not really in control. Go. Tell Sensei I'm okay."

Ben shook his head. "You're definitely not."

"You don't know what it's like!" Ash got into a fighting stance. She raised her fists. "All I can feel is her hate!"

"Ash." Ben stepped toward her. "Don't—"

Ash growled in two voices, her own and the spider's. "You killed my children!"

"Oh boy." Ben blocked Ash's roundhouse kick with his forearm, and it knocked him back a few steps. She didn't usually kick that hard. The kid wasn't just sparring this time.

"I'm not gonna fight you!" he said.

"You scared, Big Ben?" Ash said in a voice not entirely her own. She thrust a fist at him, and he dodged it, but she twisted and elbowed him in the neck. He reached out to grab her. She caught his wrist and threw him into the parked car behind him. "You never *could* beat me."

She jumped up off the side of the car, grabbed the back of Ben's head, and smashed his face into the passenger window, shattering the glass. He turned to face her and was nailed in the stomach twice by her tiny fists. He fell to his knees.

"Your world is gonna end, human," Ash and the spider said in unison. "After *Niku no Gisei*, you will regret—"

Ben grabbed her by the neck. "Get out of her brain, you parasite!"

He pressed the Onislayer to the back of Ash's head. The spider and Ash both screamed, and Ben was overcome with the smell of burning hair and melting eyes. Ash grabbed his arm and twisted. A bone snapped.

They both let go. Ben tried to crawl away, but Ash stomped on his leg. He turned to look at her. Ash's hair rose up in eight distinct spikes, all pointed at him.

From out of nowhere, Sarah Martinez seized the girl and pinned her against a car, face down, and quickly zip-tied the girl's wrists.

The spider mouth on the back of Ash's head bit at Sarah's face. She pulled out a small metallic bottle and sprayed it in the mouth. Pepper spray. The mouth coughed and screeched. Ash's hair tendrils flailed violently. Sarah blocked them with her arm.

Ben knelt down where Ash could see him. "Hey. We're going to help you, okay?"

"Child killer!" Ash said.

"Ash, she didn't give two shits about the spiders I killed while it was happening. She's just keeping you angry."

"Let me go!"

The hair thrashed at Sarah. She tried to gather it up in her hands and got one of her palms sliced open in the process.

"Ben!" Sarah shouted. "Do something!"

"Look," he said, "I know what it's like to have one of those things talking in your head. You get your emotions all mixed together. You lose track of who you are. But I know who you are. You are Ashley Ocampo. You beat me up multiple times a week. You are the strongest person I know. No demon can tell you what to do forever."

She looked at him. The hair whipped a little less ferociously. She turned away.

"Ash," he said. "You're still you."

The girl's hair settled around her. Sarah used the opportunity to gather it all up in a ponytail, zip-tie it, wrap it in a bun, zip-tie it again, and cram the bun in the spider's mouth. She pulled a roll of duct tape out of her pocket and taped over the spider parts.

"Whoof," she said, wiping her forehead. She looked at the cut in her palm, and duct-taped that too.

Ash started to cry. "I'm sorry. I-I didn't mean to hurt anybody. She made me do it."

Ben stood and immediately took the weight off his left leg, the one Ash had stomped on. He turned to Sarah. "You got here fast."

"What do you mean?" The duct tape on the back of Ash's head

stretched, so Sarah put another piece on there, for safety's sake. "You're across the street."

Ben looked at Sarah's car, still parked on the same block they were on now. "Felt like a longer rooftop chase."

"You mostly went up."

A hulking figure slammed down into the parking lot. Black claws dug into the asphalt and yellow fangs curled from its jaws. Red eyes glowed in the night. Ben could feel the rage inside his head, felt the anger rise in his chest. The inugami was in full beast mode, and it was *mad*.

"Toby!" Ben stepped forward, hands up. "It's okay! We got her!"

The beast roared. The cars around it shook, and several alarms went off. A few glasses in the patio bar across the street shattered. Sarah covered her ears. Ash just stared in horror. The inugami's eyes locked onto the girl, the one who had caused it pain.

"No! Toby! It's Ash! She's human! You don't have to—"

The inugami bulldozed through Ben and swatted Sarah away with its tentacles as it pounced on Ash.

It sunk its jaws deep into her neck.

The girl screamed.

Ben reached out. "NO!"

FIFTEEN.

Lucas shut the door on an iron crate. Inside, Toby sat and stared, his canine face as expressionless as always. The man slid his fingers along the runes carved into the bars.

Ben had seen the second floor of Lucas's barn once. He had a pretty cool setup—a bed, a kitchen, a pool table, a big TV. His illegal squatter barn condo was unquestionably nicer than Ben's apartment.

The first floor, however, was solely for the wolves, with a dirt floor, stacks of hay for beds, and ripped-up toys strewn about. One big spotlight shone down from the center of the ceiling, which left sizable areas completely in shadow. The wolves paced in and out of the darkness in a way that made Ben uncomfortable. The fact that there was no air-conditioning or windows didn't help.

"I only use this crate when they get especially wild," Lucas said. "It's etched with symbols of faith, just like your paddle thing. He's not getting out unless we let him out."

"I feel bad about this." Ben sat down on a bale of hay, then immediately stood as the wolf whose bed that was growled at him.

"It's only for tonight," Lucas said. "Give him some time to cool off."

"If you hadn't been there with that dog whistle, if you hadn't talked him down, Ash would be dead right now. I just…" Ben wiped the sweat from his brow and then wiped his hand on his shirt. "I don't know why he keeps losing it. I thought we were doing better."

"He's fueled by rage. It's the reason he's still alive after all these years." Lucas pulled a plastic jug full of water off of a high shelf. "You gotta be tough with him. Be the alpha dog. Show him you don't put up with that shit."

"I *do* put up with that shit. I put up with *all* shit. My entire life is shit."

Ben met Toby's gaze. The dog lay down and yawned. Ben focused his mind, listened for dog thoughts, but there was nothing there.

"He's not evil."

"Go home." Lucas emptied the water jug into three metal dishes. The wolves emerged from the dark and lapped it up. "Get some sleep. I've got him."

"No." Ben sighed. "I've got one more stop to make."

犬

For the first time in his life, Ben entered a police station. He was a little disappointed. If this were a movie, there would've been a thick layer of bulletproof glass between him and the person greeting him—with bars!—and two cops dragging a bank robber in the background, to add a little motion to the tracking shot. A bum or three would be passed out against the wall, clutching bottles in paper bags.

This was not that. This looked like the entrance to a hospital. Just Ben, the woman behind the big stone counter, and one fake potted plant in the corner. If not for all the cameras, Ben thought, there would've been more security at a Taco Bell drive-thru.

"Sir," the woman behind the counter said sternly. From her tone, she'd clearly said it a few times already. "You get mugged or something?"

"Uhh, no, I, uhh..." Ben glanced down at his clothes. He was still very dirty from the car chase. "I just look like this."

"It's okay, Weezie. He's with me." Sarah popped out of a door to Ben's left and beckoned for him to follow her inside.

"Is this him? He's younger than I thought." Weezie turned to Ben. "You helped my mom get a baby with no face out of her crawl space."

"Oh yeah, I remember that."

The woman filled out a blank name tag with a permanent marker and handed it to him. It just said *Dog Walker*.

"You keep killing those demons," she said.

"Yeah, you too," Ben replied, which didn't make any sense, so he ducked out of the room as quickly as he could.

The hallway Sarah led him down was also empty. Plain beige paint, infrequent narrow windows, a few motivational posters and bulletin boards. The boring hallway opened up to a wide-open office. A dozen computer desks were populated by three or four people. Sarah knocked on the desk of an overweight old man with a gray mustache, who waved to her without looking away from his game of solitaire.

"We've only got her for a couple days before she's transferred to juvie," Sarah said once they were out of earshot. She swiped a key card in a slot next to a metal door. It popped open.

"If we're gonna fix this whole situation, we need to do it now."

"How's she doing?" Ben asked, following her through the door. Sarah was walking really fast. He was having trouble keeping up.

"It's hard to say. She only talks to herself. That yōkai is still in there."

"I meant more like, 'Did my dog hurt her?'"

Sarah smiled at him. "She's got a big bite on her neck and shoulder, and a few claw marks on her arm, but I gave her a hot dog, and she's healing up pretty quick. She's got the same thing you have. The spider fixes her."

"Did she, uhm..." Ben mimed feeding a hot dog to a mouth in the back of his head.

Sarah frowned.

They stopped in front of another metal door and peered through the small one-way window at its center. Ash sat alone in a gray room. The giant wooden table in front of her made her look tiny. Bandages covered her right shoulder and left arm. She had a Styrofoam cup full of pop and an Archie comic that she was reading intently.

"She likes you, right?" Sarah said. "She'll talk to you?"

"Yeah." Ben nodded. "She'll talk to me."

犬

Ash tried to focus on the comic book in front of her, which was difficult partly because it was old and boring, but mostly because the spider in her head would not shut up.

Do not be afraid, little samurai, the spider cooed in Ash's brain. It didn't need to speak out loud anymore. Ash heard it just the same. *They cannot hold us for long.*

"I'm not listening to you." Ash rubbed her bandaged forearm. Her wounds itched.

You should listen. I am all you have.

"That's not true. Sensei—"

That old drunk dumped you over to the authorities the moment he could. The dog walker cannot even keep his dog from attacking you. Who is left? The police?

Ash poked at her neck bandage, too. Her skin felt cold under there. It hurt when she turned her neck. Shadows danced in the window on the door. There were people outside.

The moment they finish their work, they will throw you in another orphanage like none of this ever happened. You have no one you can trust.

"Stop," Ash said.

You are alone in this world.

"I said stop!"

Ash felt the spider's mouth smile.

No one loves you but me.

犬

"She said something about a 'sacrifice of meat' to Tatsuya. We should find out what that is. It sounds violent. Did you learn anything about the spider?"

Ben shook his head. "This isn't one people have heard of. Usually the spider yōkai are just big spiders disguised as people. Possession is not an official historical spider yōkai thing, but that green stain in her bedroom was definitely kakawari. I don't know. Maybe it's not actually a spider."

"How do you know about that?"

Jake was standing behind Ben. He had a black eye, and his right arm was in a sling.

"Hey, Jake," Ben said. "Glad to see you're—"

"How do you know what's in the kid's room? Have you been there? Did you see it?"

Ben opened his mouth but didn't respond fast enough.

Jake turned to Sarah. "Did you take him to the crime scene?"

"Yes," Sarah said.

"What the f—" Jake took a breath and held the bridge of his nose. "We agreed."

"Don't give me that. You were there when the girl started hovering! You saw the dojo after she escaped!"

"I don't know what I saw!" Jake got up in Sarah's face. "But we agreed to solve this case like real cops!"

"I *am* solving the case!" Sarah shouted. "You've just got your head too far up your ass to see it!"

Ben felt like his parents were arguing. He glanced in the window, checking on Ash. She turned the page of her comic with her hair.

"Open your eyes, Jake!"

"To what!" Jake shouted. "Your friend's *magic dog*? His sword that kills invisible monsters? That there's a talking spider inside that little girl's brain? Do you even listen to yourself? It's like you had a fever dream, and now you're trying to conform the world to it."

Jake and Sarah's phones both vibrated. They checked their messages.

"Foster mom's awake." Sarah put her phone away. "Great. Go do your real police work. I'll meet you there."

"Uh-uh." Jake ripped the name tag off Ben's chest. He and Sarah locked eyes, and they stood inches from each other's faces.

"You're not deflecting the issue until Ben burns the goddamn station down. You have five minutes to get him out of here before I report this to Internal Affairs, the sergeant, HR, the press, the friggin' FBI, anyone who will listen. No more dog walker. No more late-night adventures. We have a job to do. If you don't understand that, you shouldn't be on the force."

Sarah didn't blink. A beat passed. Jake turned and stormed down the hall. He crumpled up Ben's name tag and tossed it in a trash can.

Sarah took a deep breath and sighed.

Ben looked back and forth between the two of them. "Sarah?"

"We have four and a half minutes," she said.

犬

The door to the interrogation room slid open. Ben stepped into the room and gave a slight wave, trying to look as friendly as possible. He sat down at the table across from Ash. Sarah hung back, leaning against the wall behind Ben. The girl looked up from her book.

Do not believe their lies, said the spider.

"Hi," Ben said. "Sorry about your neck. Toby's, uhm…Toby's sorry too. You know Toby. He hates getting chimneys thrown at him."

Ash glared at him, giving him no response whatsoever. Sarah coughed.

"Cool. So…two things," Ben continued. "The spider in your head is this thing called a yōkai. They're all over the place, but most people can't see them. We can get it out, but we need to know what breed it is. There're about twenty different spider ones, and they all have different rules. They're more like leprechauns or genies than animals—they're like living ideas. Some of them you gotta burn out with incense, some you have to trick with a riddle. There's one that sits in school bathrooms, eats all the toilet paper, and offers kids red paper or blue paper. If you say red, it slices you up until your clothes turn red. If you say blue, it strangles you until your face turns blue."

Sarah squinted. "How do you get out of that?"

"You bring your own toilet paper to school." Ben leaned forward. "Ash, we need to know what we're dealing with here. Did any of the other yōkai at that temple call the spider by a name? It would probably be in Japanese, and they're usually pretty long."

Ash didn't blink, she just kept staring at him. Her arm prickled beneath the bandage.

"Ash?"

"I can't tell you anything," she said.

Sarah piped in. "Can't or won't?"

"The spider won't let you?" Ben bit his lip.

Silence. Ash rubbed her arm. It felt cold, like her neck. It also seemed unusually solid, like there was a layer of plastic between her skin and the bandage. Her heart began to race.

"What is the 'sacrifice of meat'?" Sarah said. "Is that still happening? Is it happening soon?"

Ash didn't hear her. Her face was warm. She felt her pulse beating in her ears as she carefully peeled back the bandage on her arm. The skin where the inugami's claws had scratched her was thin and brittle, like the top layer of crust on a croissant. She slid her fingers across it and it crumbled away. The skin beneath was black and rigid. An exoskeleton. Like a spider's.

"I'm still changing," she whispered.

"What?" Ben said.

Naive little samurai. The spider laughed. *Did you think I would stop at your head?*

"Ash," Ben said, "we're pressed for time here. If there's anything you can say, anything at all—"

"It's too late." Ash slipped the bandage back down before Ben could see. The one on her neck throbbed. "It's just too late, Big Ben."

Sarah looked at her watch. "We need to go."

Ben nodded, standing. Sarah opened the door and checked both directions as she ducked out into the hallway. Ben stopped before leaving.

"Hey..." He turned back. "All that 'Big Ben' stuff about a spaceship and a mutant pig. Is that from *Doctor Who*?"

Ash looked at him. There was no hope in her eyes, none of that spark that was always there in lucha class. She seemed immeasurably sad. "I used to watch it with my dad."

"Me too," Ben said. "We're gonna fix this."

Ash peeled up the bandage on her arm again. Shiny black carapace glimmered under the fluorescent lights. She now saw thick brown hairs, like metal wires, standing straight up from it. They stung when she put the bandage back down.

"No," she said. "You're not."

SIXTEEN.

Stoney was slow going down the stairs, so Ben took it real easy with the greyhounds, pausing at each landing so the scarred old dog could catch his breath. By the time they were outside, fifteen minutes had passed. By the time they reached the corner, Fergie had pooped twice, but Stoney hadn't even peed. Ben had to take them home regardless. He needed to be at Libby's in five minutes.

"I feel like I'm in a rut, you know?" he said, ostensibly to the dogs. "Ash is in jail. Toby's in dog jail. Kaylee dumped me. I'm not helping anyone. I'm not useful. I have...no use. I don't know. It's a lot of little things. Do you ever feel like that?"

Fergie looked at him in a way that said *No, dumbass, I'm a dog*, and then she spun in a circle seven times before pooping in the grass. Stoney just stood there panting.

Ben's phone buzzed. Another Unknown Name/Unknown Number. He was getting a lot of those lately. He muted it.

"I just thought I would know what I'm doing by now. I'm almost twenty-five. I should have something going. Steven Spielberg was twenty-seven when he directed *Jaws*. You know that? Twenty-seven! I can't even finish one script. The only thing I'm remotely competent at is helping you guys pee."

Stoney sniffed a bush and raised his leg. Instead of urine, a dark-brown liquid, thick as gravy, slopped onto the leaves in dense blobs. The dog lowered his leg.

"That's not right," Ben said.

犬

Tatsuya leaned away from the computer screen, squinting through his reading glasses. Enlarged, pixilated kanji scrolled on the dusty beige CRT monitor. He'd gotten the computer used when he'd bought the dojo, mostly to use as a cash register, and he had resented it slightly when Ben put the internet on there. He grunted.

"Anything?" Ben said, sweeping broken glass out the front door. The door was closed but still had no glass, so that didn't make much difference.

"No."

"I checked all the sites I could find that were in English, but I didn't see anything."

Tatsuya grunted again.

A piece of the ceiling was dangling above Ben's head. He reached up with the broom handle and nudged it upward. A fluorescent bulb swung loose and almost clocked him.

Sarah was sitting on the other side of the counter from Tatsuya, flipping through several different old books at once. They were also in Japanese, so she was mostly looking at the pictures.

"Maybe we're going about this all wrong," she said. "Check it out."

She held up a picture—an Edo period woodcutting of a woman in a kimono perched outside a cave, long wisps of web trailing from her chest to tiny spiders.

"*Jorōgumo*," Tatsuya said. "The entangling bride. But she is a spider that can disguise herself as a human, not a spider that possesses humans."

"Also, she breathes fire," Ben said. He dragged a chair over to where the light was dangling. "And Ash doesn't."

"That's true," Sarah said. "But what about…"

She held up another book with another picture. Another woodcutting of a woman in a kimono, this time kneeling in front of a bowl full of rice balls. Her long black hair was spiraling out in random directions except for one strand, which was feeding a rice ball to a tooth-filled mouth in the back of the woman's head.

"*Futakuchi-onna*," Tatsuya said. "The two-mouthed woman."

"Mouth in the back of her head, and she's got the prehensile hair..." Ben said. "But she's not a spider."

"Right. Do you get what I'm saying?" Sarah said. She held the two books together so the pictures were next to each other.

"They're interbreeding? Can they do that?" Ben climbed up on the chair. "They're both female."

"Yōkai are not born," Tatsuya said. "They are created. They are not animals, they are living ideas."

Sarah put the books down. "People have new ideas all the time."

"Neither of those yōkai have a weakness," Tatsuya said. "At least, not in old books. But this *is* a start."

"Ben, you said the spider was purposely keeping Ash mad, right? She's probably feeding on Ash's rage. She's probably fueled by it, like Toby."

"Toby doesn't feed on my rage...I think. Do I have rage?" Ben shook his head. "So what are you saying? We just need to calm Ash down, cheer her up, and then the spider will just, like, crawl out of her mouth? And then we can squish it?"

Sarah laughed. "I don't know, man. I'm spitballing here."

"You want me to talk to her again?" Ben reached for the swinging light bulb and missed. He watched it swing, timing it, waiting for his next attack.

"I will do it." Tatsuya stroked his chin. He set his reading glasses on the counter. "I will talk to Ashley. I won't fail her again."

Sarah bit her lip. "Could be difficult to get you in after Ben's visit, but I'll work on it. The sooner, the better. Whatever the meat sacrifice is, it could happen at any moment. She didn't give you any sort of time frame on that?"

Tatsuya shook his head.

"Nice. Okay. You guys got this," Ben said, catching the light bulb. He hoisted it back up into its fixture and reached up with his other hand to twist it. "This isn't the part I'm good at. I'll just—"

Zzackt! A shower of sparks rained down as the metal part of the bulb touched the fixture. Ben flew off the chair and onto the one section of floor not covered in gym mats, landing hard on his back. The fluorescent bulb swung back down, this time detaching completely and shattering on the linoleum next to Ben's head.

"Pinche gringo!" Tatsuya shouted. He reached under the counter and pulled out a fire extinguisher, which he sprayed at the tiny wisps of flames on the mats.

"Which parts *are* you good at, exactly?" Sarah said, laughing.

"Sorry!" Ben said, coughing. The fall had knocked the wind out of him. "I didn't think—"

"You didn't think!" Tatsuya shouted. "You never think!"

"I'm sorry!" Ben said. He shook broken glass out of his hair. "I'm just trying to clean up! Why are you mad at me?"

Tatsuya stopped spraying the fires. He looked at Ben out of the corners of his eyes. His jaw was set. His brow was furrowed. His stance shifted slightly. Ben stood, then took a step back when he saw Tatsuya's expression.

"Why am I *mad* at you?" The old luchador walked toward Ben. "I entrusted you with the inugami, and you have been losing more control of him every day. For sixty years, and hundreds of years before, he was content to be a dog. Ever since he bonded to you, dozens of people have been hurt. Some are dead!"

"That's not fair," Ben said. "They were—"

"I invite you to train with me!" Tatsuya shouted. "To teach you the arts of the luchador! And you are no better at fighting now than when we started. I trusted you with the life of my best student, my most vulnerable student, and you let the inugami maul her!"

The old luchador stopped inches from Ben's face.

"My family legacy is tarnished. My business is destroyed. Ashley is a wounded spider. I have given you everything, and you have failed me in every possible respect."

"I'm…" Ben felt a lump growing in his throat. His ears were ringing. "I'm sorry."

"Why would that matter?" Tatsuya said.

Ben opened his mouth to speak, but he had nothing. Tatsuya held his gaze, locked on to Ben. His cold glare. His undisguised revulsion. Ben turned away. He kicked the chair he'd fallen off to the side and stormed out the front door. He didn't know where he was going, didn't have a plan, he just knew that, more than anything in the world, he didn't want Tatsuya looking at him like that. He slumped down onto the curb in the parking lot, barely noticing all the broken glass beneath him. Sarah sat down next to him. She'd followed him outside.

"He doesn't mean it," Sarah said.

"No. He's right. I suck."

"You don't suck. You're just..." Sarah tried to think of something else to say, so that it wouldn't just hang in the air. She took a little too long.

"Hey, how's what's-her-face? The comedian?"

"We broke up," Ben said. "The secret identity got to be too much for her."

"Secret identity?" Sarah said.

Ben nodded. "She knew something weird was going on, and I couldn't tell her what."

"Why not?"

"Well..."

"Ben, I'm about to tell you something every guy needs to hear once in his life." Sarah knelt down on the asphalt in front of Ben and put her hands on his shoulders. She looked him dead in the eyes.

"Batman isn't real," she said.

"I know," Ben said unconvincingly.

"You don't have a secret identity. You have a weird hobby. Lying to your girlfriend doesn't protect her, it just makes your life easier, because you don't have to explain your weird hobby. You've got to tell her the truth."

"She's not gonna like it."

"Let her decide that." Sarah checked the time on her phone. "I'm late for work."

Sarah stood and ducked back inside to say goodbye to Tatsuya. Ben looked at his moped, lying flat in the spot across from him. The kickstand had been knocked off when he drove it off the roof.

He took a deep breath through his nose and exhaled through his mouth.

"Batman's a little real," he said.

犬

Sarah zoomed into the hospital lot twenty minutes later. She parked diagonally in a space and a half and jumped out of her car almost before it had stopped. Jake was already waiting inside.

Maureen Greco had been awake since yesterday, but Sarah hadn't actually seen her yet. Jake was intent on bringing in her daughter—not Ash, the older kid—and Sarah had tried to explain that this was a very bad idea, by virtue of "the woman might be full of spiders." He'd responded with a sigh.

Officer Chris was leaving the building as Sarah approached. He saw Sarah and glanced away, looking guilty.

"Hey," Sarah said. "Where you going? You're supposed to be guarding Greco."

"I got reassigned," he said.

"Son of a—" Sarah ran the rest of the way into the hospital, flashed her badge at the security guard, and jogged straight up the stairs to the third floor. As she approached Greco's room, she was stopped by two uniformed officers she didn't recognize. She tried to barge her way past them, but they held her back.

"God damn it!" she said. "This is my case!"

Jake stepped out into the hallway. He was holding a folded sheet of paper.

"Detective Martinez," he said, handing her the note, "you have been suspended indefinitely, pending review of multiple reports of mental instability and legally dubious extracurricular activities."

"Your face is dubious, you weaselly little..." Sarah read the paper. "You don't have the authority."

But the notice was legit, signed by several officials way above her pay grade. She cursed under her breath.

"This is bullshit and you know it. What did you tell them?"

"The truth. Go home. You're off the case."

"Jake, I swear to God, there are *so many* demons involved in this. If you don't—"

"These guys have orders to arrest you if you try to get past them. There's four more in the hospital room. Sarah…" Jake turned away, heading back toward the room. "Go home."

犬

Maureen Greco sat upright in her hospital bed, with four uniformed police officers watching over her. In the time since she'd woken up, her complexion had cleared and her eyes had stopped bulging. She seemed healthy enough now. Physically, anyway. Her behavior was another matter. Jake didn't know her prior to the coma, so he couldn't say for sure, but if she was always like this, he understood that kid's eagerness to get away.

Currently, the woman had a small plastic bowl full of lunchroom meatloaf in front of her, which she was meticulously smashing to a pulp with a spoon.

"Mrs. Greco." Jake coughed. The woman looked up at him. "How are you feeling?"

"Much better, detective. Thank you. Where is my daughter?" Mrs. Greco snatched the Styrofoam cup of water from her tray and sniffed it.

"I bet you're ready to go home, huh?"

She poured the water into the bowl of smushed meat.

"I am. I want to see my daughter," she said.

"Actually, we have a surprise for you." Jake signaled to the cop nearest to the door, who nodded and ducked out into the hall. "I had to pull some strings to make this happen, but um…your case is getting a lot of attention right now. If I do this, you need to start talking to me, okay?"

The woman took a loud, wet slurp of meatloaf water. Jake blinked. The three men around him didn't react at all. He supposed they'd been here longer.

The door opened. Taylor Greco ran into the room and collapsed onto her mom, burying her face in the woman's chest and wrapping her arms around her.

"Mom!" Taylor said. "I thought you were dead! They kept telling me they were looking for you and Ash, but they wouldn't say where or what happened to you, and they had no idea where you were, and I had to stay in this hotel room where they only had regular TV and the bad cereals that come in bags, and I knew if I just kept believing—"

She stopped. Her mom wasn't hugging her back. She looked up to find her mother staring at her coldly, a mask of complete indifference on her face.

"M-mom?"

"Detective." Maureen Greco nudged the girl to the side and smiled sweetly. "Where is my other daughter?"

犬

Whoever was knocking on Kaylee's door obviously wasn't giving up. She shuffled across her apartment, wrapped up to her neck in a down comforter. It was eighty degrees outside, but it was sixty at Kaylee's. She walked dogs for a living, and she made negative money doing stand-up, so she never had much, but she slept better when it was cold. Blasting the AC at night was her one extravagance. She put the chain lock on the door before opening it.

"Hi there," Ben said. "Can I come in?"

"Ben, it's two in the morning," Kaylee said. "Remember when I said you were serial-killer weird?"

"Yeah, sorry. I would've been here sooner, but I had to drive out past Mundelein on a broken moped to pick up the dog."

Kaylee noticed the leash in Ben's hand and followed it down to the floor, where a chunky little Shiba Inu was staring up at her.

"Is that Toby Paszkowski?" Kaylee looked at Ben. "Oh my God. Did you *steal* him?"

"No, uhh, his owner moved, and he didn't." Ben shrugged. "He doesn't live with me. We're just friends."

"Cool."

Kaylee shut the door. Ben tried to catch it with his hand but only managed to get his finger smashed. Toby sighed.

"Ow! I know! I know! I'm sorry!" Ben clutched his throbbing finger and shouted through the door. "I say weird, vague things! But that's why I'm here! I'm going to be one hundred percent honest with you, starting right now. I'll tell you everything! Because I really like you, and I don't want to lose you, and you're smart and funny and I'm stupid and boring and I'm garbage and you're great!"

A moment passed. Ben looked down at Toby, who gave him a withering glance.

The latch slid and the door opened wide.

"You have five minutes," Kaylee said.

"It's gonna take a little longer than that, there's, uhh…"

He held up a heavy ovular lump inside a grocery bag. Kaylee saw the word *HAM* through the transparent plastic.

"There are props," Ben said.

SEVENTEEN.

Ben explained everything: the inugami, their freelance work together, Dragon Mask, the Children of Tengu, Ash and the spider. At first Kaylee was quiet, nodding whenever Ben asked a question and giving him a "mm-hmm" or a "right" whenever he paused to take a breath. As he went along, she started to engage with him more directly, asking intelligent follow-up questions, laughing at Ben's jokes, and throwing in a few one-liners that he wished he'd thought of at the time. As his story approached the present, Ben grew more confident, acting out fight scenes with the yōkai and doing character voices. Kaylee was into it. She was taking it really well. She seemed to genuinely understand the situation.

"Hey, can I stop you for a second?" Kaylee said. "I just want to say one thing."

Ben stepped down from the coffee table and set the candles he was using as Toby and Ash down on the couch. Kaylee took a deep breath through her nose, tapping her fingers on her chin.

"Everything you just said is the stupidest thing I've ever heard," she said.

Ben nodded. "You don't believe me."

The oven timer started beeping, so Ben headed for the kitchen. Toby emerged from beneath the kitchen table, tail wagging. The dog walker slid an oven mitt over his hand and pet the inugami with it before removing a piping-hot honey-baked ham from the oven.

Toby licked his chops.

"I'm struggling to picture the person who *would* believe you," Kaylee said. "It's too violent for kids and too ridiculous for adults. Who's this for? Who's your target audience?"

"Uhh...you? C'mere, Tobe."

Ben carried the metal tray full of ham over to the welcome mat by the door. Toby followed, his eyes never leaving the meat. Ben pushed a half dozen pairs of Kaylee's shoes to the side with his foot and set the ham down on the floor.

"I mean, is this what your writing was like in college?" Kaylee continued. "No wonder you're stuck."

Ben unlocked the front door. He headed over to the window in the dining room.

"You can't just write about real life, so you couch all of your feelings and anxieties in this weird power fantasy where you're the center of a supernatural conspiracy and..."

Ben opened the window. He felt the wind with his hand and looked down.

"What are you doing?" Kaylee said. "I've got the air on."

"Third floor, right?" Ben took a few steps back. "Make sure he eats that ham."

He ran and dove out the open window. Kaylee yelped in surprise.

There was a sickening thump as a body hit pavement. Kaylee stood where she was, hands over her mouth, frozen in shock. Toby looked at her for guidance, found none, and started gobbling up the ham anyway.

Kaylee's gaze slid back to the window. She could feel her heart pounding in her chest. The blanket she had wrapped herself in dropped to the floor. Slowly, she stepped over it and tiptoed to the window, still unable to lower her hands. She didn't want to see, didn't want any of this to be happening. She leaned out and looked down.

Ben wasn't there.

The front door swung open, and Ben Carter, dog walker and apparent immortal, stumbled into the apartment on wobbly legs. His clothes were scuffed up, but otherwise he was no worse for wear. He smiled, revealing a gap where one of his front teeth ought to have been. He popped a loose tooth into the empty socket and wiggled until it stuck.

"It's not a weird power fantasy," he said. "It's a weird power reality."

Over on the floor, Toby looked up from the metal tray and burped. He'd licked it clean.

MORE PIG, he thought.

"Jesus, really?" Ben said. "That was like sixty bucks' worth of ham."

"You…" Kaylee said, almost whispering. "You can talk to him, too?"

"In my brain, yeah. I mean, he's a dog," Ben said. He stuck his finger through a hole in his shirt that wasn't there a minute ago. "It's like talking to a baby. Look, I didn't choose this stuff. It all just happened to me. I would pick you over this in a heartbeat."

Toby tilted his head at Ben. His tail went down.

"Terrific. Ben, I'm gonna need some time to process all this," Kaylee said, in a slight daze. She pointed toward the door. Her hand was shaking. "Please take the talking dog and go."

"Yeah. Okay," Ben said. He backed up into the hallway. Toby was already on his way out the door. "Can I call you tomorrow?"

"Uhm…" Kaylee noticed her hand was shaking. She held it with her other hand. "Why don't you let me make the next move?"

"Okay," Ben said.

He went and stood in the hallway. Kaylee closed the door, and Ben heard it lock.

"I think that went well," Ben said before looking around on the floor for Toby. He saw a tail swoop out of view. The dog was already on his way down the stairs.

Ben's phone buzzed, a little more rattley than usual. He pulled it out. *Damn it!* A snowflake of broken glass spread from the left side of his screen. He'd cracked it jumping out the window. Ben sighed.

He had a text from Lucas:

Found the bull.

犬

Ben's moped zipped through traffic, sticking to the bike lanes and blowing stop signs. It was the middle of the night, and a lot of bars on this strip of road were closing, so the streets were thick with cabs and rideshares and pedestrians. Ben leaned forward, willing his bike to go faster.

The moped had been maxing out at around fifteen miles per hour, ever since he'd driven it off a roof. He could almost run faster than this. He glanced in the mirror. Toby looked angry, as much as Toby ever looked anything.

"Hey, Tobe," Ben said. "This thing we're going to...you gotta control your shit, okay? No going crazy and eating people. Everybody's counting on us."

BEN HATE TOBY, Toby thought.

"What?" Ben said. "I don't hate you! Where'd you get that idea?"

BEN WANT GIRL. Toby's eyes met Ben's in the mirror. *NOT TOBY.*

Ben laughed. "Are you jealous? I can want two things. You know you're—"

TOBY BAD. TOBY BABY.

"Oh, uhm." Ben hit a red light and coasted to a stop. "Look, I didn't mean... When I said that...that wasn't meant to be...How much English do you understand?"

ENOUGH.

Toby leapt down from his basket and out onto the street, gunning it straight into the intersection. A car swerved. A semi blared its horn.

"Toby!" Ben shouted. "Where are you going?"

KILL BULL ALONE.

A tentacle of darkness whipped from the dog's back, wrapped around the next traffic light down, and flung him forward, off into the night.

"We're not— Toby!" Ben hit the gas and scooted forward. A horn honked, and Ben braked as traffic rushed in front of him.

The inugami was gone. Ben smacked his handlebars.

"Shit!"

犬

As Ben turned his moped down the dark alley, he saw a flash of bright red. A long-robed figure greeted him with open arms. Panic flooded Ben's senses, and he drew the Onislayer and leapt off his bike, running to attack the figure before it could hurt him.

"Whoa, whoa, whoa!" The robed figure removed its mask. "It's me! It's Lucas."

Ben lowered his weapon. He noticed the three wolves sniffing around the garbage cans. Toby was there too, facing the wall, deliberately not looking at Ben.

"What is this?" Ben said. Lucas handed him a second robe, along with an equally red mask.

"We're going into the actual club part of the club. You don't want to be…" Lucas gestured to Ben's general aesthetic. "You. It's a—"

"Tengu." Ben held up the mask. Its long, phallic nose protruded out a foot from its face. "It's a Tengu mask. Where'd you get these?"

"Costume shop. Are you all right? Toby got here like ten minutes before you."

"We had a fight."

Lucas poked a brick with his finger. Eyeballs opened at the center of every brick on the wall. "Like a fight fight or like an old-married-couple fight?"

"THE FOUR INUGAMI MAY ENTER," the wall shouted. "HUMANS WAIT—"

The wall stopped talking as soon as Lucas crammed a wad of cash into the one of the eyelids. The bricks before him parted like curtains, revealing a dimly lit hallway. Lucas looked at Ben, who was stuck trying to get the long red robe over his head.

"Are you sure you're up for this?"

"We just had a fight." Ben popped his head through the hole and brushed his hair back down with his fingers. "We're fine."

"The wolves tracked the bull here based on this scent." Lucas held up the horn Ben had chopped off at the temple. "I went back for it.

The odds are pretty low that he's in the kitchen, so we're going to have to enter the actual club. We're looking for a blue bull with a human face and one horn, correct?"

Ben nodded. He lifted up his robe and tried tucking the Onislayer underneath it.

"You're the one who maimed him, so I'll do the talking," Lucas said. "We find out what the sacrifice is, where the sacrifice is, and how to stop it."

The Onislayer bulged out under Ben's robes. He pulled it out and gathered up his robes to try again. Lucas snatched it out of his hands.

"Leave it. You bump into one of the yōkai with that and the whole place'll go up in flames. If the bull attacks us, we have four inugami that've been eating live cows for a month."

"But they won't eat anybody unless they absolutely have to," Ben said, loud enough for Toby to hear. It garnered absolutely no reaction from the Shiba Inu.

Ben turned to holster his Onislayer on his moped, and when he looked back, the rest of them were already inside. The bricks began sliding closed. Ben hustled forward, stepping sideways between the bricks and swinging his long red robes just in time to keep them from getting caught. The wall slammed shut.

"Toby? Lucas?"

A muffled dance beat echoed down the hall. Everyone else was already in the club. Ben fumbled with the plastic mask.

"Friend!" said a small voice. "Friend!"

Joey the cyclops boy stepped into the hall, carrying a tray full of dirty glasses. He grinned excitedly at Ben.

"Are you here to lick my tofu? I did not know you were coming! I would have brought my tofu for you to lick."

"Uhm…"

The wall behind Ben reopened. A crocodile with a metal bell for a head—or was it a metal bell with a crocodile body?—walked on its hind legs past Ben and Joey. The dog walker turned away, hiding his human face. The croc's bell head rang as it entered the club. The crowd cheered, and the music shifted to a more upbeat tempo. Through the doorway, Ben saw a leather wing and a quick glimpse of a wolf's tail. He knelt down in front of the cyclops boy.

"Listen, friend," Ben said. "It's not safe out here. Go stay in the kitchen for a while, okay?"

"Yes, friend!" Joey said, nodding so hard the glasses on his tray jingled. "I will bring you tofu! Sharing! Sharing tofu with a friend!"

He scampered off down the hall, past the door, toward the kitchen. Ben stood. He lowered the mask onto his face, adjusting the straps around his ears, and flipped up his hood.

Then he stepped into the dance club.

A gust of warm, wet air oozed into the eyeholes of his mask, blinding Ben. He squinted and rubbed his eyes with his fingers, willing them to adjust. A white light strobed to the beat of the music, which was thumping so loudly that Ben could feel it in his teeth. The dance floor was thick with gyrating yōkai of various shapes and sizes. Scales and wings and teeth flashed in front of him, as well as shiny button-up shirts and glitter. These demons were here to party.

Something clunked against his head. Ben had no peripheral vision in his stupid outfit. He felt fur and branches and mud brushing against his robes. Something smelled like manure. Manure and blood.

It was time to focus. He held the mask close to his face so he could suck in a few good breaths through the slim mouth hole as he scanned around for Lucas and the wolves.

The crocodile with a bell for a head had taken over as DJ, ringing his head to the beat on a raised platform at the back of the room. Ben pressed the sides of his hood against his ears until all he could hear was his own breathing. He felt like he was in a spacesuit. There was heat coming up through his neck hole. He was sweating buckets. How had the Children of Tengu managed to chase him around in these things without fainting? He sent out his thoughts, mind-listening for his inugami.

Toby had also been separated from the pack. He trotted along the filthy dance floor, continually being bumped and shoved and prodded by the dancing yōkai. A forked tail swatted him off his feet. He growled and staggered upright again, took a step, and was spritzed in the face by a foul-smelling mist. He sneezed, and his eyes began to glow.

Ben sensed the dog's anger. He turned toward it and smacked into a wall of flesh.

"Hey, watch it!" growled a headless man in a purple vest through the wide mouth in his belly button.

"S-sorry!" Ben said, backing up.

He felt something cold squish against his back. A twelve-foot-tall snail lowered its eye stalks, poking one into each eye hole of Ben's mask.

"Whaaaaaaat yōkai are yoooooou?" it said.

Ben ducked away from the creature's sticky, unsettling gaze, stumbling over the tail of something aquatic. A car-length fish spun around and swatted at Ben with its human skeleton hand. Someone grabbed Ben's wrist and yanked him out of the crowd.

Lucas lifted his Tengu mask and winked at Ben. They were pressed against a brick wall on the far edge of the club, away from the exit. The space opened up a bit, giving them a little more breathing room, mostly so a line could form in front of the restrooms next to them. For a brief moment, Ben wondered what a walking umbrella or a giant snail even *did* in a bathroom, but his brain instinctively canceled that thought. There were some things man was not meant to know.

"Where's Toby?" Ben shouted over the music.

Lucas cupped his hand by his ear. Ben repeated it. Lucas pointed over Ben's shoulder. The dog walker turned.

Razor-sharp fangs glinted an inch from his face. Hot breath wafted out as the inugami panted, a large pink tongue dangling from its maw. Toby was in his full monstrous form. Ben put his hand on the beast's snout. The club must've spooked him almost as much as it spooked Ben.

Lucas was already on the move, confidently dodging yōkai as he prowled along the wall. Ben noticed the wolves at waist level beyond him, leading the way. They hadn't transformed like Toby. Those wolves always kept their cool.

The music faded, muffled through the soundproof padding on the walls as the men and wolves cut left at the restrooms, into a hidden corner of the club behind the stage. Round, upholstered booths fashioned in a variety of sizes to accommodate the scales of different yōkai were spread sporadically throughout the space like bubbles. In a small booth next to Ben, a scroll with a human face was reading a different, faceless scroll to a group of winged squirrels.

"*Konbanwa*," said one of the squirrels, to Ben. He gave it a slight bow.

Lucas and the wolves strolled onward with a purpose. Ben gently led his humongous, rage-filled inugami between the booths, trying not to upset it any further. They passed a medium-sized booth, where half a dozen faceless monks silently watched a skeleton do a pole dance on its own oversized rib bone.

It boggled Ben's mind that all of this could be happening in one building. When Lucas talked about "the forums" on the internet, Ben pictured six or seven people spread out over the planet. He figured they all had about the same experience he had. All the yōkai Ben had dealt with in the last year—minus the giant ones—wouldn't fill a quarter of this place. He had pegged the scale of this whole secret world of yōkai wrong. He had thought, deep down, that he was making a real difference, clearing these things out of people's houses and workplaces, burning demons, saving lives. He wasn't. He hadn't even made a dent.

Lucas stopped, and Ben walked into him. The man gestured subtly to one of the larger booths toward the back. There, between a semitransparent pig wearing a business suit and a two-wheeled rickshaw with a human face, sat the blue bull. He had a martini glass in front of him and a toothpick dangling from his human lips. His head was tilted to the side with his one remaining horn.

The wolves ducked low and swooped around to the other side of the bull's booth like velociraptors. Ben looked down at his robes.

"You realize we're sneaking up on a bull while wearing bright red capes," Ben said.

"Bulls don't charge the color red," Lucas said. "That's just in cartoons."

The bull glanced up at Lucas right as he was saying that. The toothpick dropped from the creature's mouth moments before the table flipped to the floor and the bull barreled toward the two men.

Voosh voosh voosh! Three spears of pure darkness fired from the wolves' backs, wrapping around the bull's neck and dragging the beast forcibly back into the booth. The ghost pig gulped, sinking through the floor and out of sight.

"Easy," Lucas said. "We just want to talk."

As the wolves retracted their tentacles, Lucas put his arm around the bull, speaking in a soft voice. His body language was casual, chummy even. Ben couldn't make out what he was saying. He figured he should hang back a bit anyway, what with Toby on edge.

The inugami growled, a deep rumble, like two ships scraping together. Ben looked up. The rickshaw with a human face was sniffing Toby's snout, its two arm bars hovering on either side of the inugami.

"Hey, be careful," Ben said. "He's not in the best mood."

The cart turned to Ben, bopping Toby in the face with its arm bar in the process. It sniffed Ben, too. Ben leaned away.

"You are not a Tengu," the rickshaw said.

"Well, you're not a…" Ben couldn't remember the word for what it was. "Wooden…pull…wagon."

"True enough," said the wooden pull wagon. "We are, all of us, metaphors."

"What're you a metaphor for?"

"Nothing relevant now. I am an old metaphor from a distant land."

Toby growled more. Ben noticed the rickshaw's wheel repeatedly rolling over Toby's massive black paw as it spoke. "Watch the wheels, man."

Lucas took a step back as the bull stood up in his booth. He had a wild, angry look in his eyes. That conversation was getting heated. The wolves were standing by in case the bull tried to run again.

"What of you, False Tengu," said the rickshaw. "What do you represent?"

"Nothing relevant now. Shh, Toby," Ben whispered. "It's all right."

"Ah. The kakawari…" The rickshaw nodded with its whole body. "You serve the inugami."

It turned back to face Toby, bopping the inugami across the face again. "But who does the dog serve?"

Toby lunged forward, clamping his gruesome yellow jaws onto the rickshaw's face. The sentient object screamed in horror. Sap oozed from the breaks in its wood like blood. The inugami wrenched the plank of wood from the rickshaw and whipped its head to the side, slamming Ben to the floor beneath the lifeless face of the talking cart.

The blue bull dashed out of the booth, this time slipping between the three wolves, whose shadow whips flailed in the air around it. The bull knocked over two other tables before charging through a glowing doorway on the other side of the room. The beast that was Toby scrambled over the wreckage of the rickshaw, through what remained of the booths in its path, and bounded after the bull. Lucas and the wolves followed.

Ben shoved the dead wood off. His robes were covered in sap, and his mask had been knocked sideways. He ripped it off his face.

"Toby!"

The yōkai around him were panicking, stampeding toward all the other exits. Ben saw the three squirrels fly past carrying their scrolls. The fish with skeleton arms wriggled across Ben's chest, dragging itself forward with its two limbs. The crocodile with a bell for a head was up on the wall, ringing its head like a fire alarm.

"Toby!" Ben shouted. "Lucas!"

Lucas and the four inugami were nowhere to be seen. Ben ran for the glowing door.

He found himself in a narrow hallway, much smaller than the one he'd entered. A fluorescent bulb flickered in the room beyond. Ben's leg hit something big and heavy, like someone had dropped a mattress in the middle of the hall. He looked down.

Blue fur was matted down with red blood. A human face, stiff and empty, its disproportionate pink tongue lolling out of its mouth. Something had mauled the blue bull to death and then moved on without stopping, leaving the creature to bleed out, wedged into this dark hallway. Ben had a pretty good idea who.

"Son of a bitch. Toby!"

He tried to squeeze past, but the bull's corpse filled the hallway from wall to wall. Ben gritted his teeth. He had no choice. He hoisted himself up on top of the bull's lifeless body and crawled over it. Halfway across, a weakened rib snapped, and Ben's left leg plunged deep into the bull's exposed guts. Ben swore as he rolled down onto the floor. He pulled his red robes over his head and left them behind.

The door in front of him was half closed. Ben swung it open and found himself in the dilapidated kitchen where Joey the cyclops boy worked.

"Oh no."

Blood was splattered on the walls. The fluorescent light flickered. A block of tofu lay on the floor, surrounded by the shards of a shattered porcelain plate.

A small boy was sprawled on the floor in a crimson puddle.

A single lifeless eye gazed up at Ben.

"Oh, Jesus. Joey…"

Ben dashed out of the kitchen and into the main hallway, where a steady stream of yōkai were exiting the club in droves. Ben got sucked up into the crowd and ran along with them, between a potbelly pig on stilts and a walking paper lantern. All along the hallway, there were splashes of blood and bits of flesh, cloth, wood, and bone. A severed lizard leg. A disemboweled fox with two tails.

As Ben stepped outside, he noticed the brick wall had been smashed to pieces. Individual bricks were scattered around the alley, eyeballs at their centers still blinking.

"Toby!" he shouted.

At the end of the alley, Toby was in the process of ripping a floor rug to pieces. The rug moaned as its body tore in half. Lucas was blowing furiously at his dog whistle. The wolves had Toby surrounded, whipping at him with their shadow tentacles, which the monster that was Toby swatted away with its own.

Ben rushed toward him, waving his arms. "Toby! Stop!"

The inugami tossed the rug away and turned toward the street. He stomped out of the alley, and a small green car screeched to a stop in front of him.

Toby pounced on the hood of the car, which dented inward. The front two tires burst and the driver's glasses dropped into his lap.

Six more tentacles, two from each wolf, swooped out at Toby. Ben sprinted up to the car and yanked the driver's side door open.

"Dude! C'mon!" he shouted.

The driver looked at him, dazed, hands shaking as he fixed his glasses. He was short, bald, with a little mustache curving above his lip. He seemed more stunned than afraid. It was unlikely that he could see Toby's true form, much less the gaggle of yōkai currently fleeing around them.

"Get out of the damn car!" Ben shouted.

The man unbuckled his seatbelt and stumbled out just as the inugami smashed its face through the windshield, biting at him.

"Go! Run!" Ben shoved the man toward the sidewalk and stepped toward Toby. "Toby! It's Ben! Stop! Listen to—"

Shadow tendrils slashed at Ben, and he found himself weightless, flying through the air before crashing through an empty storefront window. He went rolling across the floor and into a metal filing cabinet. A box of papers plopped onto his head.

Ben groaned.

He pushed himself back up and climbed out the window, cutting his palm on the glass. As he did, he saw the inugami stop raging for a brief moment and lick its front paw. The wolves wrapped their tendrils around Toby again, three apiece, and slammed the beast to the ground.

Lucas spat out his useless dog whistle. "Ben! Get out here! He's losing it."

Ben staggered out into the street. He saw the little bald man crawling on his belly, away from his car, blood trailing a few feet behind him.

Toby howled and lunged forward, dragging the three wolves along with him, pounding the man into the asphalt with his front claws. The man reached around for something to brace himself, finding nothing. He screamed. The wolves each sent out one more shadow tendril and yanked Toby off the guy.

"Ben!" Lucas shouted. Ben blinked. Lucas was right next to him. "Talk him down!"

"T-Toby!" Ben said. "Look at me!"

The inugami howled again. Ben stepped toward Toby, and large jaws snapped at him. He stepped back. He closed his eyes and felt around inside his mind for Toby, finding nothing. Not even rage. Just nothing.

"I can't... I..." Ben looked at Lucas. "I don't know what to do."

Lucas sighed. "I do."

He stepped behind Ben and wrapped his arm around Ben's neck, pressing his forearm tight against Ben's jugular and holding the boy's head with his other hand.

"Sorry, kid," he said.

The inugami gagged. It fell to its knees, pawing at its neck. Ben's vision blurred. As the world went black, he saw Toby stumble forward and smash into the hood of the car.

The bald man was lying motionless in the street.

犬

Ben was already gasping in a deep breath as he woke up. He coughed. He was lying on a bale of hay in Lucas's barn. Three wolves watched him from the barn's many shadows. Toby was in the rune-covered metal crate, scarfing down what looked like a plate full of raw ground beef.

"He wasn't going to stop," Lucas said as he washed his hands in the work sink. "I had to knock him out, which meant knocking you out. Sorry about that."

Ben rubbed his neck. "How long was I out?"

"Long enough that you might have brain damage, but the meat will fix that, right? How many fingers am I holding up?" Lucas held up three fingers. "What do you remember?"

Ben saw Joey the cyclops boy, tofu smashed on the floor, his lone eye gazing lifelessly at Ben. "How's the guy Toby mauled? The guy in the car?"

Lucas shook his head. Ben closed his eyes, sighing. He looked at Toby, who looked away.

"Look," Lucas said, "one human casualty is not bad for an inugami rampage."

"It is when it's my inugami who's rampaging," Ben said.

He got up slowly and walked over to Toby's cage. Toby turned away, ears down. There was still meat on his plate. Ben knelt down in front of him.

"He can stay with me for a while," Lucas said. "I'll give him a crash course in training, out here at the barn where he can't hurt anybody."

"Take it out of me," Ben said.

Toby turned, listening to him.

"I know you can understand me. Take it out of me. I don't wanna be your little slave anymore. Take the kakawari out."

Toby stared at him, emotionless.

"Ben," Lucas said, "that's not necessary."

"I don't want this!" Ben shouted. "I don't want you! You're a goddamn monster, and I want nothing to do with you! Get this shit out of me!"

Toby opened his mouth and inhaled. A green cloud drifted from out of Ben's nostrils and into the dog's mouth. Ben fell forward and immediately threw up.

The wolves stepped forward, and Lucas put his hand up, stopping them.

The puddle of green vomit steamed as it expanded. Ben felt cold inside, empty. He threw up more.

"Ben…" Lucas said. "Regardless of how you feel right now, he'll be here when you're ready to take him back. Okay? I'll train him. You don't have to worry."

The dog walker stood on weak legs and wiped his mouth with the back of his hand. He turned away from the inugami without saying a word. He checked the time on his phone. His moped was resting next to Lucas's van, over by the big wooden doors.

"Ben?"

"Just take him." Ben brushed past Lucas. "I gotta go to work."

EIGHTEEN.

The dog walker yawned as he trudged up the steps to the greyhounds' apartment. Disconnecting the kakawari had drained him of all his energy. He felt like he was miles away, watching himself live his life on a screen. The two hours of sleep he was running on weren't helping. Maybe now that Lucas was handling any and all inugami training, Ben could actually go to bed before sunrise.

Still, with everything going on, he was looking forward to seeing the greyhounds. They could be a pain in the ass, but they were always happy to see him, and they brought much-needed consistency to Ben's life. These dogs were dogs. They did not, to Ben's knowledge, eat people.

He put his hand on the doorknob, and the door to the apartment nudged open. Ben's heart stopped. Was someone here to attack him? He didn't have his healing powers. The Onislayer was outside on his moped. He could run down and—

"Ben?"

He didn't recognize the voice. The dog walker opened the door slowly, his other hand wrapped around his keys.

A middle-aged woman in a "Greyhound Mom" sweatshirt was sitting at the kitchen table, a box of tissues in her lap. Fergie leaned against the woman's legs, panting. Ben had an anxious, guilty feeling in his gut, like a kid who'd been caught stealing. He never thought about the fact that people lived with the dogs until they were home. Ben tried to remember this woman's name. It was on the info sheet.

Janet? Janice?

"You're Ben, right?" the woman asked.

"Yeah. Sorry," he said. "The owners aren't usually home. I can come back."

He looked around, then asked a question he already knew the answer to. "Where's Stoney?"

"You've been so good to him," she said. "I wanted to tell you in person."

Ben noticed there was only one leash on the hooks by the door. Stoney's collar was sitting on the table behind the owner.

"Oh," he said.

犬

Ben made it halfway into Libby's walk before he broke down and cried. He leaned against a tree, covering his eyes. He hated crying. He hadn't done it in at least a year. In that time, he'd broken several bones, he'd been stabbed, poisoned, burned. On more than one occasion he'd lost a limb. The kakawari healed him, but the pain was still there, and he'd remained tough. He'd taken it. He *liked* being someone who could take it. Ben took a deep breath and felt his lip quiver.

He didn't know why Stoney's death was hitting him so hard. It wasn't his dog. Stoney was old. Ben knew he was old. He knew that Stoney was sick and getting sicker. Dogs didn't live that long, so this was bound to happen eventually. Ben had no reason to feel this blindsided. It shouldn't upset him this much.

He tried to remember how sick Stoney had seemed. He'd written about it in the poop sheets, right? He should have paid more attention. Maybe if he had picked up the signs sooner, he could've helped him. Maybe Stoney would still be okay.

Ben realized he'd been standing in the same spot for a while. Libby was looking up at him, tail wagging. He knelt down and pet her ears, and she rolled over for a belly rub.

"Good dog," Ben said.

His phone rang. Mrs. McClanahan.

"Hello?"

"Ben! Sorry, I'm in Lake Geneva!" Ben's boss shouted over the roar of a pontoon boat. Baby boomer rock 'n' roll played on staticky speakers. "I'm so sorry about Stoney! I meant to warn you beforehand that Joyce would be there, but I've been swamped with the Kaylee situation!"

Ben sniffed, wiping his face with his shirt. "What Kaylee situation?"

"She quit! She didn't even warn me. I'm going to need you to cover some of her dogs. I'll let you know when I'm back tomorrow. There's no time to hire a—MADISON! GET YOUR FEET OUT OF THE WATER! THE BOAT IS—Hold on, Ben."

The shouting grew muffled. Kaylee quit? Why did Kaylee quit? Especially out of nowhere like this. That wasn't like her. Ben hoped it wasn't because of him, regardless of every single bit of evidence in front of him. Maybe jumping out a window hadn't fixed everything like he'd assumed.

"Sorry," Mrs. McClanahan said, picking up again. "Kids. You know how it is."

"Yeah," Ben lied.

"Oh! How's it going with the new dog?"

"New dog?"

"Asher Lebow? Black lab, vegan treats, he's got—"

"—bad hips so I have to walk him slow." Ben finished her sentence. He felt sick again. "I forgot."

"Forgot what? To walk him? You've got another hour in his scheduled time."

"No, I mean I..." Ben trailed off. He looked at Libby, who tilted her head in confusion.

"Ben..." The boat engine in the background of the call died down. "How many walks have you missed with this dog?"

Ben leaned against the tree and slid down until he was sitting amongst the roots, knees on his chest. Libby sniffed his face. He nudged her away with his arm.

"All of them?"

"All of them?" Mrs. McClanahan shouted. "*All of them?*"

"I'm sorry!"

"He's on your schedule!"

"I haven't checked it. I haven't really looked at the new app at all! I know! I'm sorry! I've been busy! I've had a lot of real-life emergencies! I haven't really had time to—"

"We've been charging these people for a month! You *never* walked this dog?"

"I'll go there right now!" Ben stood up again. "I'll go there, and I'll, I'll leave an apology, I'll walk him, and I'll—"

"Ben," Mrs. McClanahan said, "you're fired."

Ben stopped.

"You're done. Bring me your keys tomorrow morning."

"But—"

She hung up. Ben groaned, rubbing his eyes with his fists. He felt hungover.

Libby tugged at the leash, ready to move on. Ben looked at her.

"Well, I'm not doing this for free."

He scooped Libby up with one hand and held her like a football, heading back toward home. Libby whimpered, sniffing at the grass. Ben sighed.

He set the dog back on the ground.

Thunder rumbled in the distance. The sky had gone gray. Ben was wearing shorts and a T-shirt, and Libby's house was half a mile away. He pulled out his phone and stuck it in an unused poop bag.

犬

Both man and dog were soaked to the bone by the time they ran up the steps to Libby's porch. Kaylee was rocking in a deck chair, wearing her big yellow reflector-covered raincoat, umbrella closed at her side. That was Kaylee. Always responsible.

"Libby!" She held out her hand. The mini dachshund shook off the rain once she was under the awning and trotted over. Kaylee pet the wet dog with the tips of her fingers. Ben stood by the door and wrung out his shirt like a wet rag.

"Hey," Kaylee said.

"Hey. You quit?"

"I got the call," Kaylee said. "Producers loved my audition. They want me to go out and film the spot in LA."

"What!" Ben said. He was genuinely excited for her. "That's amazing! I mean it's not unexpected, you're very good. But look at you! On the road to fame and fortune! When is it? How, uhh—" Ben looked down. "How long are you going?"

Kaylee shrugged. "It only takes an afternoon to film, but I think I'm gonna stay there for a while. Work the scene, really make a go at it."

Ben nodded.

"They gave me two tickets," she said. "Come with me."

He looked at her.

"See, I've got you figured out." Kaylee stood and kicked her wet boots against the side of the chair. "You're a spaz and a liar, because you're maintaining these two separate lives, but it's not for any logical reason. You're just unhappy with both. You're embarrassed. You're not a demon hunter. You're not a dog walker. Not in your heart. You want to write movies, right? Come to LA for a few days, check it out. Leave Toby with the luchador, leave the demons to Sarah, and—"

"Okay," Ben said.

Kaylee blinked. "Really? There's more to my pitch."

"Yeah, no, you convinced me," Ben said. "Let's do it. Let's get the hell out of here. You and me."

"You and me." Kaylee put her hands on his neck and kissed him. She felt warm. Her raincoat squeaked as he held her in his arms. Over by the door, Libby whimpered.

"We should bring her inside," Ben said. He rifled through his keys to find Libby's. "Neither of us is a dog walker."

"Ben," Kaylee said, "are you sure about this?"

"Absolutely." Ben stuck the key in the lock. "There's nothing keeping me here."

犬

Sarah sipped cheap coffee as she watched the outside of the dilapidated Buddhist temple. She was on the third hour of sitting in her car, staring at a building, and it was starting to feel a little pointless. Still, someone had to work this case to its conclusion, and if Jake insisted on doing it wrong, Sarah would go it alone. She was unemployed. It wasn't like she had anything better to do.

Criminals—the human ones, anyway—always returned to the scene of the crime. To double-check, to clean up, to steal more things. Whatever. This was the hub of whatever vast yōkai conspiracy the spider was involved in. If anything were to happen, it would be here.

A mangy gray cat stepped from the shadows of the temple, eyeing the cars and pedestrians with caution. Sarah sat up. She tried to remember what she'd learned about cat yōkai. Didn't they have two tails? Or a flaming tail? So many of these things were partially on fire, and yet the primary way of killing them was also fire. The cat glanced in her direction, and Sarah ducked down behind the steering wheel. After a moment, she peeked back up again.

The cat flicked its one tail, hocked up a hairball, and went on its way down the sidewalk. Sarah relaxed.

"Normal cat," she muttered.

A beat-up red Honda Civic with tinted windows pulled up in front of the temple. A man stepped out of the shadows where the cat had been. He wore blue robes, with prayer beads hanging loosely at his wrists. He was a little too tall, his head was too large, and his arms were too long. He was a child's drawing of a man. Sarah watched and waited.

The man went to the car, took a quick look from side to side, and then he swooped into the passenger-side window like a Slinky going down stairs.

"Bingo," Sarah said.

She started the car and followed the Civic.

The ride was mostly uneventful. The Civic was slow, and Sarah had to pull over and coast in the right lane a few times to put a little distance between them before she continued. They headed east, clear across the city, then north up Lake Shore Drive. As the stench grew, Sarah realized where they were going.

The Civic came to a stop in the parking lot of a closed seafood restaurant. Sarah parked across the street. The gangly monk exited the vehicle, along with a furry red guy and some kind of a sky-blue elephant.

The giant chicken carcass loomed two stories overhead, waves crashing against its rotting flesh and yellowed bones.

"Sacrifice of meat..." She put her shirt over her face to block the smell. It didn't help. "How did we not think of this?"

NINETEEN.

Mrs. McClanahan's home office was up in the suburbs, far from the actual working area of Windy City Waggers. Ben stood on her back deck, hands in his pockets, too embarrassed to make eye contact with his boss, who was sitting in a deck chair with an ancient Windows laptop. Ben hadn't actually been up here since he'd interviewed for the job...three years ago? Four? It had been a while. The three kids running in the sprinkler looked older. He was pretty sure one of the girls had been in a high chair last time.

"I've got Julie taking over on Fergie," Mrs. McClanahan said, typing on her phone. "Aidan's got Libby, at least for the rest of the week."

"Who's Aiden?" Ben said.

"You never met him. He's new, he's still in school. Something with video games? You kids and your art degrees..." Mrs. McClanahan pointed at the keys hanging from Ben's belt and made a *gimme* motion. "Your last check will be in the mail on Friday."

She looked up from the screen as Ben detached his key ring. "I'm really disappointed in you, Ben."

He plopped the keys in her hand.

"So am I," he said.

犬

Back at Lucas's farm, the four inugami finished picking the last few bits of meat from the cow they'd just devoured. As they trotted back into the barn, each carrying a rib to gnaw on, Lucas doused the carcass in gasoline and lit it up. One advantage of living so far outside the city: easy cow disposal.

The fire raged behind him as he entered the barn. The three wolves had curled up in their respective corners. Toby was in the middle of the floor.

"Toby," Lucas said, whistling. The Shiba Inu trotted over. Lucas knelt and opened the door to the magic crate.

"In." He nodded toward it.

Toby stared at him.

"Get in the crate," Lucas said. "Now."

Toby didn't move. Lucas inhaled through his nose.

He grabbed Toby by the scruff of his neck and slammed his face into the dirt floor before throwing him full force into the crate. The little dog smashed into the metal bars in the back, upside down. His eyes glowed red and his fur turned black. Tentacles speared off of him toward Lucas then stopped at the opening, blocked by the magic of the runes carved into the bars.

The wolves all looked up from their bones. Lucas shut the door quickly, locked it, then leaned in close to Toby's face.

"You're not with Ben anymore. You are not gonna pull that shit with me," Lucas said. "Fun time's over. I am the alpha here! This is my pack! If I give you an order, you do it."

Toby growled. Lucas stood, cracking his back. Smoke from the bovine bonfire wafted in, smelling for all the world like barbeque.

"Get some rest, all of you," he said. "We're leaving tomorrow morning."

He hoisted himself up the ladder to his loft space. Toby pawed at his cage, whimpering. The wolves watched him for a moment, ears twitching in his direction, before going back to their bones.

犬

Ben sat crouched on the curb, hidden behind his moped, as Sarah pulled into the lucha dojo's parking lot. She waved to him as she exited her vehicle, and he stood as she approached. He was holding the Onislayer.

"Ben!" she said. "Great! You're already here. Listen, you're never gonna believe this. I figured out what the sacrifice of meat is."

She grabbed him by the shoulders.

"Poultry Zone."

His eyes lit up as she said it. "Oh my God. Why didn't we think of that?"

"I know! I saw a bunch of demons gathering at that seafood restaurant. I don't know what the actual sacrifice is, but at least we know where it'll be. I'm sneaking Tatsuya into the station tonight to meet with Ashley. He's pretty confident he can separate her from the spider, but I need you to stand guard while he does it."

She tapped the Onislayer with her shoe.

"Once the spider's out of the girl, we can either question it or kill it or hold it hostage. We'll help the kid first. What do you think? C'mon, I'll give you the details inside."

She started for the door, but Ben didn't follow. He glanced at his moped.

"Ben, he's not going to yell at you again. Man up. We've got work to do." She noticed something was missing. "Where's Toby?"

"He, uhh, he lost control. I couldn't stop him," Ben said. "Lucas is going to keep him for a while. Give him a crash course in obedience. Get him back to a base level of domestication."

"You *gave* him to Lucas?" Sarah shouted. "*Lucas?* Ben, that guy has been using you since day one! All he ever does is separate you from your friends and neg you!"

"He's training me," Ben muttered.

"Yeah, *clearly* he's doing a real bang-up job. He wears a fur coat in July! He lives in a barn! He's a lunatic! He is going to skin that dog and grind up his bones and snort them. What are you even talking about?"

"Sarah, it's all right," Ben said. "He's kind of a dick, but he's an inugami expert. He's got three of 'em. Toby will be fine. Besides, I'm going on vacation."

She squinted. "You what?"

"Kaylee killed it at her audition. She's flying out to film a commercial tomorrow, and she's bringing me with to help write and pitch her sitcom. I'm going to LA!"

He paused, trying to will her into meeting his level of excitement. She didn't.

"Ben..." Sarah held the bridge of her nose. "We're kind of in the middle of something here. You can't just leave."

"Why not?"

"Why not? *Why not?* This is all! Your! Fault!" Sarah punched Ben in the arm after each word. He flinched. "You brought Toby back from the dead, and now there are demons everywhere! You let the spider get away, and now it's in Ash's head! This whole damn shit show is because of you!"

Ben rubbed his arm. "You always say it's *not* my fault."

"I was being nice, Ben! I thought you felt guilty! I thought you cared! I defend you to everybody, because *Hey, give him some credit! He's a good guy! He's trying his best!* And then the moment the opportunity presents itself, you fly off to Hollywood to get rich and famous!"

"I'm only going for a few days," Ben said.

"We need you here."

"Why? What's my part of the current plan?" Ben stepped toward her. "When you picture it going down, what am I doing at the police station?"

"Guarding the door."

"Could that be done by a chair propped against the knob?"

"Ben—"

"You don't need me! I don't have powers anymore. Tatsuya knows the yōkai, you're the detective, Toby's with Lucas. You're about to cure Ash. It's all good! Everything's copacetic."

Sarah glared at him.

"Astronauts say that. It means—"

"I know what copacetic means. What do you want me to say to you?"

"Sarah," Ben looked away. "I don't belong here. You're all better off without me."

He handed her the Onislayer.

"Give this to Tatsuya. Tell him I'm sorry. I'll text you later to see how it went with Ash. Keep me posted."

"You know what, Ben?" Sarah said, holding the Onislayer to his neck. "If you're not gonna help, fuck off."

She turned and went inside the lucha dojo, slamming the glassless door behind her. It rattled like a shopping cart.

Ben started toward the dojo, then stopped. His moped was sitting there behind him, with his backpack in the basket, all packed full of clothes and ready to go. He heard talking inside, which soon became shouting.

The former dog walker hopped on his bike and drove away.

犬

Ben pulled up to the departures gate at O'Hare International Airport, with his moped's basket full of luggage. Kaylee clutched him tightly around the waist. Cars rushed past all around them, honking at the small, painfully slow scooter. Ben hopped up onto the curb and leaned the moped against a stone pillar. He and Kaylee gathered up their things.

"Hey!" A woman in a neon-yellow vest stomped toward them, waving an orange lantern. "You can't park that there!"

Ben thought for a moment, then tossed his keys to her.

"Keep it!"

He turned toward the entrance to the airport and grabbed Kaylee's hand. She smiled.

"I've always wanted to do that," he said.

TWENTY.

Weezie looked up from her magazine as the door to the police station opened. Sarah Martinez walked in with her hair tucked back in a tight bun, wearing her old uniform from before she'd made detective—sans badge. She was leading what appeared to be a homeless Asian bodybuilder in handcuffs in front of her. Weezie put her magazine down as Sarah approached the desk.

"Not much of a disguise, Martinez."

"It's mostly for the cameras." Sarah gestured subtly toward the four security cameras pointed at her at this exact moment. "We need to talk to the kid again."

"Who's this?"

"I am a criminal," the giant hobo said with great import. "I have forgotten honor and committed a crime."

"She's cool, Tatsuya."

"I am a luchador," Tatsuya said. He snapped his handcuffs with a quick jerk of his arms. "And I cannot play a *rudo* this blank. Who is this man that I am? What crime did I commit?"

"Can you let us in?" Sarah said.

"I could lose my job." Weezie thought about it. "Is it a spooky thing?"

"Would I be here if it wasn't?"

The door opened again. Sarah turned and slammed Tatsuya against the wall in a way that hid both of their faces.

"No! I regret my crimes!" Tatsuya said.

Sarah peeked over her shoulder. Jake entered the station flanked by two uniformed officers. Between them walked a middle-aged woman with red hair. Maureen Greco walked at an odd pace, like her legs weren't speaking with each other.

"Oi oi!" Tatsuya whispered, also peeking. "Is that—"

"He brought the foster mom here." Sarah sighed. "Jake, you absolute dumbass."

犬

Ash sat alone in her windowless gray cell, scratching at her ankle bracelet. The man who'd strapped it onto her had been very friendly, making it seem as normal as possible for a ten-year-old to be getting a security tracker, but there was only so much he could do.

In a couple of hours, Ash would be transferred into a group home downtown. Her feelings were mixed. She'd had a pretty bad experience in the months between her parents dying and her stay in Mrs. Greco's house. Sure, she was looking forward to not being in jail, but also...

She knocked on the brick wall behind her with her knuckles, which was slathered in the same gray paint as her room at Greco's. All the murder, all the drama, and she was in the same prison in a different location. Nothing really changed. She was always alone, always some scary lady's pet.

She reached up to feel the mouth on the back of her head and found nothing but hair. The spider had been dormant since that cop lady brought Big Ben to see her, but it was in there, silent and waiting. Ash would know if it was gone.

The foot beneath the bracelet felt numb. Ash took off her shoe and wiggled her toes. Three of them, big toe to middle, plopped off her foot and back into her shoe. In their place, two pointed black claws emerged, stretching the opening on her foot until the human skin flaked away and revealed the ends of two enormous spider legs.

Her foot bulged, then her ankle. The tracking bracelet stretched to its limit. Ash tugged her pants leg down, twisted the end of it, and tied the cuff of her pants in a knot. She slid her shoe back on over the spider claws.

Did that really happen? She was afraid to look again.

It's time, said the spider in Ash's head.

"Time for what?" Ash replied.

Just as the door to the cell opened, Ash felt her leg split apart longwise inside her pants. She held it together at the knee, leaning casually against the desk in front of her with her other arm.

Jake walked in, giving Ash's room the once-over before two uniformed cops came in. Between them was Mrs. Greco. She smiled when she saw Ash. Her teeth were wrong.

"My daughter," she said.

Jake crossed his arms. "Ma'am, say what you need to say."

Mrs. Greco had never called Ash "her daughter" in her life. This was all wrong. Ash felt the same burning tingle in her right leg, which also began to split apart.

Ash spoke. "Mrs. Greco..." The thing wearing her foster mom's face gazed at her expectantly. "I'm so sorry."

"Why, whatever for?" Mrs. Greco smiled sweetly.

"Are you ready to talk, kid?" Jake said. He pulled out a notebook from his coat pocket. "She's alive, everyone's alive, it's all fine. You're not in trouble, okay? I just need to know what's going on. Let's close this case together."

Ash rubbed the bandage on her neck. The skin beneath the tape tore away like tracing paper. "You need to leave."

"We have so much to talk about," Mrs. Greco said.

Ash stared past Mrs. Greco and directly at Jake. "You need to leave right now or you're going to die."

犬

Sarah and Tatsuya ducked down the hall, trailing after Jake and the cops. Both had dropped all pretense of a disguise. Tatsuya removed his knit cap, scratching his hair. After decades of wearing a luchador mask, he liked to keep his head free. Sarah stopped at Chris the beat cop's desk and knocked on it. He looked up from his computer.

"Hey," she said. "Since when are you on the night shift?"

"I'm not," Chris said. "I, uhh...I don't know. I felt like I had to come in tonight. Aren't you suspended?"

"Did you know Jake was going to bring Greco here?" Sarah said.

"No. He transferred me," Chris said. "How would I know that?"

Sarah looked in the direction of Ash's cell. There was another locked door between her and Ash for which she didn't have the key.

"I've got a very bad feeling about this," she said. "You gotta get us through that door. Tatsuya can fix this."

Tatsuya gave Chris a nod, still scratching.

"I—" Chris stopped.

His eyes grew big, and he coughed. He coughed again, then wheezed, then stood, trying to catch his breath. The four or five other cops in the room turned and watched. Sarah patted his back. He spat into his hand.

A live spider, drenched in spit, wriggled in his palm.

犬

Ash's head spun around, and her spine audibly cracked. Mrs. Greco and the two beat cops to either side of her began to shudder, their bodies spasming. They closed their eyes and their heads lolled back. Their mouths opened.

"Awaken, my children," said the spider.

Dozens, hundreds, and then thousands of spiders poured from the humans' mouths. A wave of liquid arachnid filled the room, flowing out of the three hosts, who deflated like empty plastic bags onto the floor. Jake screamed, reaching for his gun.

He stopped and clutched his head as the mother of all migraines threatened to split his skull in two. The spiders. He could see the spiders.

Ash stood. Both her pants legs split, revealing four black carapace-encased spider legs, the remaining bits of human skin still flaking away. The spider legs stretched out and bent upward, raising the girl's body six feet off the floor. She raised her human hand and peeled away the bandage on her neck, revealing more shiny black exoskeleton underneath. The human mouth smiled behind Ash's hair, which clutched the walls and ceiling like webs.

The cell was quickly filling up with tiny spiders. Jake was already up to his ankles. He unholstered his gun and aimed it haphazardly, wonder what exactly he was supposed to shoot. He dropped it and climbed up onto a chair. He turned to the creature that was once Ash.

"W-what are you?" Jake said.

"The future," said the spider.

犬

Sarah cussed like a sailor as a flood of living spiders gushed from Chris's mouth, a steady flow of skittering darkness draining onto the floor as his body collapsed. She backed away, stomping at them. Tatsuya cracked his knuckles, then reached down and hoisted up a heavy metal desk. He grunted as he lifted it to his chest.

"*Arañas!*" He raised the desk up over his head. "You have revealed yourselves at an inopportune time! Prepare for squishing!"

Wham! The desk crashed onto the ground, taking a good chunk of the spiders with it. The survivors oozed like wet tar around the edges of the desk, flowing toward the old luchador. Sarah came up behind Tatsuya with a fire extinguisher and blasted foam and CO2 at the unsquished demons.

When the fog from the extinguisher cleared, only two random cops remained in the room. The rest had fled in the chaos. One, Sarah had talked to at a few meetings. He could definitely see the spiders. The other was just young and probably too shocked to move.

"You guys all right?" she said. Both cops nodded. "We need to…"
She trailed off.

Tatsuya smashed a stray spider under his shoe, then noticed Sarah staring at what remained of Chris. He put a strong hand on her shoulder. She dropped the empty fire extinguisher onto the floor.

"Sorry. I knew him, you know? He was a nice guy," she said, collecting herself. "He didn't deserve this."

Boom!

The moment of quiet was shattered by pounding on a metal door.

Boom! Boom!

Muffled shouting could be heard through the door at the end of the next hallway.

Tatsuya raised an eyebrow. Sarah picked the extinguisher back up and held it like a bat. One of the cops picked up a chair. The other unholstered his gun.

More shouting. Gunshots.

"Ashley!" Tatsuya ran for the door.

The door groaned. A few spiders scurried from the edges.

"Wait!" Sarah shouted. "Don't—"

The metal door exploded into the hallway, colliding with the old luchador before clanking against the wall and onto the floor. Another wave of arachnids surged from the open doorway and out into the hall, fully encasing Tatsuya's prone form.

The spider wave poured out into the open office where Sarah and the two cops stood. One cop threw his chair, to no effect, before being overrun by spiders. The other dropped his gun and bolted for the exit, finally coming to his senses. Sarah climbed up on top of a desk. The spiders filled the room, several inches deep. The floor was made of spider lava.

A figure emerged in the doorway.

The girl's lower half was now completely arachnid. Four three-foot-long spider legs clicked delicately on the linoleum tiles, baby spiders scattering with each step. A shiny black spider's abdomen dangled behind the creature, thick hairs protruding in sporadic clumps along its surface. The bite wounds on Ash's still-human torso had grown dark and solid, as though the transformation had progressed quicker there. The girl's head was twisted around 180 degrees. The spider mouth bared its fangs.

Sarah chucked the fire extinguisher at the creature, but the spider caught the canister with its prehensile hair and squeezed, bending the metal inward. As it approached Sarah to return her attack, Tatsuya's head emerged from the sea of spiders.

"Ashley!" he shouted. "Fight it!"

The spider stopped. Ash looked down with her human eyes and met Tatsuya's.

"Sensei..." she said. Tears welled up.

"You are stronger that her! I can help you, but you must—"

The spider screeched like a banshee and slammed its head into the wall, stunning Ash, before skittering past Sarah and down the hallway toward the exit. The wriggling mass of spiders went with it, flowing out of the room in an instant. The cop who'd been overrun by spiders was lying flat on his back, staring up at the ceiling in shock as a few stragglers skittered out of his shirt. Tatsuya's leg was trapped beneath the metal door, which had pinned itself between the wall and the floor upon impact. Sarah started toward him.

"No! Go!" he shouted, waving her away. "Save Ash!"

Sarah nodded, then hustled down the hall after the spiders.

Jake emerged from Ash's cell. His shirt was torn, and he had his gun cocked and ready. His hair was sticking up on one side. His former partner's elderly luchador friend was lying on the floor in front of him. The old man nodded to him.

When Sarah reached the lobby, she saw Weezie hiding behind the front desk. The back half of the flood of spiders wriggled its way out the front door. Sarah gunned it after them, bursting outside. She slid across the hood of her car and hopped into the driver's seat and started the engine.

She knew exactly where those spiders were going.

犬

Passengers bustled through the airport terminal, dragging suitcases and small children along with them. Ben tried to lean back in his small metallic airport chair, but the chair had no give, so he just scooched down, resting his head against the back with his butt hanging off the edge of the seat. He yawned.

Next to him, Kaylee had headphones on and her eyes closed. She'd wanted to get there super early to go through security—because she was Kaylee—but they had actually gotten through pretty quickly, so they had to sit for two and a half hours. Ben squirmed. He looked at his phone again, but he had no job and no friends, so nothing on there had changed.

He lifted up one of Kaylee's headphones. "I gotta pee."

She gave him a thumbs-up without opening her eyes, and he ducked toward the restrooms.

犬

Ben washed his hands. There was a long row of sinks in the airport bathroom, running parallel to the stalls and urinals. He was alone in there, save for one man standing at a urinal in the back corner. The man had been there when Ben came in, and he was still there now. That was a long time to pee. Maybe he was a nervous pee-er.

The guy glanced at Ben in the mirror, pushing up his glasses. He looked familiar.

Ben had a flash of memory. The man Toby had mauled in the street, who, when Ben had last seen him, was bleeding out, crawling on his stomach, holding in his own guts like a wounded soldier. Bald head, same glasses. That had been two days ago.

"That's impossible," Ben muttered.

The man bolted toward the exit, and Ben tackled him against the wall. They tumbled into a trash can, sending it clattering to the floor.

"Stop!" Ben said. "I just—"

The man elbowed Ben in the neck and then stood, picking up the trash can and smashing it onto Ben's face. Ben rolled to the side and groaned, rubbing the cheek where the trash can hit. Wet paper towels scattered as he got to his feet and punched the man in the stomach.

He went to punch him again, but the man caught his arm, yanked Ben toward him, and then shoved him back into the stalls. Ben smacked into a stall door and slid to the ground. The door he'd hit squeaked partially open. The man stomped toward him.

Ben kicked the stall door, and it collided with the man's nose, shattering his glasses and breaking the frames with an audible snap. The man stumbled back into the wall and soundlessly shifted forms—a squirrel, a mailbox, a stone goose, back to a man. He blinked, shaking his head.

"Tanuki!" Ben said.

The man snarled, high and shrill, bestial. He bared fangs that hadn't been there before.

Ben stood and raised his fists. He had to focus. He had fight training. He was a lucha samurai, operating at *nearly* a fifth-grade level.

The man pounced at him. Ben sidestepped and grabbed the guy's wrist, redirecting his momentum left. A crack echoed through the restroom as the man's skull collided with the granite countertop around the sinks. As he flopped to the floor, he transformed. Libby again. A snake. A little boy with one eye, his small kimono soaked in blood.

"What...Joey?"

Back into the man with the gruesome injuries he'd sustained from Toby's attack, and finally, the raccoon-like tanuki, bleeding from its forehead.

Ben backed away from the unconscious yōkai. Why would it pose as the cyclops boy? And the wounded human? And Libby? Why would it—

"Holy shit." Ben gasped. "He set me up."

He barreled out of the bathroom, knocking the briefcase out of a businessman's hands. Papers fluttered in the air. Ben's flight to LA was already boarding. Kaylee was standing in line with both of their bags.

"Hey! Hurry up, we're boarding." Kaylee noticed the bruise on Ben's face. "What the f—"

"I have to go." He grabbed his bag off her arm and slung it over his shoulder.

"What?"

"Lucas is working with the tanuki!"

"The tah-nookie?"

"The raccoon thing that was spying on me! Toby didn't just lose control at the yōkai club, Lucas sprayed him with that inugami catnip stuff to get him all riled up, and the tanuki disguised itself as the bodies that would make me feel bad enough to break the kakawari!"

"What part of that sentence was supposed to make sense?" Kaylee said.

"Lucas has been lying to me this whole time! He set me up and he stole my dog!"

"Ben..." Kaylee sighed. "We're boarding. We're leaving. We're going to LA!"

"Kaylee—"

"None of this is your responsibility anymore! You said so yourself! This is your chance to make a clean break! It's time to go."

"Kaylee—"

"You don't have to do this! You're gonna be a writer! This is your dream! Let the others—"

He kissed her. For a moment, it all went away. But only for a moment. Ben looked her in the eyes.

"It's not about me," he said.

犬

Outside the terminal, a tow truck driver slumped into the driver's seat of his truck and tossed a set of keys onto the seat next to him. A hand reached in through the open window and snatched away the keys. The driver saw the empty seat and checked his pockets.

"Hey!"

The rusted green moped he'd just collected whizzed off the back of his truck and bounced onto the tarmac, skidding side to side as it landed.

Ben swerved across traffic, ignoring the honks of the oncoming cars, and pulled onto the highway, heading back toward the city.

He hoped he wasn't too late.

TWENTY-ONE.

Freshwater waves crashed against the giant chicken corpse as the spider that once was Ashley Ocampo scaled its side. The transformation had spread to her upper half, and one of her human arms was now two spider legs. Soon the girl would be a memory, a template to be overwritten, and only the spider would remain.

The carcass swayed as the spider reached the top, perching itself at the tip of a rib bone the size of a telephone pole, which had been stripped white by a year of sun and erosion. All Ash could do at the moment was watch and listen and smell, and right now she wasn't sure which sense was worse. It was probably the smell. The thing *reeked*.

"Are you ready?" shouted the Tall Priest.

The other yōkai leaders—Iguana Elmo, the Tall Priest, the woman with eyes on her arms, and the sky-blue anteater—had gathered on the roof of the seafood restaurant on the shore. They were all standing in a line, holding aloft a long metallic ramp. The spider turned to regard them, which meant Ash looked up. Storm clouds gathered overhead. Ash saw a flash of lightning.

The spider raised its three upper appendages toward the heavens. "Now!"

The other yōkai dropped the ramp, and it slapped into the side of the carcass with a wet thud. There was a sound like rain, but it came from below as a solid black mass of spiders poured up from the restaurant and onto the roof. The skittering shape flowed across the metal ramp and onto the gargantuan carcass, where the spiders swirled across each and every bit of exposed meat and bone, covering the surface of the dead chicken in a thin but complete layer of hungry arachnids. The carcass seemed to sparkle as the last few gaps in the spiders closed. It would almost be beautiful if it wasn't completely disgusting.

"Feed, my children!" the spider in Ash's body shouted. "Feed!"

The coating of arachnids pulsed as they began feasting on the rotten flesh. A bolt of lightning charged across the clouds. Blood-red lightning. Ash had never seen that before. There was a weird muffled quality to the thunderclap that came seconds later, like the sound was coming from a different room in the sky.

The spider began chanting in Japanese.

"*Niku no shiro. Atarashī sekai. Niku no shiro. Atarashī sekai.*"

The yōkai on the roof chanted along with her. The chicken carcass withered and grew thinner as the spiders fed. Ash watched in horror as each bit of rotting meat was nibbled away by thousands of tiny mouths.

And then, just as it seemed that the spiders had stripped every last bit of flesh off the bones, the meat began to grow back. Purplish red flesh filled in the gaps between bones and tendons, and an invisible heart began pumping blood back into the chicken's long-since-decomposed veins.

The bones began to move. The meat around them shifted.

The chicken began to rise.

犬

Lightning struck the road in front of Sarah, and she shrieked, swerving around it as she zoomed up Lake Shore Drive. Ahead, the rotting carcass that once was a giant chicken rose from the waves on its two-story putrid drumsticks. It looked…healthier than the last time she'd seen it. Sarah leaned forward to look up through her windshield.

The electrified clouds above the chicken began to swirl. The enormous rib cage tilted inward, bone by bone, to form a conical shape—a pointed dome made of bones, spiders, and meat.

犬

"The worlds of the living and the dead shall merge!" the spider shouted. "No longer will we hide in the shadows. Lift the veil, my children! Lift the veil!"

The spider laughed maniacally into the sky, then gasped in confusion as the chicken carcass below her suddenly stopped moving. The winds died down. The clouds slowed their swirl. The processes at work seemed to have stalled.

"My children?" the spider said.

"Futakuchi..." The Tall Priest stretched his neck and torso up to where the spider stood atop the half-transformed chicken. "I told you."

The spider glared at him.

"There is *always* a price," he said.

The spider looked down at her children. Millions of spiders, fat with putrid meat, resting on the bones below her.

"*Niku no gisei...*" She understood.

Ash felt the spider's resolve fade. The hair around Ash's face lowered.

"The meat is the catalyst," the Tall Priest said. "But it is only a sacrifice if you mourn it."

The spider nodded. Ash tried moving the fingers on her one remaining human hand. The pinkie twitched.

The Tall Priest watched the spider closely, reading her. "We can find another—"

"Get back on the roof," the spider growled.

The Tall Priest nodded, lowering himself down. The spider took a deep breath, then exhaled. She twisted her arm, and Ash's human skin peeled away as two new spider arms grew. The spider's eight limbs were now entirely arachnid.

"We've come too far," she said. She began to chant once more. "*Niku no shiro. Atarashī sekai. Niku no shiro. Atarashī sekai...*"

The clouds resumed their rotation. The wind kicked up again. The chicken bones below shifted. A red glow bubbled up at the center of the storm.

Boom! The spider leapt down from the carcass just as a red flash of light filled the sky and a bolt of lightning came screaming down onto the dead chicken. The spider landed on the roof amongst the other yōkai, not bothering to look back as her own arachnid children were flash-fried and left smoking and sizzling on the electrified corpse. The others backed away as she stood, shaking dust and embers off of her exoskeleton.

"It's done," she said. "The new age of yōkai has begun."

In the distance, there were screams.

犬

Kaylee rested her head against the complimentary airplane pillow. She closed her eyes as her plane lifted off the runway and coasted up over the city. Her body leaned as the plane banked right.

She had given Ben every opportunity. She had bent over backward for that guy, and where did it get her? She was done. Kaylee was living for Kaylee from now on. She opened her eyes, and every single other passenger was staring at her. Some of them were taking pictures with their phones. No, wait. They were looking out the window behind her. Kaylee turned.

Down below, cars swerved off the roads. People ran out into the street. Several buildings were on fire. An air raid siren went off. And there were...other things. Creatures of unusual shapes and sizes. A swarm of flying animals swept a train yard. An enormous human skeleton was climbing one of the skyscrapers downtown. The eye at the center of Wrigley Field blinked.

The pilot clicked onto the loudspeaker. "Ladies and gentlemen, you're about to experience a little turbulence. Nothing to worry about."

The window grayed out as the plane flew up into storm clouds.

"What is going on down there?" Kaylee said.

"Hell if I know," said her complimentary pillow.

犬

Mrs. McClanahan paced back and forth across her front yard as she ranted into her phone. Her children raced around a kiddie pool, each trying to push the others into the water.

"Aidan, can you just walk the greyhound *and* the dachshund?" She sighed. "I lost two walkers in one day. I'm trying to keep this—"

The two girls worked together to force the little boy into the pool. They had him by the arms with his face dangling an inch from the water.

"MADISON!" Mrs. McClanahan shouted. The kids looked at her. "Play nice with your br—"

A flash of fangs and stripes burst out of the kiddie pool, powerful jaws snapping at the children. A fish the size of a horse—with the head of a tiger—flopped out onto the lawn, rolling around and gasping for air.

Mrs. McClanahan gathered up the screaming kids and dragged everyone inside. The tiger fish wobbled toward the house, knocking over a picnic table.

犬

Lucas Alcindor yanked open the two big doors to his barn. A herd of cattle grazed peacefully on his lawn. Some were headless, some had no skin, some were merely living skeletons, and none had been there the night before.

"Huh," he said.

犬

Libby the mini dachshund leaned against the front window to her apartment, yapping at a squirrel. The squirrel sniffed the acorn in front of it and then pounced at the window at supernatural speed, latching on with the suction cups on its arms and legs and scraping at the glass with the sharp teeth that protruded from the second mouth on its belly.

Libby scurried away and hid under the dining room table, whimpering.

犬

Ben zipped along the edge of the highway. A ten-foot-tall human head—bright red, with arms sticking out of its cheekbones and legs sticking out of its chin—climbed up over the side of the barrier and jogged out into traffic. Ben barely noticed it, having seen those a couple times before, until the car next to him blared its horn and veered right, nailing the median and almost crushing Ben in the process. He weaved around it. Every other car going in that direction honked and swerved. Ben heard a scream.

Down in the city park below, two joggers were in a fistfight with a tree. The tree's branches held melon-sized orange fruit. Each had grown to look like a very detailed, very wrinkled human face. Beyond them, a family shooed a monkey with a white humanoid mask out their apartment window. In the next unit over, a man with twenty-foot arms and legs was crouched, listening to the people next door with his oversized ear pressed against the wall. He winked at Ben through the window. A woman entered that apartment and screamed, dropping a big bag full of groceries.

"They can all see them. Everyone can see them." Ben leaned on the gas, and his moped sputtered with effort. He shook his head. "That can't be good."

His phone buzzed in his pocket. Sarah was calling. As he went to swipe up and answer it, another car spun out of its lane and into the shoulder. Ben zigzagged around it, dropping his phone in the process.

"Damn it!"

As he considered going back for it, several giant centipedes with rams' heads skittered out of that car's windows. Ben shuddered.

"I'll get a new phone," he said.

犬

Ten minutes of driving through anarchy later, Ben pulled up to the front of the lucha dojo. He shouldered his way through the door and found Jake, Sarah's former partner, sitting behind the counter and drinking a Pocari Sweat. Ben squinted at him.

"Hey," he said.

"Hey." Jake wiped his mouth and twisted the cap back on his bottle.

"Is, uhm…is Tatsuya here?"

"He's in the back, getting ready."

Ben nodded. This was the longest one-on-one conversation he and Jake had ever had. "Can you see the yōkai now?"

"Yeah," Jake said. He walked toward Ben. "I can see them. Listen, Carter…if I had known these things were real, I would've gone easier on you."

He held out his hand. Ben shook it.

"But I still don't like you as a person."

"Fair enough," Ben said.

The door to the locker room opened, and Tatsuya limped into the room, his ankle wrapped in a bandage. He had a cane, and that alone made him look ten years older.

"Tatsuya!" Ben said. "I know you're sick of hearing me apologize, so we can do that later. I just need the Onislayer."

The old luchador looked at him. "Why would I have the Onislayer?"

犬

Sarah hung up as Ben's phone went to voicemail again. She parked right in front of the giant chicken. Or whatever it was now. The bones and meat of the enormous carcass had bent and twisted into four walls, topped off by a curved, pointed roof made of tendons and sinew. A single tall tower rose from the center, several stories above the water. The giant chicken carcass was now a castle made of meat. The metal bridge still ran from the roof of the seafood restaurant to the only entrance into the castle, which was…

"Unquestionably the chicken's butt," Sarah said out loud. "God, I hate these things."

She stepped out of her car and raised the Onislayer in front of her as she marched toward the entrance to the meat castle. There were sirens and screaming in the distance but no immediate signs of danger. Still, this was ground zero of…whatever this was, and they wouldn't leave the place unguarded with the butt door wide open.

A red blur shot across the road and upward onto the wall of the seafood restaurant. A furry red yōkai perched on the bricks like a frog. It opened its mouth.

A pink tongue shot out toward Sarah like a bullwhip, and she swung.

Voosh! A severed, smoking piece of tongue tumbled into the gutter. The creature on the wall howled, sucking its wounded organ back in. It leapt down and bounded across the sidewalk toward Sarah. She stood with one foot in front of the other, bracing herself. The creature pounced at her, and at the last possible moment, she sliced upward.

Voom! Two halves of the furry red yōkai dropped to the ground on either side of Sarah, with burning tufts of fur scattering in the air around her.

"Okay." She laughed, choking up on the Onislayer's hilt to get a better grip. "Okay. I get it. That feels really good."

Something grunted to her right. She turned and saw a small sky-blue elephant standing before her. It pressed the tip of its trunk against her forehead.

犬

Sarah awoke in bed, confused. Wasn't she just…somewhere? She could've sworn she was in the middle of something. Her hands gripped the covers tightly, almost like she was holding—

An arm wrapped around her. She flinched momentarily, then relaxed.

"You all right?" Ben said. "It's still early."

"Yeah," Sarah said. She was at home, in her bed, with her boyfriend. Everything was all right. "Just a weird dream."

TWENTY-TWO.

Sarah chewed up a big bite of the pancakes Ben had just made for her. It felt nice to be in her apartment, with her boyfriend and their dogs, eating breakfast like normal people. Dozens of Chicago Police tchotchkes littered every corner of the room, but that was the status quo. That was normal too.

"We've got that big award ceremony at six," Ben said, slipping a few bits of eggs under the table to the dogs. Toby and Magnum both sat up straight, tails wagging. Ben thought Sarah didn't notice, which only made it cuter. "They're still going to give you a medal, but I managed to talk the mayor out of making you give a speech. We can have Tatsuya talk. He likes that."

"A medal?" Sarah said. She rubbed her forehead.

"For saving the city from all those crazy demons? They've been planning this for weeks. Are you okay? You still have that headache?"

"Yeah. Right here." She poked a spot in the center of her forehead. She went to take another bite of her breakfast and decided she was done. She pushed the plate away.

"I don't know. I just feel off. Something's not right. Wasn't I mad at you for some reason?"

"You're just nervous. We've got all day to ourselves, so we can veg out and binge movies together."

Sarah nodded. Her skull throbbed. She got up and went over to the couch, flopping down into the cushions face-first. It seemed softer than usual. She had a very good couch. The dogs followed her, and Ben followed them. He sat down next to her.

"Maybe for lunch we can go to that pizza place you like, where they let you play with the extra dough like Play-Doh."

Sarah laughed into the cushion. She looked up at Ben. "What am I, six years old? Wait. Are you talking about Papa Gino's? That place closed twenty years ago."

Ben blinked. "Of course it did. I only meant, uhm—"

"Why would I ever have told you about that?" Sarah sat up. "What day is this? What's the exact date?"

Ben squinted at her, thinking. He swallowed, then stood. He looked very serious. "I'll tell you what day it is. It's the best day of our lives."

He knelt down in front of her and pulled out a ring. It looked exactly like her mother's.

"Oh, that is a *bit* much!" Sarah shouted past Ben to the room in general. The dogs tilted their heads. "Those pants don't have pockets. Where was he even keeping that ring?"

"Are you..." Ben stood back up. Tears welled up in his eyes. "Are you saying no?"

Sarah pawed around on the couch until she found the TV remote. She stood in front of Ben.

"Can you put your hand on my forehead for a second?" she said.

"Sure," Ben said, doing so. "But I don't—"

Sarah pressed the remote against his arm. The world shifted, and the sky-blue elephant squealed as the Onislayer singed its trunk. Sarah took a step back as the yōkai released its grip on her head. She spun her weapon around and was about to slice it into the creature's neck when—

Phoof! A glittery cloud of golden dust burst from the elephant's trunk. Sarah coughed, covering her face. When the glitter cleared, the yōkai was gone.

"There'll be no more of that!" Sarah shouted, waving the golden dust away. She pointed at her head. "*This* is off-limits! No one thinks my thoughts but me! You got that?"

She wiped the Onislayer off on her pants and continued on

toward the meat castle.

犬

Ben dropped into the seat of his moped and bounced a little too far down. A spring and a screw tinkled out onto the parking lot. He frowned. A familiar gruff voice called out to him.

"Gringo!" Tatsuya shouted. The old luchador hobbled out of the dojo on his busted ankle. "*Uno momento!*"

"I need to go," Ben said. "I can help Ash, but I need to get Toby first."

Tatsuya stopped next to Ben. Across the street, a woman was fleeing from a rat with a man's face. He watched them for a moment before speaking.

"Why did you give the inugami to Lucas?" Tatsuya paused. "Instead of me?"

Ben sighed. "You never really wanted Toby anyway, right? You quit drinking when you gave him to me. Lucas was the alpha wolf. He knows inugamis better than anyone."

"Ben..."

"I was afraid of you. Okay? Fine! I admit it!" Ben said. "You yelled at me, and I'm a coward. I tried to run away and fly across the country without telling you. But I—"

Tatsuya raised his hand, stopping him. "You are nothing like me when I was young..."

Ben looked down.

"And you are *exactly* like me when I was young. He says he is alpha wolf?"

Ben nodded.

"Alpha wolf is not a real thing. It's what, eh... *pendejos* say to be *pendejos*. It is a fake thing for jerks. You understand?" Tatsuya's ankle ached. He switched to the other hand with his cane. "Have you ever seen a wolf pack? The leader is not the biggest, toughest wolf. A wolf pack is a family, and the leader is the oldest male. The leader is the dad. He leads them out of love. Sometimes he's tough, sometimes he's not. Sometimes..."

The woman across the street was now beating the human-faced rat with a stick. Tatsuya shook his head.

"The inugami…he knows you are not a dog." He put his hand on Ben's shoulder. "Don't be an alpha. Be a dad."

Ben smiled. He started the engine on his moped. He gestured to Tatsuya's ankle. "You should get that looked at."

The old luchador tapped it with the cane.

"Later," he said. "I also have things to do."

犬

Sarah stepped up to the entrance to the meat castle. The moist avian skin hung loose at the edges of the doorway. Before her stretched a blank, solid wall of darkness. Warm air wafted from inside. She had a very clear vision of finding a dead possum inside the shed behind her parents' house when she was a little kid. It was funny how smells brought back memories like that.

A drop of rancid chicken blood on her neck yanked her back to the present. She held the Onislayer between her knees and pulled out a handkerchief, wiping the yuck from her skin.

"Guess what, chicken butt?" she said, tying the cloth over her face. "You're going down."

She raised the Onislayer and strode confidently into the dark. The floor beneath her feet crunched unsettlingly with each step. After a few seconds of confident striding, she stopped. Nothing had attacked her immediately. A dim red light glowed softly up ahead, and Sarah headed toward it, slower now. She had to keep her guard up.

She stepped out from a pitch-black hallway and entered a large central chamber. A single red paper lantern hung twenty feet up, casting the room in a monochromatic haze. Pillars of rib bones curved up to the center of the ceiling, held together by undulating meat, with black rot growing in its folds like moss. It was like when Pinocchio got eaten by a whale in the cartoon, except everything was decomposing and covered in bugs. Sarah glanced down at her feet. The floor was wriggling. That explained the crunching.

She was so viscerally disgusted that she thought she might lose her mind. She was also, for the moment, alone. One big room. No obvious path onward. She could check the walls for hidden doors, but the last thing she wanted to do was *touch* anything.

Someone was watching her. She could feel it.

She closed her eyes and listened. The handkerchief reflected the sound of her own breathing back at her, so she held her breath.

She stood in silence.

Listening.

Waiting.

A slight tremor in the air behind her. She turned and swung.

Voosh! The Onislayer burst into flames as it sliced through something solid. A long human arm—too long—rolled across the floor, scattering the bugs. Beyond it, the rest of the body also landed, flopping down like a sack of flour. A dozen eyes on the surface of the arm blinked at random.

Sarah took one gasping breath and exhaled. The body wasn't moving. She approached the bundle of cloth and hair with caution, keeping her weapon between it and her. One leg was exposed; the rest was hidden by cloth. The leg, also covered in tiny eyes, was half as long as the arm, which was weird. The eyes all turned to regard Sarah.

The eyeball woman shot upright and pounced, swiping at Sarah with the talons on her remaining overlarge hand. Sarah dodged and stumbled back.

The woman howled, swiping again. Her claws slashed against the Onislayer, which glowed with sparkling embers upon impact. The woman attacked once more. Sarah ducked it, and she plunged the Onislayer deep into the inhuman woman's stomach. She screamed as the flames consumed her, and she fell to burning pieces upon the insect-covered floor.

A monkey wearing a plain white porcelain mask leapt onto Sarah's back. She grabbed it by the scruff of its neck, threw it in front of her, and sliced it in half, wincing at the heat from the burst of flames.

A blob of sludge flew past her face. Then another. The sludge hit the floor and sizzled, oozing deep into the floor meat. Acid!

A ten-foot-tall man, fully nude save for the layer of gray fur covering his entire body, spat acid into his hand and tossed the blob across the room at Sarah. She blocked this one with the flat side of the Onislayer, grunting as the splash hit her arm. She charged at the furry man and lopped off his legs at the knee. He fell onto his back, and Sarah stabbed him through the chest.

She scanned the room as the fire from the furry man added much-needed light. Yōkai of all sorts were crawling from the folds in the meat around her. A human leg with a cyclops eye. A huge black bird in a kimono. A snake with legs. A clock with eyes. A sentient bale of hay with thin, loose arms made of straw, dragging its round body across the floor. These and a dozen others were inching toward her, each keeping an eye or three on her magically charged weapon. Sarah removed the Onislayer from the furry man's corpse and held it in front of her. She stepped around in a defensive circle, holding her ground in the fading light.

"All right, you mythological creeps," she said. "You want a fight? Let's—"

Sarah made eye contact with a Buddhist monk, the one she'd tailed here yesterday. He smiled. She tried to look away, but her eyes were locked on to his, as if they were no longer taking orders from her. As she gazed at him, his head rose upward and upward until she was craning her neck, leaning, sitting, bracing herself up with her elbows, until finally she was flat on her back. Creepy crawlies wriggled around and beneath her.

The Tall Priest pounced, pinning her to the floor with his clawed hands. His head wobbled from side to side on his impossibly elongated neck. He wrenched the Onislayer from her hand and tossed it away, then held her down again. His hand felt hot. In that brief moment, the blade had burned him.

"Get off of me!" Sarah shouted.

He held her gaze again. She froze. The demons encroached from every direction, blotting out the light.

Sarah screamed.

犬

Lucas hefted the last box into the back of his van. Each of the three wolves were chowing down on the remains of a different cow yōkai. Bovine corpses littered the field around them. In the shadows of the empty barn, Toby watched from his magically secured crate. A small, sputtering engine approached from the road.

Ben wobbled to a stop next to Lucas's van. Lucas brushed off his hands and shut the van doors.

"You lied to me," Ben said.

As he stood, the handlebars of his moped popped off in his hand. There was an audible clank as the chassis dropped to the ground. The front tire bounced off into the field. Several important-looking pieces of the engine clattered out. Gasoline dripped from a crack in the fuel tank.

Ben and Lucas each silently edged away from the broken vehicle.

"You said you were going to help me," Ben said, continuing like none of that had happened. "You weren't even training me, were you? You were just using me to get to Toby. You had your little shapeshifting tanuki spy tailing me and making me feel bad about everything. What's with the cyclops boy with the block of tofu? Is that even a real yōkai?"

"I met one of those in Japan, years ago," Lucas said, laughing to himself. "It's cute, right? I thought you'd get all protective of a creature that's somehow actually weaker than you."

"You sprayed Toby with that inugami catnip stuff in the club so he'd lose it." Ben took note of the locations of each of the three wolves, who were still busily gnawing on bones and meat. "Make me rethink things. How'd you *really* get those wolves?"

"It was a lot harder than taking yours." Lucas stepped toward Ben. "I *barely* lied to you. You were so insecure, so ready to be told you could leave. I only gave you an excuse."

Ben looked at Toby. Was he really that insecure? The inugami sat upright and stared at him from inside the unbreakable crate. Ben couldn't read Toby's expression, and he realized, at that very moment, he was looking to a dog for approval.

"You lost authority over Toby a long time before I showed up. I only staged that thing in the club so I could take him before anyone died for real. You should be thanking me! I'm bailing your ass out! Pouncing on the cop in the gym was real. Attacking the spider girl was real. I tried to talk you into giving him up earlier, but you couldn't take a hint!"

"You stole my dog!" Ben shouted.

"Like *I'm* the bad guy! I'm the hero of this story! I've been handling inugami for years! I'm *actually* good at this! You are a ticking time bomb of disaster. Do you know how frustrating it is to watch you suck so bad at my job? Jesus Christ! All that whining and failure! Why would Toby ever listen to *you*?"

Toby was still silently staring at Ben. The former dog walker closed his eyes and sighed.

"Look at this." Ben gestured to all the dead cow yōkai strewn about the lawn. "Look around you. Have you seen what's going on in the city? I passed three unrelated talking mailboxes on my way here. One of them gave me directions. We got caught up in our own drama for like a day, and the apocalypse happened. We can stop this."

Lucas shrugged. "That's not my problem."

"Everything is everyone's problem! The world is a dumpster fire! Please. Lucas, my friends are in trouble."

"That's your business," Lucas said. "I don't know how to make it any more clear to you that I was just pretending to like you."

"Fine. Screw you, too." Ben moved toward the barn, where Toby sat. "I'm taking Toby, and we're—"

Lucas slapped Ben across the face with the back of his hand. Ben fell to the grass. He groaned. His lip throbbed, and he had a metallic taste in his mouth.

"You can't have that dog, kid," Lucas said. His whole demeanor had changed. The front of affability was gone. "You had your chance and you blew it. Walk away."

Ben stood. He spat blood. As he prepared to swing back, Lucas pulled out his dog whistle and blew. In an instant, a powerful set of jaws locked onto Ben's shin. One of the wolves had him pinned. The other two were up and growling. Lucas stepped forward and slugged Ben in the stomach.

The former dog walker fell back, coughing.

"Not so tough with no kakawari!" Lucas punched the air a couple times. He whistled again, and the wolf released Ben. All three wolves lined up in front of Lucas. The man in the fur coat pointed at the empty road.

"Walk away," he repeated.

Ben held his wounded leg, then wiped his bloody hand on the dirt. He stumbled back to his feet, slower this time.

"I'm not leaving without Toby," he said.

"Then you aren't leaving," Lucas said. One of the wolves barked. Lucas held it back. "You had a perfect out, Ben. What the hell are you still doing here?"

"Right now?" Ben wiped his bloody lip. "Distracting you."

Lucas thought for a moment. He whipped around to face the barn. Toby was missing. In his place: a hole in the ground.

Tentacles of darkness wrapped around Ben and yanked him up into the sky, then back down to the ground, next to another hole, ten yards from where he'd been standing. He landed on his feet, blinking and confused. Next to him, a fat Shiba Inu shook the dirt off its fur.

The dust cloud slowly faded. The wolves growled. Toby growled back.

Thunder rumbled overhead.

Lucas reached up to put his dog whistle to his lips, but he didn't have it. He checked his pockets. Ben held up the whistle, smiled, and tossed it back over his shoulder. Lucas sneered.

"You okay?" Ben asked Toby.

The dog snorted.

"Can you fight all three?"

Toby glanced up at him. His eyes flashed red.

"All right." Ben got in a fighting stance. "I'm with you."

"Take 'em down!" Lucas shouted.

The wolves charged.

TWENTY-THREE.

The three wolves stormed across the lawn in a V-formation, ears back, fangs bared. Toby rushed forward to meet them, the faint outline of his shadow form darkening the space around him. Ben scampered behind the dog at half his speed.

The wolf out in front leapt at Toby. Shadow tentacles whipped out from Toby's back, caught the wolf in midair, and hurled the lupine assailant into and through the side wall of the barn. The other two wolves pounced on the Shiba Inu, and they all rolled together, a shifting ball of claws and teeth and shadows.

Ben threw himself into the pile, grabbing one of the wolves by the fur and ripping it away from the fray. The wolf spun around and clamped its jaws onto Ben's forearm with a snarl. The shadow tentacles on its back flailed as Ben struggled, and the wolf sank its teeth deeper into the man's flesh. He screamed.

Several tendrils wrapped around the wolf's neck and yanked it away, back toward the dog pile. As the tendrils faded back into Toby's fur, the little dog dodged a bite, spun to the side, and shoved one of the wolves away with his body before chomping on the leg of another. The wolf who'd been thrown into the barn came rocketing out of the doorway before launching itself back into the fight. Ben stood, holding the skin on his arm closed with his other hand.

Toby was holding his own in the inugami battle, but just barely. There were too many of them. Ben wasn't sure how to help fight three wolves without *immediately* dying. He wished they'd had time to reconnect the kakawari. If only he'd—

Lightning ripped through the air and crashed onto the field beyond the barn. The clouds in the blood-red sky above were tearing their way east, rotating in a spiral from a specific point in the city. This cataclysmic event, whatever you'd call it, was getting bigger, getting closer.

Ben and Lucas exchanged a look. Lucas bolted for his van.

"Hey!" Ben shouted.

Toby fired off two tentacles, snagging two of the wolves by the legs and slamming them together. The third pounced on him, biting at his neck and coming away with a hunk of fur and blood. Toby bit back, piercing the wolf in the snout. He barked as the wolf backed away. The other two attacked from behind, the first biting Toby's haunch to distract him, the second pinning him to the ground. He rolled to the side and swatted at the wolf with his shadow whips before being pinned by another.

Each time the Shiba Inu freed himself, another wolf was already on him. Two pinned him at once, and then the third joined in. The wolves encircled him, holding him down with their fearsome claws and taking quick, unblocked bites at his furry flesh. The shadow around Toby grew darker. His eyes glowed as red as the sky.

Whoom! All three wolves were blown back as a flurry of tentacles filled the air. Shadows thickened into solid fur as the monstrous shape around Toby expanded and hardened. In Toby's place stood a grotesque parody of what once was a Shiba Inu.

The beast reared back its head and howled.

The wolves turned from one to the other, acknowledging this display of aggression and coming to silent agreement. Their eyes also glowed. Their gray fur faded to black and stretched against their skin as their bodies grew. The wolves' already large claws speared into the ground as they sprouted into foot-long ebony blades. Fangs slid out from their mouths and past the edges of their jaws. Their eyes burned as red and luminescent as Toby's. When the transformation was complete, three monstrous inugami surrounded the beast that was Toby, towering over his previously intimidating frame.

Toby blinked. His ears and tail lowered in fear.

The wolf creatures leapt upon him.

Just as Lucas started the engine and shifted into drive, the door opened. Ben grabbed two fistfuls of coat and yanked Lucas down into the dirt. The van coasted in a circle before crunching on top of Ben's moped. More gas spurted out of the moped's fuel tank. The van was still running. Both men stood.

"What the hell is wrong with you?" Lucas shouted, fixing his coat as he paced around Ben. He picked up a piece of wood that had been thrown from the barn, and before Ben could respond, Lucas nailed him in the face with it. The dog walker dropped to the ground.

"You little prick." Lucas kicked him in the stomach. "You need to learn to stay out of other people's shit."

The cluster of fighting inugami stomped past, knocking him to the side. Toby managed to break free for a moment before the wolves caught him in their tentacles and whipped him into the barn, through one wall and out the other. A full third of the roof crashed down onto the hay-lined floor below.

Lucas watched this, and then glanced back down at Ben, who wasn't there. He turned.

Ben clocked him in the side of the head with both fists. Lucas raised the piece of wood to strike, but Ben caught it. They struggled. The wood lowered, and the sharp end pressed against Ben's neck. Lucas smiled.

"Lot harder than fighting little girls, huh?"

Ben grabbed Lucas's wrist and twisted. Something popped inside the man's arm. He dropped the piece of wood.

"You ain't half the man Ash is," Ben said.

He yanked Lucas toward him and headbutted him right between the eyes. Lucas's world exploded into stars. He blinked, his nose oozing blood as he swayed on his feet. Ben gently pushed him to the ground, then winced at the pain in his wolf-bitten arm.

"Toby!" he said. "C'mon! We're leaving!"

The beast that was Toby tumbled backward through another part of the barn, causing that wall to fall and another section of the roof to cave in. Only the front wall was somehow still standing. The beast's jet-black fur was spotted with bloody red patches. The other three inugami bounded out of the rubble after him. One bit his back leg while another plunged its teeth into his throat.

"Hey!" Ben shouted. He ran toward them. "Stop!"

Tentacles from the backs of all three monstrous wolves wrapped around Toby's neck. The former dog gagged, and the dark mass of fur and muscle faded back into shadow, retreating into his body until he was a Shiba Inu again.

Ben grabbed one monstrous wolf by the flailing tentacles, which was like sticking his hands in a barrel of sharpened eels. He yanked as hard as he could, slicing his palms without moving the lupine beast an inch. The wolf turned to see what was happening, and Ben ducked under its snout, getting between it and Toby.

"Wait!" he said. "Stop!"

A second monstrous wolf bit his leg, and he kicked it away. The third had Toby pinned. Ben moved toward it, and the wolf growled. The first wolf barked in his ear. Ben spun around and raised his hand. The wolf chomped down, its powerful jaws enveloping Ben's entire arm up to the elbow. The dog walker screamed. Blood oozed between the wolf's teeth.

The other two wolves were ready to tear into the wounded Shiba Inu, who lay silent in the dirt. Ben raised his fist to punch the wolf attached to his arm.

He stopped. The wolf growled.

Ben closed his eyes, blocking out the unspeakable pain. He took a breath, and then stared into the wolf's eyes. He stood up straight, maintaining eye contact. The wolf stopped growling.

"That's enough," Ben said sternly. "Drop it."

The wolf glared at him, then glanced at its two brothers. They were also frozen in their tracks. Toby whined softly.

"He's going to die if I don't help him," Ben said. "You know Toby. You like Toby. You can kill me after if you want, but you have to let me save him."

The wolf just stared. Ben didn't blink. Across the field, Lucas got to his feet, clutching his broken and bleeding nose.

"Please," Ben said, softer now. "He's my dog."

A moment passed. The wolf's ears tilted into the wind. It blinked. Slowly, gently, it unclenched its jaws, and Ben's arm dropped limply to his side. He'd been bit twice on the same arm. His bone was visible above the elbow. He felt like he might pass out at any moment, but he made sure not to show it.

"Good boy," he said.

The other two wolves backed away as Ben knelt before Toby. The dog whimpered softly, blood gurgling in its throat.

"Hey bud," Ben said. "Wake up. You gotta kakawari me again."

He reached into his pocket with his working arm and pulled out a sandwich bag with a single hot dog in it. The Shiba Inu's eyes opened slightly.

"Kakawari us. Eat the meat. We'll both feel better."

The wolves trotted closer. One sniffed the hot dog, and Ben pulled it away. He held the meat in front of Toby's face. The dog turned his head away. Ben sighed.

"I didn't mean that stuff I said to Kaylee. *You* are the most important thing in my life. You're my best friend." He paused. "I love you."

Behind Ben, Lucas laughed. "He's an inugami, Ben. He's a dead dog brought back to life to commit murders."

"That's not the point," Ben said.

The whole time they were mind-linked, Toby never had a single complimentary or affectionate thought toward Ben. On several occasions, including earlier this week, the inugami had tried to eat him. But that wasn't the point with dogs. You don't love a dog because it loves you back. Hell, you don't love *anything* to be loved back. You do it for the act itself.

You do it because you can.

"Toby," Ben said. "I won't leave you again."

The dog looked up at him. He opened his mouth, and a green gas oozed up into Ben's face. Ben inhaled and tried not to cough, but did anyway. He held his breath to keep the kakawari in, and he opened the sandwich bag. The hot dog slid onto the ground next to Toby. As Ben got to his feet, a vicious wound opened on his neck, gushing blood onto his shirt.

"Crap!" he gurgled. More wounds opened on his leg and stomach, identical to Toby's injuries from the wolf fight. "I didn't know it worked like that!"

He fell on his face, shaking uncontrollably. The little dog turned its head and gobbled up the hot dog lying in the grass. The injuries on both man and dog sealed up, but only to a point. Ben's neck wound closed, but the wounds on his stomach did not. He and Toby still had torn flesh and exposed bone where the wolves had bit Ben's arm.

"Son of a bitch." Ben sat up, then fell back. Blood soaked into his shirt. "One hot dog's not enough."

Ben and Toby both lay in the grass, too hurt to move. The monstrous wolves glanced from one to the other, thinking as a group.

"Well." Lucas walked closer, still holding his nose. "I'm not gonna look this gift horse in the mouth." He whistled. "Kill them."

The wolves regarded him. One tilted its head.

"Kill 'em!" Lucas shouted.

The wolves just stared. He stomped over and kicked the nearest one in the side. "That is an order! I said—"

The wolf snapped at him. Lucas stumbled back, shocked.

"Hey! Don't you—"

The wolf snapped again. The others stepped toward him, tails down, ears back.

Lucas fell back onto his butt, then scrambled up to his feet. He pointed at the nearest wolf. His hand was shaking.

"D-Damn it! I'm the alpha here!"

The wolves growled, fangs bared.

Lucas frowned. He looked ready to shout at the wolves again. Then he turned and fled to his van. All three wolves followed.

Lucas ripped open the door and climbed inside his vehicle. As the van bounced under his weight, Ben saw a spark between the undercarriage of the van and the gas-soaked frame of the moped trapped beneath it.

"Wait!" he said.

The wolves were blown back as Lucas's van erupted in a white-hot ball of flame. Bits of metal and rubber rained from the air around them. A large piece of sheet metal with three wolves painted on it sliced into the ground in front of Ben's face.

The last remaining barn wall rocked on its base. A shadow fell on

Ben and Toby as a thousand pounds of burning wood careened down at them.

Ben hugged his dog close.

犬

Sarah struggled against the yōkai's constant grasp as they dragged her up a flight of flesh-and-bone stairs into another room. It was smaller than the vast chamber below, and the meat on the walls was significantly more decayed. Thick sheets of spiderwebs draped from ceiling to wall like curtains.

The yōkai stopped in the center of the room. The Tall Priest stood behind Sarah and kept his clawed hands on her shoulders. A three-foot-tall fish with humanoid arms and legs held the Onislayer, wrapped in a bundle of cloth so it wouldn't burn him. A dozen or so other creatures stood with them, all watching the far wall. All Sarah could see were webs and shadows.

"A human invaded our fortress," the Tall Priest said. "It bears an enchanted weapon. Dodomeki and Akaname are dead, among others."

"The dog walker?" said two female voices at once.

"No."

The shadows shifted. Shiny black exoskeleton revealed itself in the dim lantern light. Eight legs, each the size of a fence post, carried a fat segmented body across the floor and up to Sarah with a speed she never would have imagined.

The spider had grown significantly in the last hour. Its head alone was at least two feet across. The creature was entirely arachnid, and all traces of Ash's human body were gone except one: at the center of the spider's forehead, the girl's human face stared unblinking at Sarah, nearly lost amongst a haphazard cluster of blank brown eyes.

"The cop." The spider clicked its pedipalps together as Ash's human mouth moved. The two spoke in unison. "Are any others coming?"

Sarah thought before speaking. She glanced at the Onislayer. Just a little too far to grab.

"Ashley—"

"Don't call me Ashley!" shouted both voices. "I am not Ashley anymore!"

"I'm here to help you," Sarah said.

The spider and the girl laughed. "You do not even know me. I do not need your help. Look at me! Gaze upon my true form!"

The spider leaned in toward Sarah, who forced herself not to cower in fear.

"It is too late. We are one now. It is far, far too late."

The spider looked up at the ceiling. All the other yōkai did the same, so Sarah did too. The bone pillars turned, and the meat parted with a wet slurp, revealing the swirling red clouds in the sky.

"Soon," the spider and the girl said, "the merging of the worlds will be permanent. No more will the yōkai be confined to the shadows, invisible to all but a few damaged humans. Your time as rulers of this earth is at an end, and there is nothing you can do. Your world has become ours."

"Ash—"

"Ash is gone!" the voices shouted. The ceiling sealed back up, and the spider skittered into Sarah's space again. This time, she couldn't help but flinch.

Ash's human face smiled. "Who else is coming?"

犬

Ben opened his eyes. He didn't *feel* crushed beneath a barn, but he'd been wrong about things like that before. He looked up.

A solid wall of wood hovered above him, held aloft by a series of shadowy tentacles. The monstrous wolves around him dug their paws into the ground, visibly straining under the weight. One was panting. Ben set Toby on the grass and stood, then winced and knelt back down as the wound in his gut tore a little wider. The wolves eased the wall over to where the rest of the barn had settled and dropped it. Flaming rustic wood came clattering down.

"Uhm...thank you," Ben said.

He pet the jet-black mane of fur around the nearest wolf's neck. It felt cold and a little slimy. The wolf grunted in a way that said it didn't approve of being pet but wasn't going to eat Ben immediately.

Someone coughed. Over near the burning van, Lucas rolled, wheezing for air. His face was badly scarred. Half of his beard and one eyebrow had been burned away. Wisps of flame curled above his coat. Smoke rose all around him. He gave a weak, wet whistle.

"Inugami…" He gasped. "Miya…Help me…"

Ben held his stomach as he scanned the horizon. Bodies approached along the road, some too large and some too small to be human. A countless horde of yōkai marched out from the city. The clouds were whipping ever faster through the crimson sky.

"We need to go back," Ben said.

The burned-out husk that was once Lucas's van collapsed onto the charred clump of moped metal beneath. Both were still in flames. Even if Ben and Toby weren't too injured to stand, even without every yōkai in the Chicagoland area in their way, even if they *had* a car, they were a two-hour drive from the Poultry Zone. Ben turned to his dog.

"Do you think you can—"

A burst of green gas hit him in the face. The wolf who'd released it closed its mouth. Ben looked at the wolf, coughed. He squinted. His eyes felt dry and gritty, like his eyelids were made of sandpaper. He rubbed one with his fist, and it came away with green dust.

LEADER, thought a gruff unfamiliar voice inside his head.

Ben felt the wounds on his arm, leg and abdomen begin to heal as the wolf's life force was added to his. Below him, Toby shook the blood off his fur.

Lucas watched this happen from across the field. His eyes glazed over, and he sighed as he slumped face down in the dirt.

"Wait!" Ben stood and backed away from the wolf as the last of his wounds closed. "N-no. Don't. We already—"

Another cloud of gas discharged in front of Ben's eyes. He waved it away and winced. His head felt like it was full of rocks, all rolling around and scraping against the inside of his skull. His stomach flipped upside down inside his belly, and he fell to his knees before vomiting a torrent of bright-green sludge.

He knelt there in a daze, only vaguely aware of the puddle of steaming yuck slowly expanding onto his pants. Disparate visions overlapped in his head. Two miles away, a skunk foraged near a rotten log. A car engine started in the next town over. The yōkai approaching in the distance chatted casually about the destruction of human civilization. Several rats scurried from the rubble of the fallen barn. He could catch those. As a young pup in the forests of Japan, Ben had hunted mice and rabbits from dawn to sunset, until the coat-wearing human brought him here.

"No!" Ben said, shaking his head. He growled. "Rrrr... No! It's too much."

LEADER, thought a second unfamiliar voice.

Ben saw himself from three different perspectives, kneeling in barf with a fire raging behind him. The vision made him dizzy. The third wolf walked toward him, and Ben smelled his own fear.

"Stop!" he barked. His voice sounded wrong to his own ears. Too rough, too far away. "No! No, no, no, it's too much, it's too much, I can't do it, you can't—"

The final wolf opened its mouth and gassed him. Another set of thoughts smashed Ben's brain like a sock full of quarters. Pain and hunger and loyalty and the smell of meat and the feel of the sun on his fur, anger and fear and joy and sadness, decades and centuries of lives, of loves, a kaleidoscope of scents and sounds and feelings and memories whirled behind his eyes.

He watched the flames dance above the van through six lupine eyes, and he remembered the way the wolves had been treated. A trap, ropes and wooden spikes in the Japanese forest. A kindly old monk, poisoned. Dead. A woman in Ohio, robbed of her treasured pet at gunpoint. Years spent traveling the country in cages, in the back of a hot van. Violence. Cruelty. Confinement. Starvation.

Lucas Alcindor lay face down a few feet from the van. His jacket was still smoking. He did not move, but by his scent, he was alive. The pack would not miss him. Ben opened his eyes, and the addition of another perspective made him throw up again.

LEADER, thought a third voice.

Ben stood. The four inugami faced him. Lightning illuminated the sky. Four visions of himself conflicted with the reverse angle, then all five perspectives consolidated into one. He could hear everything, smell everything. Liquid kakawari dripped from Ben's nose and ears.

It was a struggle to keep his eyes open, like in a dream. Or a nightmare. Thick green tears clumped at the edges of his vision. He looked at Toby.

LEADER, thought the dog.

A shadow fell on Toby, solidifying as he transformed back into a monster. Ben turned away. Beyond the fire, beyond the encroaching hordes of yōkai, the Chicago skyline rose from the horizon, backlit by a raging red sky.

Coils of black fur wrapped around Ben and hoisted him onto Toby's back. The dog walker spit a hunk of slime into the field and watched as the blades of grass around it dissolved.

"Okay," he said. "Let's go."

The human and his four-inugami hunting party howled as they charged toward the city.

TWENTY-FOUR.

Sarah stood silent at the center of the meat-and-bone room, held in place by the Tall Priest. The other yōkai waited for a signal. The spider clicked its appendages thoughtfully as it considered what to do with this human woman. Sarah hadn't given any answers to their questions. She obviously didn't intend to.

"Dodomeki was a friend," the Tall Priest said. "I am happy to kill this human if we do not need her."

"No..." the spider said in two voices. "She can be a strong host for one of the other symbiotic yōkai. Sanshi, the three worms...Haimushi, the lung moth...Hishaku, the wolf of the spleen. How is your spleen, human?"

"One of the best," Sarah said.

Ash's human face smiled slightly. Something heavy landed downstairs in the lower chamber of the meat castle. Muffled shouts echoed through the floor of flesh.

"What is that?" said the Tall Priest. "Who did you bring here?"

Sarah listened. More impacts. More shouting.

"From ancient Japan..." she said with great import. "He has traveled thousands of miles to become the greatest fighter of them all. *Rudos...demonios...*"

The yōkai around her began to shift in place as they nervously watched the stairs. The sounds grew closer. Ash watched Sarah.

"Guard the entrance," said the spider. A bear wearing a sedge hat and a clock with a human face went to the doorway and stood on either side. A high-pitched scream sliced through the air. A body fell down the stairs.

"Tonight, you face a *true* warrior," Sarah said. She felt the Tall Priest strengthen his grip on her shoulders. "Prepare yourself! For the UWA heavyweight champion of the world! And face the wrath…"

The room fell silent.

"…of Dragon Mask."

Ash's eyes grew wide.

A hulking figure tore through the wall next to the staircase. He was shirtless. Faded dragon tattoos drenched in the drippings of undead chicken meat wrapped around his strong, wrinkled chest. Dragon Mask laughed maniacally from behind his white-and-red luchador mask.

"Sayonara Slam!" he shouted as his elbow tore into the behatted bear's neck, bringing both man and bear to the floor.

The old wrestler rolled, and without skipping a beat, grabbed the clock with a face in one strong hand and slammed it hard into an exposed wall bone. Springs and gears went flying.

He glared at the small fish man, who had the Onislayer cradled in his arms. The aquatic creature shrieked, dropped the weapon, and scurried down the stairs and out of sight. Dragon Mask grabbed the Onislayer and flung it in Sarah's direction. The blade sliced through a sentient tree man, who erupted in flames as Sarah caught the handle of the weapon.

She spun, and before the Tall Priest could react, she severed his hands from his wrists with a single stroke.

The Tall Priest reared back, screaming, his head bobbing on his long prehensile neck as he raised his handless arms in horror.

Another monkey wearing a white mask gunned it across the room toward Dragon Mask, brandishing a knife. The wrestler dodged his simian foe's attack and redirected the monkey into the burning stump that was once the tree man. Porcelain mask shards littered the room as face hit wood.

"Seize him!" shouted the spider and Ash. Ash's voice was enraged, but her face was not. She looked nervous. "Catch him! Destroy him! Tear the wrinkled flesh from his bones!"

"Ashley!" Dragon Mask shouted mid-battle. He punched a seven-foot caterpillar in the face. "I can help you, but I cannot save you. Only you can free yourself! Are you ready?"

A swarm of crows sent him flailing backward, where he tripped over a living record player. He hoisted the sentient Victrola over his head and hurled it into the crowd of yōkai.

"We are one," said the spider and Ash. "You have—"

"—no power here," said the spider, alone.

Dragon Mask smiled, his perfect white teeth glimmering through the mask hole.

"Old fool!" the spider shouted before nailing the luchador in the side of the head with what could only be described as a sucker punch. "Your words are as weak as your frail body!"

Dragon Mask stumbled from the blow and then winced, lifting his bad foot off the floor. The spider noticed the bandages around his ankle. She sprang forward and smashed his injured foot into the floor with her terrible spider claw.

The old luchador howled in pain.

犬

The Tall Priest snapped at Sarah, then again, biting at her face as his head dangled on a drooping twenty-foot neck. In his rage, all of the humanity had drained from his face. His eyes grew dark, and he bared his fanged teeth with an animalistic ferocity. He bit at her again. Sarah swiped at him with the Onislayer, but his head swung back and then forward. His jaws clamped onto her forearm.

"Aahh!!" She tried to hit him with her blade, but he had her arm pinned.

The Tall Priest snarled.

Blam! Blue-black blood splattered onto Sarah as the Tall Priest's head exploded into brains and giblets. The vested yōkai's long, prehensile neck went slack as its whole body slumped to the floor. Sarah unclamped the priest's lower jaw from her arm. She turned.

Jake was standing in the doorway to the stairs, holding a smoking gun. He gave her a nod, then was attacked by a small creature with a wooden mallet.

The bug-eyed creature had long white hair, black skin, and a beaklike mouth. It clocked Jake in the nose, then the chest, pushing him back into the stairway. Sarah rushed forward and took a swing at it. The creature caught the blades of the Onislayer in its wooden mallet, where they stuck in deep.

"Ha-HA!" cackled the mallet-wielding yōkai. "You'll find that I, Kanazuchibō the Hammer Priest, am not so easy to—"

Sarah stomped on his chest, yanked the Onislayer out of his mallet, and stabbed the tiny creature through the neck, decapitating him. He burned away like embers on the wind. It was a brutal action, more than Jake had ever seen from Sarah. He coughed.

"Hey," Sarah said. "Get up."

"Sarah," Jake said, "I need to—"

She held up her hand. The yōkai hordes were quickly approaching.

"Apologize later," she said before running toward the crowd and swinging her blade, slicing through three of them in one go. Four more were on her before the burning bodies landed.

Something hissed behind Jake. More demons were heading up the stairs.

He fired at them. *Blam! Blam!*

犬

The spider kept Dragon Mask pinned to the floor, with his busted ankle twisted painfully to the side. The yōkai raised a claw to the luchador's chin and lifted it up, exposing the naked white flesh beneath his mask. It pressed the claws against his neck, then hesitated. The luchador glanced into Ash's eyes. She was watching him.

Dragon Mask dove to the side, and he muffled a scream of pain through his mask as he twisted his ankle free. He rolled on his shoulder and then flipped upright, using his momentum to smash a sentient pile of wood to pieces with his arm. A flying squirrel swooped through the pile of wood and onto the luchador's face. Dragon Mask grabbed it and ripped it away.

"Ashley!" he said, drop-kicking the squirrel. "You know that I do not drink! Do you know why?"

The spider stomped toward him. He caught the arachnid horror by its two front legs and held it back. His feet slid then stood firm. His muscles bulged.

"For thirty years after my father died," the luchador said, grunting, "I was drunk. Every moment I was Dragon Mask. Every day, I woke up and I followed my father's stupid immortal dog as it wandered north, as it ignored me as though I were nothing. I had nothing, I was nothing, and I was drunk. Always drunk."

He shoved the spider back just in time to block an attack from a nude headless man.

"When the inugami chose Ben and I finally quit, I thought I could not be Dragon Mask! The drunk and the luchador, the two were one! My fight was over!"

He punched the headless man in the stomach, and the man split into three smaller headless men. The old luchador sighed and kicked one, bracing to fight the other two.

"This girl is mine!" said the spider.

More and more yōkai were coming up the stairs, down through the opening in the center of the ceiling, in through the folds in the walls of meat. Most were heading immediately toward Dragon Mask, who fought them off while talking. Across the room, Sarah was swinging wildly at another batch of demons, lighting up the room with each successful stroke of the Onislayer. Jake made his way toward her as he ran out of bullets. He tossed his gun at a small gray-skinned boy, who caught the pistol in his mouth and swallowed it whole. Jake shuddered.

"When the spider took you," Dragon Mask said, "I came very close to drinking. Why wouldn't I? I could not help you without Dragon Mask, and there was no Dragon Mask without tequila. I was afraid I would lose what I had. But I will tell you this…"

He held back the largest of his foes, a seven-foot tall hairy human foot. With his other hand, he undid the straps on his mask and pulled it away. Tatsuya smiled.

"Some things are just worth fighting for."

He let go of the foot and was completely overrun by yōkai. Ashley watched, helpless inside her arachnid prison, as the animals, objects, and humanoid creatures all swarmed onto the old luchador. A single tear rolled down her cheek.

"Ashley..." Tatsuya faded behind a wall of demons. "Why do you fight?"

犬

Traffic was at a standstill on the northbound Tollway as the good citizens of Chicago fled their demon-infested city. People had started getting out of the cars and were standing around in the middle of the street. Mrs. McClanahan was among them. She leaned against the side of her minivan, taking a breath of fresh air away from her kids, who were all shouting at each other in the back seats. She should call her mother, she decided, and try and explain what was happening while she had a moment to herself.

She pulled out her phone and then dropped it, screaming as four enormous, monstrous wolves trampled over her van. The beasts vaulted from her car to the next, leapfrogging their way across the river of cars as they stormed toward the city. The smallest of the beasts had a man on its back. Mrs. McClanahan recognized him, but it seemed impossible.

"Ben?" she said.

The dog walker threw up again off the side of Toby's back. His whole body had a migraine. Pain pulsed through his every muscle at an irrhythmic beat. He was so overflowing with kakawari that he could see it in his hand, green ooze pulsing inside his veins. A squirrel pranced across a lawn two blocks south. Too much perfume in that car. Jackhammering three miles away. Someone in one of these cars had fast food. French fries!

"Focus..." Ben snarled.

The skyline was bigger now. The eye of the swirling clouds had shifted left. They were getting closer. Syncing his mind and spirit with four inugami had left Ben a shambling mess, but in bonding with him, they also bonded with each other. They'd been analyzing threats and coordinating routes as one singular neural net the whole way here. Ben was definitely going to die from this, but he had to admit they were making good time.

Three of his five points of view zeroed in on a white shape clinging to the side of the overpass.

MAN BONES, thought a wolf.

"Man bones?" Ben grunted.

BIG MAN BONES, thought another wolf.

"What?"

The single white shape became four. Then the four shapes became four fingers as a gargantuan human skeleton pulled itself upright, leaning over the highway and cackling at the tiny motorists who fled in terror. Its jaw, which was the size of a Buick, bobbed up and down like a ventriloquist dummy's.

Ben, the wolves, and Toby all focused on the same thing for once, and that helped clear Ben's head. He sensed their need for guidance. In the span of a millisecond, they all worked out a plan. The giant skeleton reached out with its skinless hand.

Tentacles whipped from Toby's back, snagging the hand and pinning it to the street. The three wolves bounded up the skeleton's arm. Two of them leapt onto its shoulders. The third scrambled over its head and onto a nearby roof. It whipped out its tentacles and wrapped them around the skeleton's neck.

The two wolves on the shoulders each seized a collarbone with their fur whips and then jumped downward, yanking the skeleton down with them. Bound by the third wolf, the colossal skull popped off the skeleton's body like the head of a dandelion. The wolf holding it dropped it, and it clunked into the pile of giant bones now littering the streets below.

The three wolves scurried up the buildings and concrete pillars around them until they were back on the highway with Ben and Toby. Ben gave them each a quick pet behind the ears.

Deep, booming laughter echoed as the headless skeleton rose again, reattaching its skull to its spine like it was screwing on a bottlecap. It moved towards the pack. The wolves growled.

"No! No time!" Ben snarled. He and Toby turned away. "Let's go!"

Toby continued running away from the skeleton, and the wolves followed after him, narrowly avoiding the titanic yōkai's grasp. The skull roared.

Ben tasted something weird in his mouth. Meaty but dry. He looked back. One of the wolves had a giant, still-wiggling finger bone in its mouth.

"Drop it!" he growled.

The wolf did so reluctantly, and the pack bounded onwards into the setting sun.

犬

The shapeless mass of yōkai piled onto Dragon Mask. Clawing at his arms, biting at his chest, bludgeoning him with wooden fists. Sarah swung the Onislayer one last time before a living statue knocked the blade from her hand. She and Jake stood back to back as the demons closed in.

Ash observed it all, her eyes darting around the room. The spider wiped the blood on its claws onto a clean wall bone.

Tatsuya's luchador mask was thrown from the crowd, and it flopped limply onto the floor.

"N-no..." Ash said. Her face shifted, exposing a gap in the exoskeleton by her left cheek.

"Quiet, meat," said the spider. "You don't need him. You only need me."

"No," Ash said, firmly.

Crunch! A small human hand punched free from the giant spider's head, sending exoskeleton and gobs of bright orange spider brains into the air.

The arachnid horror wobbled.

"Need...me..." it gurgled.

"I don't need you!" Ash shouted.

Crunch! Another hand smashed out of the head. Ash reached down and wrenched her face free from the exoskeleton. She tore into the hard shell, ripping away chunks of spider skull like she was peeling a hard-boiled egg.

As the spider slumped onto the floor, Ash hoisted herself out and crawled onto the floor. She was covered from head to toe in thick, goopy orange gunk, still wearing the prison scrubs she'd been given at the police station. All of her fingers and toes were still there. She still had her ankle monitor. Fat lot of good *that* did her. No voice in her head. She lifted up a handful of her hair, and it fell like hair should. She was free.

The spider was dead.

Several of the yōkai pummeling Tatsuya turned and saw her, crouched in a pile of their leader's guts. A black-furred creature with long legs started toward her, as did a frog man and a pale woman with no eyes. Ash picked up the luchador mask and put it in her pocket. She grabbed one of the spider's legs with both hands and twisted, tearing it free from the body.

As the furry creature lunged for her, she nailed it in the stomach with the severed leg. She ducked under the leaping frog man and jumped onto the eyeless woman's chest, wrapping her legs around the woman's waist and punching her until she fell. Ash snapped the woman's arm behind her back then turned to the frog man with rage in her eyes.

"Leave," she said.

The frog man fled down the stairs.

"Sensei!" Ash shouted. "I'm coming!"

A living broom hopped at her. She grabbed it, spun it around her back and hurled it back into the crowd. A man-sized rat creature bounded at her, hissing. She dodged his claws twice, then grabbed him by the neck and slammed him to the floor. She stood.

"Shooting Star Elbow Drop!"

She jumped up and then drove her elbow into his spine, finishing him. Beyond the yōkai, Tatsuya lay motionless on the floor. His eyes were closed.

"Sensei!"

The world shook. The building swayed. A large strip of wall meat peeled from the bone, and Ash dove to the side to avoid its landing. The lights of downtown Chicago shone in from the new window.

"Our fortress!" shouted the sentient broom.

"Its corporeality was tied to the spider, who has been slain by her human host!" said a pair of talking sandals.

The yōkai began to flee and disperse. Ash used the commotion to work her way to Tatsuya. She knelt by him and lifted his head off the floor.

"Sensei!" she said. "I'm here. I'm here! I'm fighting! C'mon!"

He was beaten and bloodied. He didn't react to her presence, but he was breathing. He was alive. Ash looked around for an exit. The stairs were clogged with yōkai. Dozens remained in the chamber. She saw Sarah and Jake, still both punching different yōkai. Jake had a swollen purple bruise on his face.

There was no clear way out. Ash didn't think she could carry her sensei alone. A man with the head of a cat pointed at her.

"It was her!" he hissed. "She has doomed us! Get her!"

The yōkai swarmed. Ash held Tatsuya.

She couldn't save him. There were just too many.

A cacophony of howls echoed throughout the chamber as four monstrous inugami barreled into the meat castle. The wolves immediately got to work mauling and maiming as many yōkai as possible. One pounced on the talking sandals, shaking them in its jaws like a rope toy. Another grabbed two monkeys and smashed them together with its tentacles. The third smashed its way into the crowd of yōkai by the stairs and just went *hog wild* with the biting.

A piece of the floor peeled away as the meat castle continued to disintegrate. The yōkai began to clear the room. The pack saw Sarah, with a pig yōkai pinned beneath her, punching it repeatedly in the face. Ben blinked, remembering he was Ben. He tumbled off Toby's back like a rag doll and clambered toward her.

"Sarah!" he said. She looked up.

The dog walker was drenched in green slime, which was actively seeping out of every orifice of his body. His eyes darted around uncontrollably, sometimes in two directions. His teeth seemed longer, pointer. His fingernails had turned green.

"What *the hell* happened to you?" Sarah said.

"Climb on one of the wolves," he said. "I can get everyone out of here! I'm sorry I left! I shouldn't have abandoned you guys!"

"Ben, you're...you're barking at me." She looked concerned. "Do you think you're talking?"

He closed his eyes, focused. The wolves all gathered behind him. Toby remained locked in battle with a giant frog made of mud.

"Get...on..." Ben growled.

He dove past Sarah, pouncing on a tiny squirrel yōkai. Ben chomped down on its back and then violently shook his head, snarling.

"All right, we're leaving." Sarah turned and grabbed Jake—who was losing a fight with a sentient fan—and shoved him toward the monstrous wolves. He looked the nearest one in the eye. The wolf glared back.

"Uhh, what," Jake stammered. "I'm not—"

"Jake, get on the goddamn wolf!" Sarah shouted.

She stomped over and clutched him by the waist, hoisting him up next to the wolf. Black tendrils of fur wrapped themselves around Jake and carried him the rest of the way onto the creature's back.

The slice of floor meat beneath Tatsuya peeled away as Ash dragged him toward the wolves, her hands cupped under his armpits. Below, water rushed into the first floor of the castle from all sides. Sarah grabbed the Onislayer right before it dropped into the drink and then hurried over to help Ash. The two of them hefted the old luchador up behind Jake. It took a couple tries. He was very heavy.

"Oh God," Jake muttered, frozen in horror as the unconscious wrestler slid behind him. "It's cold. The wolf is so cold. Oh Jesus."

"Men, huh?" Sarah said. Ash smiled.

Suddenly, all around them, yōkai began to scream, grasping their heads—or what passed for heads—as they were wrenched toward each other by an unseen force. Yōkai slammed into yōkai, umbrellas on bears, trees on clocks, talking feet on walking mouths, sentient objects and anthropomorphic animals alike collided into a writhing, screaming mass of demons. Rotted meat peeled from the walls and ceiling, wrapping itself around the mass, shaping it. A structure began to emerge. Eight jagged legs, each the length of a flagpole, bent and twisted from the center, spearing themselves into the remaining floor. The mass pinched in at the middle, with a fat, pointed abdomen drooping behind the legs and a face emerging at the front. Eyes, fangs and pincers, all molded from the bodies of live yōkai.

Ben looked up from his prey, his face caked in squirrel blood. The mud frog Toby had pinned melted into sludge, which slid through the cracks in the floor into the lake below.

The All-Spider rose, the top of its shifting form scraping the bones on the ceiling. A dozen voices spoke in unison.

"Ashleeeeeeeeeeeeeeeeeey…"

Sarah was up on the second wolf, reaching down for Ash. The little girl gasped when she heard her name and understood what was saying it.

"Get her out of here!" Ben snarled.

Tentacles swirled from the third wolf and ensnared Ash, plucking her off the floor and onto its back as all three wolves sprinted out a hole in the crumbling wall.

"Wait!" Ash shouted.

A cacophony of voices wailed from the All-Spider as Ash faded from view. Ben shambled toward the creature, his gait awkward and halting, like his legs weren't communicating with each other. He spat green goo, which burned away a three-inch hole in the floor meat. Toby stepped next to him, in full inugami glory.

The All-Spider peered down at them.

Toby sniffed the air. Ben sniffed too.

Both growled.

犬

The three monstrous wolves bounded down the side of the castle, meat disconnecting from bone beneath their paws with each step. The entire structure was gradually sinking into the lake. The main level, with the chicken butt door, was already underwater. All around them, the yōkai who hadn't been absorbed into the All-Spider were scurrying out of the building and into the city. A turtle with a pot on its head snapped at Ash as it ran past.

They all settled in the parking lot next to the seafood restaurant. Jake and Tatsuya were dropped off next to an empty white van. Jake sat Tatsuya upright and leaned him against the side of the van then stood, unsteadily. He couldn't bring himself to look at the wolf who'd saved him. He checked the old luchador's pulse.

Sarah hopped down by herself, careful not to let the Onislayer touch the wolf. She wasn't completely certain on the science of it, but the sword probably burned good guy demons on impact, too. How would it know?

As the final wolf set Ash on the ground next to Sarah, the other two turned to race back inside. Ash frowned, bouncing from foot to foot. This was wrong.

"Take care of Sensei!" she said.

Sarah turned. "What?"

As the wolf went to follow its brothers, Ash grabbed onto its fur and was yanked upward. She dangled from the side of the wolf as the pack scaled back up the outside wall of the crumbling meat castle.

"Hey!" Sarah shouted. "Ash! Are you crazy?!"

She started toward the castle and stopped as something roared behind her.

A massive human skeleton climbed out from between two apartment buildings across the street. It stood, towering over the surrounding buildings, tearing down the power lines in front of it with a single swipe of its arm. It was twice as tall as the nearest trees, it was angry, and it was staring directly at her.

"Okay." Sarah choked up on the Onislayer's hilt. "That's a big one."

The skeleton charged.

犬

The All-Spider moaned in a dozen voices as it turned to follow the inugami, which leapt from one bone to the next with the dog walker on its back. The meat of the floor had mostly peeled away, leaving only a support structure of bones on which to stand. The space below had flooded completely. The water was still rising. Each moment, another strip of rotting poultry dropped from the walls and ceiling.

The spider swung its massive front leg, and Ben and Toby ducked it in unison before separating and landing next to each other on one of the larger support bones, crouched in the same canine pose. The inugami's eyes flashed red. Ben's did too. Both howled, and the mass of live yōkai that made up the spider's body shuddered at the sound.

Shadow tentacles speared from Toby's back and stabbed at the spider in quick, staccato strikes. *Thip thip thip thip thip!* The yōkai on the surface squirmed in pain. Ben rushed down the bone toward the spider's nearest leg and threw himself at it, ripping away a rooster in a kimono with his teeth.

The All-Spider reared back, away from the inugami's fur whips. It swung its leg at the inugami, who ducked under the attack, only to be clobbered by the second leg swinging right behind the first. The beast tumbled into the rising water. The spider shifted and directed its attention at Ben.

As Ben snarled and bit at the spider's leg, the many yōkai before him reached out, with their legs, claws, wings, and fins, and together, pulled Ben screaming into the mass.

For a moment, there was silence.

Voosh! A shadow tentacle whipped up from the water and into the wriggling wall of yōkai. Ben emerged, yanked by the tentacle around his wrist. He slid down the bone, halfway across the castle before he snagged an outcropping. He swung his other arm, grunting.

The Shiba Inu on the other end of that tentacle burst from the water and flew toward the spider's head. The little dog closed its eyes, and it popped inside the tightly-packed clump of living creatures with an audible slurp.

The All-Spider stumbled, one of its eight legs dipping into the water. Dozens of voices wailed in pain as the full form of the monstrous inugami burst from the top of the spider's head, a human-sized rabbit creature in its jaws. Several yōkai fell into the water, freed as the spider was weakened.

Two massive spider claws rose up on either side of the inugami before grabbing him by the head and hurling him down onto a bone, which snapped upon impact. The whole collapsing castle groaned.

Toby tried to stand, but the All-Spider stomped on him. It raised its foot. Toby stood, roaring. The spider stomped again. And again. The spider turned to the side to crush the human, too, but Ben was already running full-speed along the edge of the castle. The All-Spider rotated, following him.

As Ben ran, his paws—*feet*, his feet kept shifting in place. He was going forward, but also up. Inside, but also outside. Something clung to his fur. Ben coughed, tripped, fell to his knees. His eyes went blank as green sludge—darker than before—oozed out of his mouth and nose. He threw up again, and just as his eyes cleared, the spider's claw slammed down on top of him.

The All-Spider leaned hard on both man and dog, bracing itself with its other six legs. The bones beneath Ben crunched apart, and more of the castle floor tore away. Ben gurgled up more green sludge before submerging under the water. Toby crumpled as Ben's fresh injuries transferred to him, and he plunged into the water too.

"Dieeeeeeee…" moaned the many yōkai.

Ben's face rose briefly from the water. His eyes were glowing.

"Now!" he snarled.

Two monstrous wolves swept into the ruined castle from behind the All-Spider. As they soared toward the other side of the room, their fur tentacles snagged two of the spider's back legs. The enormous arachnid roared in many voices as it flipped head over heels, crashing through most of the remaining floor and splashing down into the lake.

The wolves landed on the thick, round bone making up the outer structure of the castle, the only piece of flooring that remained. They used their tentacles to scoop Ben and Toby out of the water. Toby was back to being a Shiba Inu. He shook the lake water off his fur.

The All-Spider flailed and undulated, losing its shape as the yōkai began to disperse, broken free by the water. Most swam toward the bone. Some sank to the depths. Many floated lifeless on the surface.

Ben sat, his feet dangling in the water, staring straight ahead. The green fluid oozing out of him was nearly black. He watched himself, with concern, through three sets of eyes. All of him was looking at Ben, which meant Ben wasn't looking at all. The voice in his head, the main one, the running visual commentary that made him who he was, grew quieter and quieter until only the pack could be heard.

LOSING HIM.

TOO DEEP.

LEADER.

BEN.

Toby nudged Ben with his nose. The man growled, saw who it

was, and shook his head. He took a deep breath and exhaled. A black-green tear slid down his cheek. He looked up. There were only two wolves standing with them.

"Where's Taka?" Ben closed his eyes, tried to focus on the perspective. "No."

The third wolf stood across the water, on the other side of the bone circle. A small figure climbed down from its fur.

"No!" Ben howled.

Whoosh! The All-Spider rose from the water, still screaming. Fallen yōkai were sucked back into its shifting form even as others tumbled away.

Ash stepped away from the wolf. The bone floor had submerged a few inches. Her ankle bracelet floated next to her shin. She glared at the loose, vaguely spiderlike cluster of yōkai that had once possessed her.

"Ashleeeeeeeeey..." murmured the many voices of the All-Spider as it leaned toward her.

"Hold it back!" Ben shouted.

A flurry of shadow tentacles whipped from the wolves, grasping at the All-Spider, and failing, as the looser structure and the wet yōkai made it impossible to get a grip on. Each time the wolves caught a creature, two more splashed up from the lake and filled its place. Toby barked.

Ben swung his arms out, fingers-first, like he too was using his tentacles. He saw his own hands, realized what he was doing, and stopped as his eyes filled with green-black darkness and the silent thoughts overwhelmed him once more.

Toby nudged Ben. No reaction. The dog whined.

"Ashleeeeeeeey..." said the voices.

The spider continued to move toward Ash, unaffected by the wolves' attack. It stopped with its face inches from the girl's.

"I didn't get it until now," Ash said without looking away. "I knew you needed me to live, but I didn't understand what you wanted. For a while, I thought it was revenge on Ben, on *all* of humanity, for killing your children. And then you killed them too. Then I thought, maybe it's about all the yōkai? There's a bigger picture here. She loves her people. But look at this. Look at you. Do these things look happy?"

The All-Spider stared back at her with uncomprehending eyes, made from several sentient drums and a few turtle shells.

"You're just a bully. That's all. There's no goal. There's no end to it. You are nothing but blind rage. You're a virus looking for a host and a target, and I'm done listening to you."

The yōkai began to slide from the All-Spider like melting snow. The remaining ones moaned. "Ashleeeeeeeey…"

The girl placed a hand on the center of the All-Spider's face.

"Hold still."

She made a fist, and she punched the mass of yōkai with all her strength.

Voom! Water burst upward in a ring around the All-Spider, then rained down as whatever magic holding the creature together vanished in an instant. The bone below Ash dropped, and she yelped as she was dunked up to her waist in Lake Michigan. She reached for the wolf. Fur tentacles wrapped around her arms and waist and pulled her up onto the monstrous inugami's back.

The wolf leapt up onto the quickly dissolving clump of yōkai that, moments ago, had been the All-Spider's head, and then bounded through the collapsing multitude beyond, which tumbled into the lake with each step. All around, beasts and tools and furniture and limbs were breaking free and either diving into the water or flying off into the night sky. The wolf landed on the other side, where its two brothers stood, patiently awaiting a command from their leader.

Ben was up to his knees, eyes open, mouth curved in a frown. His eyes were pitch black, same with his nails, and nostrils, and teeth. He looked like a pillowcase full of hot tar had been run over by a truck. Toby was on two legs, paws on Ben's waist, head in Ben's hand, nudging the man repeatedly with his nose. The last remaining wall of meat drooped above them.

Ash climbed down from the wolf, back into the water. She waded over to the dog walker.

"Ben!" Ash said. "C'mon! We're gonna be underwater in a second!"

She grabbed the man, shook him. He didn't react. He was staring past her, over her shoulder.

"I'm not..." he grunted, forcing the words. "I'm not who I should be."

Ash followed his eyeline to an airplane in the distance, lights blinking in the darkness as it headed east, away from O'Hare. She held his hand.

"Ben," she said. "You're still you."

Ben looked at her, the little girl waist-deep in the lake in the middle of the night. He felt fur in his other hand. Toby's head was the only part of him out of the rising water. He pressed his cold nose against Ben's palm. Ben turned to the three wolves.

"I'm here," he said.

The castle finally tilted sideways, and the floor gave way entirely. The four inugami gathered up the two humans and bounded up onto the last remaining pillar of bone. They climbed around to the other side, out in the open air, before leaping onto the seafood restaurant's roof and then down the fire escape into the small walkway behind the building. They set Ben and Ash down on the pavement. The air around was very warm. An orange glow emanated from the parking lot. Demons fled in all directions, no longer concerned with Ben and his friends. It had been a rough night for them, too.

As the wolves and humans all came around the corner, they found a giant skeleton—the one that Ben and the four inugami had fought earlier—crumpled into a pile, lifeless and burning at the center of the parking lot. Sarah was standing on its shoulder, hacking away at its skull with the Onislayer. Most of her uniform shirt had been torn away. She was missing a shoe. She turned, wiping sweat from her brow, then jumped down to meet the others. Ash saw Tatsuya, safely hidden behind the white van with Jake, and she ran to him.

Ben smiled at Sarah, his teeth blackened with kakawari. Behind him, waves crashed upon the shore as the last of the meat drifted slowly downward.

"Well," Sarah said. "That should help with the smell."

Stars shone through the clouds as the sky began to clear.

TWENTY-FIVE.

The lake had fully consumed the meat castle by the time fire crews and paramedics arrived on the scene. The yōkai had dispersed, save for a few stragglers. A pile of enormous, lifeless human bones crackled and smoked in the center of the parking lot. Jake was explaining the situation to the beat cops who'd taken the call. As the most reluctant believer, he was the only one who really could.

Sarah helped the EMTs load Tatsuya's stretcher onto the back of an ambulance.

"Thanks, guys," she said, patting one on the back. "I know you're busy tonight."

Ash climbed into the vehicle after the stretcher. "I'm going with him."

Sarah nodded. "You gonna be okay?"

"Yeah." Ash smiled. "Take it easy, cop lady."

The doors swung closed.

Ben Carter sat on a bench, his back to the lake, hunched over the bucket he had locked between his legs. Toby sat next to him, back to being a regular-sized dog. The three wolves lined up before them. They each pressed their forehead against Ben's, then Toby's, before prancing off down the street.

Sarah sat down next to Ben. "Are we just going to let three demonic wolves go off on their own?"

Ben watched the mystic beasts vanish into the night. "Do you wanna stop them?"

He inhaled sharply, then vomited a torrent of emerald bile into his bucket. When he looked back up, the green coloration in his skin and eyes was already beginning to fade.

"There goes the extra kakawari." Ben chucked his bucket of puke into the water. "Just me and Toby again. Which is good. I was starting to go full feral. I bit one of the EMTs."

"They told me," Sarah said. Across the street, a sentient trashcan had stolen one of the firefighter's helmets. Four men in reflective coats were chasing it as it hopped around in a circle, giggling. "Everyone can see them now? The demons?"

"I guess so," Ben said. "That part doesn't seem to be going away."

Sarah nodded. "Good for business, at least."

He looked at her. "What business? We both got fired."

"That is true. I have an idea, a thing we can do for money, but I don't want to tell you yet. Do you trust me?"

"Yeah, of course."

She smiled. "Just like that?"

"Yeah." Ben smiled too. "Just like that."

They sat, listening to the waves, not actively doing anything for the first time in a month. It was nice. Toby climbed up into Ben's lap, and Ben put his arm around Sarah without really thinking about it. She leaned back against his arm.

"When I first got here, I fought this little blue elephant guy," Sarah said. "He stuck his trunk on my forehead and it made me, uh…hallucinate."

"Oh yeah, that thing. That's a…" Ben snapped his fingers, thinking. "Baku. It's actually a tapir, not an elephant. They eat dreams, and while they do it, you go into like a fantasy-sequence trance as it feeds on your brain. There's an alien flower that does it to Superman in this one comic. Wait."

He sat up and looked at her. "What'd you see?"

"What do you mean?"

"It's supposed to be, like, your greatest hopes and desires made manifest. What did the baku show you?"

Sarah took a long time to answer. "Cop stuff."

"Cop stuff." Ben raised an eyebrow. "That's it?"

"Yeah. Big promotion. The mayor gave me the key to the city. That sort of thing."

Ben stared at her, scanning her face for signs of lying, but with Sarah he could never tell.

"Carter!" Jake beckoned to Ben from across the street. The police had more questions for him.

"Speaking of cop stuff…" Ben set Toby to the side and stood.

"Hey, Ben?" Sarah said. He turned back. "Why'd you come back?"

Ben just smiled and walked away. Sarah sighed. Toby was staring at her with a judgmental look he usually reserved for Ben.

"Shut up," Sarah said, petting him.

犬

Tatsuya opened his eyes to see his star pupil standing over him. He was in a moving ambulance. Two medical workers were bandaging his wounds.

"Ashley…" he said, putting his hand on hers. "You are not a giant spider."

She laughed, wiping her eyes. She'd been crying, and she was trying to hide it.

"This is better, no?"

She nodded. She reached back in her pocket and pulled out a red-and-white cloth. She held Tatsuya's luchador mask out to him.

"I saved your mask."

He took it, studied the seams with his thumb. "I used to have a drawer full of these. I bought them in bulk when I first started, forty years ago. This is my last one."

"Ben got Toby back, too," Ash said. "They'll come see you at the hospital later."

"The inugami was my father's legacy," Tatsuya said. He handed the mask back to Ash. "This is mine."

She held the mask in both hands. It felt heavier somehow. Tatsuya grunted as he sat up, which the EMTs didn't look happy about. He looked Ash in the eyes.

"How would you like to be a *true* warrior?" he said.

犬

Ben limped up to the door to his crappy apartment. Toby walked past him, heading two doors down to Ben's elderly neighbor's apartment. The inugami scratched on the door, and the old woman answered.

"Toby!" the woman said as the dog's tail wagged. "I was wondering where you were. Your bacon's already ready."

Toby trotted inside. The door shut.

Ben looked down for a moment, then entered his own apartment alone.

He stepped out of his shoes, threw his barf-drenched shirt on the floor, and flumped down onto his bed. Long day. Long year. After a moment, he sat up, yanked open the drawer at his bedside, and pulled out the old flip phone that he used whenever he broke or lost his iPhone. Which, in his line of work, was surprisingly often. He plugged it in, typed in the activation code, and let it charge.

There was a scratch at the door. Ben went and opened it.

Toby nudged a paper plate full of bacon into Ben's apartment with his nose. He picked up a single slice with his mouth and gently set it at Ben's feet, then pushed the plate over to his never-before-used dog bed and curled up with the rest.

Ben smiled. He picked up his bacon slice and set it next to his phone.

"Thanks, Tobe."

The phone rang loudly, a midi of a song Ben hadn't liked in ten years. No caller ID. He answered anyway.

"Ben!" It was his mother. "Where in God's name have you been? I've been calling you for weeks!"

"Hey, Mom," he said. "Sorry. I think it's been coming up 'Unknown Number,' so I haven't been answering."

"It's probably the international calls. You know it costs me five dollars every time I call you?"

"Right, uhm…" Ben rubbed his forehead. "Sorry. Where are you?"

"Brazil. My big retirement present to myself? My Amazon river cruise? Ben, what's going on? You forgot I was out of the country for a month?"

Ben had known that at some point. It was all she had talked about last Christmas, but his mom and sister lived all the way up in Minnesota, and he'd had a bit of a situation here. He looked at Toby. The bacon was gone. The dog burped.

"Yes, I know. Sorry. I, uhh, I just woke up. How's the vacation going?"

"Ben…" his mom paused. "I'm getting married!"

Ben stood. "What?"

"His name is Alvar Encantado. We met on the cruise. He's such a gentleman! I'm so excited. I didn't want to tell you with a text."

"You're getting *married*? Who is this guy?"

"He's Brazilian. He's a musician. He's artsy, like you and Becky. You guys are going to love him."

"Mom—"

"Hang on, I'm sending you a picture so you can see. I think he looks exactly like the man who plays Zorro. The new one."

Ben looked at his phone. He got a "Loading…" message, and then the image slowly drew itself onto the screen, one line of pixels at a time. Stupid ancient cell phone. He saw his mom wearing BluBlocker sunglasses, the kind that went over regular glasses, and a big floppy sun hat. The man next to her wore a straw hat, flat on top, round brim, and an all-white suit. His skin was pink. Too pink. Newborn baby pink. His head looked off. Couldn't be…

Ben squinted at the pixilated image on the tiny screen.

The man had a long snout, a permanently smiling mouth, and two wide-set black eyes.

Ben had been to the aquarium when he was a kid. He lived in the world. He knew a dolphin when he saw it, and the man standing next to his mother was, without a doubt, a dolphin.

"What?" he said.

DOG WALKER II
SHADOW PACK

ABOUT THE AUTHOR

Jack McGuigan is the author of the *Dog Walker* novels and the writer of *Agents of Paradox*, a comic book. In his youth, he made movies under the pseudonym "John McGuigan" that can be found on the internet. He lives in Chicago with his family. Everything he writes is true, except for the parts he makes up.

If you liked this, leave a review on Amazon! Reviews help readers find our books, which gives Jack more time to write new ones.

Sign up for our mailing list at GorillaHouseBooks.com for news and updates!

Website: **GorillaHouseBooks.com**
Twitter: **@JackMcGrak**
Email: **gorillahousebooks@gmail.com**

Ben and Toby will return in
"Dog Walker III: Wedding Siege"

Made in the USA
Middletown, DE
28 June 2019